THE
BIG
EMPTY

TITLES BY ROBERT CRAIS

THE
BIG
EMPTY

ROBERT CRAIS

G. P. PUTNAM'S SONS

New York

PUTNAM
— EST. 1838 —

G. P. PUTNAM'S SONS
Publishers Since 1838
An imprint of Penguin Random House LLC
penguinrandomhouse.com

LIBRARY OF CONGRESS CATALOGING-IN-PUBLICATION DATA

Names: Crais, Robert, author.
Title: The big empty / Robert Crais.
Description: New York : G. P. Putnam's Sons, 2024.
Identifiers: LCCN 2024027689 |
ISBN 9780525535768 (hardcover) | ISBN 9780525535799 (ebook)
Subjects: LCGFT: Thrillers (Fiction) | Novels.
Classification: LCC PS3553.R264 B54 2024 | DDC 813/.54—dc23/eng/20240628
LC record available at https://lccn.loc.gov/2024027689

Printed in the United States of America
1st Printing

Title page photograph by DmytroPerov/Shutterstock

for Martin Rast

and

Christiane, Monika, and TC.

Welcome to the pack.

Acknowledgments

For her support and herculean assistance, then and now: Carol Topping.

This novel began with my former editor, Mark Tavani. Thank you, my friend.

Daphne Durham assumed the editorial reigns with grace, insight, and love for Elvis Cole and Joe Pike. Her encouragement, suggestions, and unrelenting enthusiasm kept me on the rails and running true. Thank you.

Boss production editor Claire Sullivan and copy editor Rob Sternitzky had my six, and saved me from myself innumerable times. They had large shoes to fill, and did. Pat Crais, C/E Emeritus, approves. No higher compliment could be paid.

Thanks to my publicists, Kim Dower and Katie Grinch, for getting out the word, and Aranya Jain for helping everyone do everything, especially this author.

Aaron Priest and Lucy Childs, Lauren Crais, Wayne and Trey Topping, Shelby Rotolo, Diane Friedman, Max Sherman, and Steve Volpe all helped in ways large and small. And, always, Randy.

THE
BIG
EMPTY

Bad Mother

Sadie Given woke from a troubled sleep, the stupid phone babbling like an angry turkey, gobble-gobble, gobble-gobble. Sadie had fallen asleep on the couch in their tiny single-wide, and the instant she woke, Sadie knew she was late. She snatched up the phone as she stood.

"I'm sorry. I'm leaving now."

Anya said, "You're late."

Anya gave her an icy fifteen-year-old's tone with just enough hurt to make the tone sting.

Sadie hopped toward the door, slipping on her sandals.

"I know, I know, I'm sorry, baby. I'm coming."

"It's getting dark. I'm the last one here."

Sadie glanced to the windows and saw purple shadows.

"Where are you?"

"The skate park, Mom, where I said. I texted you like five times. Why didn't you answer?"

Found her keys and purse by the door, let herself out, and fumbled the keys locking their mobile home. She always seemed to be rushing. Rushing to get Anya to school, rushing to work, rushing to pick up Anya, rushing to make dinner, rushing to eat, rushing to her second job, rushing to give Anya the life and opportunities Sadie never had.

"Anya, stop. I'll be there in, what, ten minutes? I'm sorry."

"More like twenty. This is stupid. I'll walk."

Anya could be a pain, but Sadie felt terrible. She had made Anya promise to wait. She had made her promise not to leave with her friends. And now she was rushing again because she'd fallen asleep.

"I messed up, okay? I'm coming."

Sadie turned from the door, stumbled, and fell down the three wooden steps her ex-boyfriend built after he got out of prison back when she was still stupid. Her phone and keys went flying and Sadie landed hard in the gravel, scraping her palms and shredding her knees.

Anya's tiny voice saying, "What was that? Mom?"

"Shit."

Darker now, the deep purple sky turning to a midnight blue specked with stars.

Sadie found her phone and keys, and climbed into a dreary fourteen-year-old Honda the color of twilight. Her right knee hurt. Blood spotted the knee of her jeans like tiny black flowers.

Ruined.

Anya, still talking.

"Hello? Mom? Are you there?"

Sadie started the car and powered toward the road, kicking up trailer park gravel and dust.

Anya's voice saying, "Hell-lowww?"

Sadie took a deep breath, held it like the girl on TV said, and visualized her throbbing headache being carried away as she exhaled. It didn't work. It never worked.

"Hell-lowwww? Anyone therrre?"

Sadie steered onto the old highway and sped toward town.

The skate park was five miles from their home, but only a quarter mile from school. Anya could've ridden the school bus home, but, no, of course not, she went to the skate park with friends. To work on homework and study together, Anya said, which was bullshit. Sadie had given her mother exactly the same crapola when she was fifteen and went to the skate park, and all she'd done was smoke weed, make out with boys, and ruin her life. She wanted more for Anya.

"Mom?"

Sadie said, "I fell. It's nothing. I'm coming."

She veered left when the road forked and passed the old drive-in theater, picking up speed.

Anya said, "Fell? Fell how?"

"I tripped on the steps. It was stupid."

"Were you drinking?"

Sadie's grip on the wheel tightened.

"Stop."

"Did you get high? Is that why you forgot me?"

Sadie took another deep breath. She held it.

Please work.

"I didn't forget you."

"Then where were you?"

Now the tone was a whine.

It was hard, just the two of them. And the guilt, oh Lord, the guilt was enormous.

Sadie was seventeen when she had Anya. She had been arrested eight times after Anya's birth and had served eleven months at the Century Regional Detention Facility. Sadie had lost custody of her child to the state, gotten her back, and currently worked sixty-five hours a week split between two jobs, one paying minimum wage, the other paying minimum plus tips. Sadie had been straight-edge sober for three years, two months, and sixteen days, and attended meetings three times a week, despite working two jobs and raising Anya. Sadie Given had turned her life around, made a home with her daughter, and didn't owe anyone anything. She didn't date, saved what money she could, and had a plan for community college. Maybe next year. Maybe.

Anya gave her the tone again.

"I'm waiting. Where were you?"

"Home."

"*Our* home?"

"Stop!"

Anya stopped, but Sadie kept going.

"I fell asleep. I was sleeping. Maybe if you didn't watch TV all night, I could rest."

Sadie cringed even as the words tumbled out and knew she had blown it again.

Anya said, "This is bullshit. I'm not waiting any longer."

"I'm almost there."

"I don't care. Good-bye."

Sadie pressed the gas and glanced at the mirror. Checking for sheriffs. Habit.

"Anya. I can see the school. I'm two minutes away, not even."

"Go home. I'll walk."

"Don't you dare."

"Maybe you won't forget me next time."

"Anya!"

Anya hung up.

Sadie tossed her phone onto the passenger seat, so angry she wanted to slap the attitude off Anya's ungrateful face, but her rage instantly vanished and she felt only shame. And guilt.

Anya was everything. Her baby. Her love.

The school flashed past. Sadie made a last turn and saw the skate park ahead, a dim, shrouded concrete playground wrapped by trees and chain-link fences.

Closer.

Closer.

There.

Sadie pulled into the gravel parking area. Anya should've been waiting in front, but wasn't.

Brat.

Sadie beeped the horn twice, and held it the second time. She opened her door, stood from the car, and shouted.

"Anya! I'm here."

The skate park was deserted.

Sadie studied the hamburger stand and buildings across the street, didn't see Anya, and peered up the road into deepening darkness. If Anya was walking home, Sadie would've passed her. She hadn't, which meant Anya wasn't going home. She was probably going to one of her stupid friends or hiding nearby to torture her mother.

"Damnit, girl."

Sadie beeped the horn three fast times, beep, beep, beep. She called again.

"Anya, you stop it and come here!"

Nothing.

She beeped the horn and called louder.

"Anya!"

Nothing.

Sadie slid behind the wheel and slowly pulled away. She was furious, but her anger was tempered by fear. She didn't want her daughter walking along the dark, unlit roads.

Sadie followed the old road past small homes set on an acre or more, deep yards dotted with horse trailers, and empty land. She grew angrier and more afraid, but finally more afraid than angry.

Night fell hard in a rural area. The sky turned bright with stars, but the land grew black.

Sadie peered into passing shadows and fields, but didn't see Anya.

Then her eye caught a glint of light.

Sadie tapped the brakes.

The glint came again, a flash of dim light behind shadows on the far side of a field.

Sadie stopped and got out of her car. She wanted to call Anya's name, but didn't.

Sadie ran to the darkness as fast as she could.

PART ONE

1

Elvis Cole

Picture the detective alone in his office on a lovely spring day in Los Angeles. He is four floors above Santa Monica Boulevard, leaning back in his chair, feet on his desk, smiling. He is smiling because he is speaking with Lucy Chenier, an attorney who lives in Louisiana. The detective speaks with her every day. Sometimes, he speaks with her twice a day. On this day, he's certain he'll speak with her three times, and the thought makes him smile. A detective in love is insufferable.

Lucy said, "Are you bored?"

I said, "I'm never bored when I speak with you."

"I ask because it isn't even ten a.m. your time, and you've called twice. Don't you have work to do?"

"I'm between clients."

"That explains it."

"I had an idea."

"Okay, wait. I'm due in a deposition in ten, no, nine minutes."

"Let's take a trip this summer. The two of us. Or, if you want, Ben can come. Someplace you've always wanted to see."

Ben was Lucy's teenage son.

Lucy hesitated.

"Are you serious?"

"Don't I have great ideas?"

Lucy said, "This summer?"

"Check your calendar. A week, ten days, I don't care. If you can find the time, let's do it."

I was listening to Lucy think when my desk phone rang. It was one of the old hardwire Mickey Mouse phones and I liked it a lot. Prospective clients found it interesting and pushy cops found it annoying. Win-win. I was speaking to Lucy on my cell, so she heard the ringing.

I said, "Ignore it. It'll go to voice mail."

"Get it. If we go where I'm thinking, you'll need the money."

"I'll get rid of them. Hang on."

I lowered the cell and answered the Mickey.

"Elvis Cole Detective Agency. Superior detection at affordable rates."

A young female voice said, "Is this Elvis Cole?"

"Yes. Can you hold? I'm on another line."

The voice charged ahead as if she hadn't heard me.

"This is Dina Wade, Traci Beller's assistant. Traci would like to speak with you as soon as possible."

I said, "I'm on another call."

Dina Wade blurted.

"But it's Traci Beller!"

I said, "Okay. I give. Who's Traci Beller?"

Dina Wade sounded uncertain.

"The Baker Next Door?"

"Sorry."

"Her website, The Baker Next Door. Her socials. Traci has eight-point-two-million followers across her socials. You haven't heard of her?"

I had no idea who she was talking about.

"Oh. *That* Traci. Hang on."

I lowered the Mickey and returned to Lucy.

"Ever heard of Traci Beller?"

"Who?"

"The Baker Next Door."

Lucy hesitated.

"Oh, sure! The muffin girl."

I said, "The muffin girl."

"She's a baker, but she's best known for muffins."

"She bakes muffins."

"She makes cute videos of herself baking. They're short and fun. I've seen some. She called you?"

"Her assistant. She's on the other line."

"Ben will be impressed. A lot of kids in his class follow her. That's how I know about her. She's terrific."

Ben was a junior in high school.

I said, "Want to hang on?"

"For the muffin girl? Two minutes."

I lifted the Mickey.

Dina Wade was saying, "Mr. Cole? Mr. Cole, are you there?"

I said, "Sorry. How can I help you?"

"Traci specifically asked me to call. She'd like to speak with you about a private matter."

"Private matters are my specialty. Put her on."

"She'd rather see you in person. Today, if possible. Actually, now."

"I'll be here the rest of the morning. She can drop by whenever."

"Actually, she can't. She's filming today."

"Whenever she's not filming."

"Traci has zero free time, but my driving app says your office is only thirteen minutes away. If you're here in twenty, we'll pay you one thousand dollars whether you take the job or not."

"Hang on."

I picked up Lucy.

"Traci wants to meet. She'll pay me a thousand dollars whether I take the job or not."

"My. Aren't we the big shot detective?"

I smiled even wider.

"Impressed?"

"Studly, I couldn't be more impressed, and it's not because of a lousy thousand bucks. Tell me about it later."

"Love you."

"Love."

I hung up, copied Traci's address, and left to meet the muffin girl.

2

The address Dina Wade provided led to a pretty Tudor Revival home on a treesy residential street between Runyon Canyon and the Hollywood Bowl. The blue bay windows, bright green lawn, and redbrick drive were bright, well tended, and welcoming. Small cars and electric scooters lined the curb, so I pulled into the drive. A young woman with short black hair and dark-frame glasses hustled from the house as I parked.

"Mr. Cole, hi, I'm Dina. Here's the money, like we agreed."

Dina Wade pushed a check into my hand. I counted zeros and tucked it away.

"I'm three minutes early. Do I get a bonus?"

Dina Wade steered me toward the house without laughing.

"We're running behind, but I carved out twenty minutes for you and Traci to talk. We should hurry."

The living room felt crowded with two women by a rack of women's clothes, another huddled over her phone on a couch, and a man and a woman sorting through a bag of camera equipment. Dina towed me through the room without introducing me.

I said, "Why the rush?"

"Traci drops a new video every day, which means seven videos a week. She shoots them back-to-back, so the grind on shoot days is horrendous."

"She shoots them here?"

"Of course. In her kitchen."

Dina led me into a room that had been repurposed into a production studio. A sleek table topped by three large monitors filled a wall and two twenty-something men wearing headsets manned the table. They were watching multiple images of a young woman adding ingredients to a large bowl. The woman wore a simple flower-print shirt and faced us across a center island in a homey kitchen.

I said, "Traci?"

"Uh-huh. This is Miles, our director. This is Tad, our editor."

Miles glanced over his shoulder.

"Hey."

Tad adjusted a dial on an audio panel.

"Hey."

Traci Beller was twenty-three years old, but she could have passed for sixteen. She had a round face, short brown hair pinned at the sides, and large brown eyes. Her eyes sparkled when she grinned and her grin was infectious.

Dina said, "Between shoots, product development, meetings, marketing, and promotion, there aren't enough minutes in the day."

"What's she making?"

"Sour cream muffins with chocolate ganache centers."

A tall man with spiked, graying hair entered behind us and stood next to Dina. He squinted at the monitors and frowned at his watch. A Patek Philippe.

"She's behind."

Dina said, "She's wrapping five now. It's five, right, Miles?"

The tall man didn't wait for Miles to answer.

"She should be finishing six. Why are you behind?"

Miles shrugged.

"She's off."

The tall man said, "What do you mean, off?"

"Distracted, maybe. Not on point. Off."

The tall man crossed his arms and stood even taller. He looked impressive.

"She has to be in the Palisades by one and Woodland Hills by three. We cannot be late for this. Especially the Palisades."

Dina leaned close and whispered.

"Traci's opening two new storefront locations. We're expanding to fourteen by the end of the year."

The tall man made a hiss.

"If I can secure the investors."

Traci scooped a spoon of what looked like cinnamon from a large glass jar, held it toward the camera until the scoop loomed huge on the monitors, and abruptly lowered her hands. She visibly slumped.

Tad pressed a button. Traci's voice came from a speaker, but I also heard her in the next room.

She said, "I'm not feeling it. Sorry."

Tad glanced at the tall man.

"See?"

Miles keyed a mike.

"No worries, Trace. Just pick it up and keep going."

Traci Beller stared at us from the monitors.

"Has Mr. Cole arrived?"

The tall man said, "Who?"

Traci repeated her question.

"Dina, is he here?"

Dina opened a door in the far corner of the room and motioned me over.

"Elvis Cole, Traci Beller."

I stepped past Dina into a kitchen as Traci Beller came from behind the cook island. She wore black tights cut at the knee and open-toed sandals. She brightened when she saw me and put out her hand.

"I'm so glad you came. Thankyouthankyouthankyou."

She pumped my hand as she thanked me and abruptly crossed the kitchen.

"I have a gift for you."

She scooped up a pink shopping bag and opened it to reveal four fist-sized muffins.

"I don't know if you're gluten free or vegan, but I baked these this morning. Sour cream zaatar, salty caramel, honey mustard pistachio, and double chocolate cherry."

They looked fantastic and smelled even better.

I said, "They're beautiful. Thank you."

The tall man appeared behind us and didn't look happy.

"The Palisades in two hours. You need to dress. You need to finish the shoot."

Dina said, "I gave her twenty, Kev. It'll work. It's important."

Kevin scowled as if he'd seen me for the first time and didn't like what he saw.

"Twenty for what? Who is this?"

Dina said, "Traci's guest. Mr. Cole."

"Why is he here?"

Traci took my arm.

"We're fine, Kev. Twenty and done. I promise."

Traci grabbed a gray backpack and tugged me toward a set of French doors that led to her backyard.

I said, "What if we need twenty-one?"

Dina said, "Talk faster."

3

Traci led me across a used brick patio to the shade of a blossoming pear tree. Dina stopped at the doors, giving us space. Kevin circled behind Dina, glowering over her shoulder.

Traci lowered the backpack and took a breath.

"Whew. We've been shooting since four a.m."

"Do all these people work for you?"

She grinned.

"Crazy, right? I began posting content in high school and it sort of took off."

"Videos of you, baking?"

Her grin widened and she dimpled.

"Me, baking. Now Kevin manages my business and Dina manages my schedule. Who knew?"

Traci Beller wasn't beautiful like a model or an actress, but she had a fun, friendly, best friend quality I liked a lot. Her eight-point-two-million followers probably liked it, too.

I said, "We have nineteen minutes left. Do I have time to eat a muffin?"

Traci giggled and looked even younger. Then she glanced at Kevin and led me farther away.

"Did Dina give you the check?"

"She did. Thank you."

The enormous brown eyes turned serious.

"A friend at the *Times* says you're good at finding people."

"I could pretend to be modest but why bother?"

I waited for Traci Beller to smile, but she didn't. I cleared my throat.

"Who would you like me to find?"

"My dad. My father disappeared ten years ago next month."

She took a pale blue check from the pack. It looked like the check Dina gave me only the amount was larger.

"I'll pay you five thousand dollars now and another five when you find him or proof of his death. I'll cover any and all expenses and any additional monies needed during the search. That's the job. Say yes."

She held out the check.

I glanced at the house. Kevin was speaking to Dina and didn't look happy. Dina was shrugging and glancing at Traci.

Traci ignored them and pushed the check toward me.

"This is on top of the thousand."

I touched her hand to lower the check.

"The thousand is enough for now. When you say disappeared, what do you mean?"

She hesitated, as if deciding how to explain.

"My dad owned a heating and air-conditioning company with my Uncle Phil. The day he disappeared, he was making service calls out in Rancha by Calabasas."

"I know where it is."

Rancha was a rural community at the western end of the San Fernando Valley. It was in L.A. County, but outside the LAPD service area.

I said, "Was your father making the calls alone or with your Uncle Phil?"

"Alone, which was totally normal. They split the work."

"Okay."

"He called my mom after lunch, told her he was running late, and we never heard from him again. So it was like, poof, he vanished."

I tried to pretend I didn't know where this was going. When healthy adult males went missing, they almost always did so voluntarily. This happened so often the court had a term for it. Voluntary absence.

I said, "Do you have reason to believe his disappearance wasn't voluntary?"

"Of course I do. He loved us. He was a wonderful father."

"Besides that."

"I don't need besides that. What I need is for you to find him."

She shoved the five-thousand-dollar check at me again and I touched it away.

"I assume your mother went to the police."

Traci removed two folders from the backpack and offered one embossed with an LAPD seal.

"For all the good it did."

I took the LAPD folder and she held out the second.

"My mother had him declared dead as soon as she could. OhmiGod, I was furious."

If a person was missing for five years, the state of California would grant a presumption of death if certain requirements were met. This usually meant hiring a private investigator to show a good-faith effort had been made to locate the missing individual. The firm's name, Byers & Ryan, was embossed on the cover.

"I know Byers & Ryan. They're good."

"Not good enough to find him."

Kevin called from the house.

"We need to get going here."

Traci's voice held an edge when she answered.

"In a minute."

I thumbed through the folders. The police report was thin. The Byers report was thick with contact lists, search results, and documentation. Jessica Byers was one of the finest investigators I knew.

Traci watched me hopefully.

"There's a lot of information here. I thought you could look at it. I thought, I don't know, maybe you'll see something they missed."

Like I was magic.

"The presumption of death was granted?"

She rolled her eyes. Exasperated.

"I was so mad. I still can't believe it."

I felt bad for her. The presumption wouldn't have been granted if Byers had found proof of life, evidence of death, or a reason to believe her father might still be found.

"If your father didn't leave voluntarily, the options aren't good. You understand this, right?"

Traci wet her lips and glanced away.

"I get it. He might've been murdered or committed suicide or something awful. But he would've come back to us if he could. He didn't abandon us."

She wet her lips again.

"I know ten years is a long time. I know it'll be difficult to find him after so much time, but what's ten years to the World's Greatest Detective?"

"That was a joke I made to a reporter."

"Please read the reports. Maybe you'll think of something they didn't. Maybe you'll just try harder."

The weight of her hope was enormous.

"None of his friends or family has heard from him?"

"Not since he vanished."

"So nothing has changed since these reports were written?"

The large brown eyes flashed.

"Me. I have eight-point-two-million followers and endorsements and merch and bake shops and money. My mother gave up, but I won't. I'm going to find him."

Kevin stepped past Dina and stood in the door. Impatient and irritated.

Kevin said, "Traci, let's go. Everyone's waiting."

I said, "Not now."

Kevin glowered and stood taller.

"We have to lock this location, Traci. It's the Palisades. A potential investor is coming."

I raised my voice.

"Don't make me come over there."

Kevin slammed the door and Traci gripped my arm.

"Presumed dead doesn't mean he's *really* dead. I won't believe he's dead or living another life somewhere until someone proves it."

She offered the check again.

"Be that someone. Please."

Her commitment and determination were awesome.

I glanced at the folders.

"I can't promise I'll find him or learn anything you don't already know, but I'll take a look."

A bright hope lit Traci Beller's face.

"Perfect. Wonderful. Here, I'll give you my private cell. Text or call me directly."

"I'll need you to call Jess Byers at Byers & Ryan. Give her permission to discuss the case."

"I'll call right away."

Traci pushed the check again, but I still refused.

"Stop shoving the check at me. I won't take more money unless I see a way forward."

She studied me for a moment and flashed the dimples.

"I hope you'll take the muffins."

"The muffins, I'll take."

"Good. Eat while you read."

I took the folders and the muffins and left.

4

Twenty-two minutes after leaving Traci Beller, I was back in my office, eating a muffin, and reading the missing persons report. The sour cream zaatar was amazing.

Georgina Beller reported her husband as missing the day after he failed to return home. A grainy photo of Thomas Jacob Beller, age forty-one, topped the first page. The man in the photo had a wide face, small nose, and Traci's expressive brown eyes. Faint bags beneath his eyes made him look tired and his hairline was receding, but the resemblance between them was clear. The usual identifying information followed, so I skipped to Georgina's initial report.

Her statement confirmed and expanded on what Traci told me. Ms. Beller had spoken with her husband twice during the day, once at midmorning and again in the afternoon. During the second call, he told her he was running behind, dreaded the drive home at rush hour, and not to expect him until late. This was the last time she heard from him. Mr. Beller had not responded to calls and texts from her or his business partner, Mr. Philip Janley, and Ms. Beller feared her husband had been in an accident. A database search by the police produced no results. Beller had not been arrested, admitted to an area hospital, or bagged in the morgue. A BOLO on his van was issued and Glendale tossed the case to the Missing Persons Unit, but armies of cops didn't roll code three, a manhunt didn't ensue, and nobody lit the Bat Signal. The BOLO yielded nothing.

I ate a second muffin and opened the Byers report. Salty caramel. Delicious.

Jessica Byers had spent twelve years as an investigator for the L.A. County DA's Office before she went private with a former FBI agent named Deb Ryan. Their report was sixty-seven pages. Jess had interviewed twenty-six of Beller's friends, relatives, and last-known contacts. Everyone thought the world of the man and nobody had heard from him. Jess had run a VIN search for his van and even discovered a fifth contact in Rancha when she interviewed Beller's clients, a counter attendant at a hamburger stand where Beller bought lunch, but no clues to Thomas Beller's whereabouts were found. The probate judge had drawn the only possible conclusion. Since the man had been missing for five years and could not be found, Thomas Beller was as good as dead whether he was actually dead or not. Goodbye, Dad.

Byers & Ryan had done everything I would have done and probably more. Traci Beller didn't like it, but I saw no gaping holes, missed opportunities, or cut corners.

I put the report aside and let myself out onto the balcony. The sky was hazy, but a blue line of ocean was visible at the end of Santa Monica Boulevard. I returned to my desk and googled The Baker Next Door.

Traci's home page featured an ad for an upcoming cookbook, links to appearances, links to buy merchandise, and an archive with hundreds of her videos. I clicked at random and watched her make a bacon–cornbread–black olive focaccia. The video was thirty seconds of ingredients plopping into bowls, mixing, stirring, and pouring. Exclamation marks and measurements flashed. 1 cup, ½ cup, 1 tsp.

Traci beamed as she bit into the finished bread. She looked happy. I read her official bio.

Traci Beller grew up with her mom and dad in a modest ranch-style home in Glendale. Her bio contained old photos of Traci baking. Here was five-year-old Traci on a stool to reach the counter, flour smudged on her face. Here was six-year-old Traci and Thomas taking a cake from an oven. Here was her dad taking a bite of a muffin she held. A legend read: *I miss my dad. Baking is love.*

I closed my laptop and flipped through Byers's report.

> Mr. Beller was described by his family, immediate friends, and business associates as a good husband and devoted father (see attchd A). Mr. Beller had no criminal history, no known medical condition, and was not under the care of a physician or mental health professional (see attchd B & C). The undersigned found no history or evidence of substance abuse (see attchd D) or inappropriate debt (see attchd E).

Probate judges weren't interested in theories or speculations, so Jess had offered none, but I'd written enough probate reports to know that much of what Byers learned had been omitted. I dialed her personal cell. Byers answered on the third ring.

"Sorry. We're not hiring."

Jess was one of those people who thought she was funny.

"You couldn't afford me. Did Traci Beller call?"

"She did. I'll send a copy of the report."

"I have it. Solid work, like always."

Jessica laughed. She had a husky laugh I liked.

"Of course it's solid, dork. You don't have to suck up. How can I help?"

"Was he having an affair?"

Byers sighed. She wasn't comfortable discussing private cases.

I said, "This is us, Jess. I won't repeat it to the family."

She sighed again.

"Not according to his friends. And I didn't find anything in his email, finances, or phone records to suggest otherwise. Georgina and I reviewed his email together. Nothing."

"No problems at home?"

"Nope. Never complained about his marriage or family. No drama."

"So he drove out to Rancha, worked all day, and decided on the spur of the moment to blow past Glendale and keep driving."

"For all I know, yes. Or no. What we have here, my friend, is a mystery."

"So all roads led to Rancha, but none led out."

"Plenty led out. I just didn't find them."

"Traci doesn't believe he ran."

"I know. I'm sorry."

I flipped to the timeline and read from the page.

"His last client said he complained about driving home at rush hour and hurried to finish work."

"Which speaks to intention. Yeah, I know. But just because he told his client he was going home doesn't mean he headed home."

"You think he ran."

"I found no evidence he ran or didn't run. I have no idea where he went."

Went. I didn't like it and didn't like where it led.

"So you believe he ran."

"Don't you find it interesting, a then-eight-year-old panel van filled with AC parts never turned up?"

I said, "Yes."

"Like maybe a certain someone's kept his van under wraps so he won't be found."

"You can be a real drag, you know?"

"Anything else?"

I flipped through the report to the interview summary of Beller's fourth client, Samantha Mason.

"Samantha Mason. The last client he saw."

"Yeah?"

"Maybe he mentioned stopping off for dinner somewhere, or another stop he had to make."

"Are you asking if I asked her?"

"Yeah."

"Of course I asked. He griped about the traffic and wanted to get going. She didn't like it. She thought he was rude, so he apologized, but that was it. She said he seemed anxious."

"About the traffic?"

"I would guess, but who knows?"

Byers paused.

"I feel bad for Traci. I do. But it is what it is."

I nodded, but neither of us spoke. She probably didn't see the nod.

I reread Samantha Mason's summary during the silence. The first three clients and the counter attendant described Beller as friendly and talkative. Only Samantha Mason described him as anxious and rude. I wondered if running late was all there was to it and whether Samantha Mason had said something Jess hadn't included.

I said, "Do you still have your interview notes for his contacts in Rancha?"

"Should. Want the files if I can find them?"

"Please."

"You're going to try to find him, aren't you?"

"Traci gave me muffins."

Jessica laughed.

"I'll look around and send what I find."

"Have Deb look. She'll find it faster."

Jess laughed again, called me a jerk, and signed off.

Taking a case ten years cold was almost always a loser. Witnesses were difficult to locate and clues were as tough to find as an honest politician. I should've said no. I should have walked away. I had an uneasy feeling about what I might find, but I didn't.

I wasn't sure if I could help Traci Beller, but I wanted to try.

5

reread both reports and tried to come up with a plan of action. The World's Greatest Detective needed a World's Greatest Plan, but a plan didn't present itself. This was likely because I had no clues.

Like most people, Beller had never been arrested or served in the military. He had never been fingerprinted or swabbed for DNA. Department of Justice databases could be searched based on physical characteristics, but unless the subject was missing a limb or possessed distinctive tattoos, the number of five-ten, one-eighty, brown, brown, balding Anglo men numbered in the tens of millions. Beller might've turned up dead in Seattle or been arrested in Lexington, but without his fingerprints or DNA in the database, he wouldn't be identified. Beller could've told the locals he was Boris Badenov and nobody could prove different.

I was considering Beller's lack of fingerprints when my thoughts returned to his van. Byers had run a VIN search five years ago, but his vehicle could've found its way to an impound lot, repair shop, or junkyard in the interim so I called an insurance adjuster named Keri Wenn and asked her to run the VIN.

I said, "Can you check Mexico, too?"

"I can check, but they're not as stringent as us."

"Give it a shot."

I was on a roll when my cell phone rang. The caller ID showed BEN CHENIER.

I said, "Hey."

"Mom said you met Traci Beller?"

He sounded impressed.

"I did. Went to her house and everything."

"That's so cool. Traci Beller!"

A director named Peter Alan Nelson was a friend. Peter was among the top five highest-grossing filmmakers of all time. Ben had been to his home and his movie sets and met movie stars, but Ben had never sounded this impressed.

He said, "Is she hot?"

Ben was sixteen.

I said, "She's personable."

"Dude, she's hot. And funny. Take a selfie with her and send it to me."

"Won't happen."

"Are you working for her?"

"Top secret."

"You're working for her. Send a selfie."

He was carrying on like this and I had never heard of Traci Beller until three hours ago.

I told him I had to get back to detecting.

The Byers report included an addendum page listing the twenty-six people Jess interviewed. Five were located in Rancha, eight were family members, and thirteen were grouped as Beller's friends and associates. All I could do was ask the same people the same questions they'd already been asked and hope for a different answer. Maybe they had forgotten their old answer and would make up a new answer and I could pretend it was a clue. A made-up clue wouldn't help find Thomas Beller, but Traci would think I was making progress. An actual clue would be even better.

I copied the list and phoned Traci. I expected her voice mail, but she answered on the second ring. Faint voices murmured behind her.

She said, "Did you read the reports?"

"I read them and spoke with Byers. She's good, Traci. If you doubted her work, don't."

"Meaning what? You can't find him?"

Zero to frantic in no seconds flat.

"Meaning the same leads will give me the same result. I need new leads."

"Oh. Okay, sure. How do we get new leads?"

We.

"First, it's possible he's reached out to an old friend, so I'll ask. You can help."

"Nobody's heard from him. I would know."

"Probably, but Byers checked five years ago and five years is five years. I should check again. You can help by asking these people to speak with me."

"Okay. Which people?"

"A list of the people Byers interviewed is in her report. Did you keep a copy?"

"I have copies. I'll take care of it."

Her voice was muffled as she spoke away from the phone.

"Dina! C'mere."

"Also, look over the names. If you think of anyone else I should speak with, let me know."

"Got it."

She mumbled to Dina again.

I said, "Second, I'd like to look through your father's possessions."

"Like clothes and stuff?"

"Old yearbooks, scrapbooks, diaries, letters. Old calendars. Like that."

"I have some cuff links and things. I kept an old jacket. His Dodgers cap. Lemme think."

"Not clothes. Things personal to his interests and friends. Like hobbies and clubs. Things that might lead to a clue."

"I don't have anything like that."

"What about your mother?"

Her voice turned cool.

"No. She got rid of him."

"She didn't keep anything?"

Colder.

"She told me to take whatever I wanted. Everything else, anything that reminded her of him, she threw it away. She couldn't get rid of him fast enough."

Traci fell silent.

I said, "I'm sorry."

"It's okay."

"So she kept nothing."

"I don't know. She had some stuff in the garage, maybe."

"I want you to understand. I'm reaching. The odds are ten million to one I'll find anything, but no new leads means no new answers."

She sighed.

"Okay. I hear you. I'll ask."

"Also, I'd like to speak with her."

"My mother?"

"Is there a problem?"

"In case I wasn't clear, which I was, my mother doesn't like talking about my father. Also, she thinks I'm stupid for hiring you. She doesn't approve."

"If you don't want me to speak with her, I won't, but, in case I wasn't clear, which I was, clues are in short supply."

Traci was silent for several seconds.

"When do you want to see her?"

"Today?"

"She's a teacher. She's working."

"Whenever she likes."

More silence. As if Traci had to steel herself.

"I'll call you back."

She hung up before I could respond. I eyed the muffin bag and considered the remaining two muffins. I debated eating a third. I was still debating when Traci called back.

She said, "Oh. My. *God.*"

"She won't talk to me?"

"She will, but you should've heard her. OhmiGod. Is five okay? She said you can come at five."

"I've got a Zoom with the president at five, but I'll cancel."

"You're funny, but don't be funny with my mother. She isn't happy. When she's unhappy she can be difficult. I'm warning you."

"Charm. Charm is my middle name."

"She wants my Uncle Phil to be there. I said fine. You probably want to talk to him anyway, right?"

"Phil as in your dad's business partner?"

"Yeah, that's right."

Philip Janley was the Jan in Bel-Jan Heating & Air. He and Thomas Beller had met working construction after dropping out of college and eventually went into business for themselves. Phil Janley had been Thomas Beller's best man and closest male friend, but I didn't want to ask Georgina uncomfortable questions about her marriage in front of him.

I said, "I don't know, Traci. It'll be awkward. I should see them separately."

"I was scared she'd say no. I can't call her back and say Phil can't come. She'll freak. She might not let you into the house."

I didn't like it, but the list of things I didn't like was long. One adapted.

"No worries. I'll figure it out."

"Phil's great. Trust me. She'll be nicer with Phil there. She might even help."

"This is too good to pass up."

"I'll set it up. And Mr. Cole—"

"Elvis, Ms. Beller."

"I was scared you wouldn't help. I know this is a long shot, so thank you. Thanks for reaching."

"Good luck in the Palisades."

"Good luck finding clues."

I gathered the reports and the muffins and headed for Glendale. The muffins rode shotgun.

6

Georgina Beller lived alone in a small, gray stucco house two blocks south of the Ventura Freeway. Her home was similar to the other houses lining her street, all with sparse yards, few trees, and short driveways leading to two-car garages that weren't wide enough for two cars. An aging Toyota Corolla filled the drive and a pale blue van with BEL-JAN HEATING & AIR on the side was parked out front. I parked across the street and walked to the door. The freeway sounded angry.

A thin woman in her fifties with dark brown hair and fragile skin opened the door. Georgina Beller wore a loose flower-print dress, colorful bracelets, and glasses. I smiled, but she looked at me as if I'd come for an overdue bill. I smiled wider.

"Ms. Beller, Elvis Cole. Thanks for speaking with me."

I offered a card, but she ignored it.

"Let's get this over with."

Her living room was neatly furnished with a cloth corner couch, mismatched chairs, and lamps on little tables. A flat-screen TV hung between matching bookcases opposite the couch. A short, burly man with a red face and sorrowful eyes was on the couch, but stood and came around a coffee table to greet me. The crown of his head was shiny, but wiry red hair threaded with gray still grew on the sides.

"Phil Janley. Tommy and I had the business together. He and I went back even before Georgie."

Janley grinned at Georgina as if he expected her to smile. She didn't and Janley looked awkward.

"Anyway, happy to help if I can."

I said, "Thanks. I'm sure I'll have questions."

Georgina said, "For Christ's sake, Phil. Please."

She didn't want me in her home, but she'd agreed to cooperate and now she regretted it.

"The man's been gone for almost ten years. He's gone. And now this nonsense with Traci, hiring you. She's wasting her money."

I tried to look understanding.

"I know this is painful. I wish it weren't."

"It's not painful. It's infuriating. What does she think? You'll ask a question I haven't been asked? She'll find him and he'll come home? This is madness."

Phil spoke gently.

"Georgie, c'mon."

Her eyes flashed, but Phil only spoke softer.

"She needs to do this, so let's not stand in her way."

Georgina Beller wavered.

I said, "Time passes and perspectives change. The questions might be the same, but sometimes the answers are different."

She seemed to relax.

"I don't consider myself a rude or unkind person, Mr. Cole. This is about Traci, not you."

"I understand."

"Good. Now, she tells me you want to see Tommy's things."

"Whatever you kept, yes."

"You will find nothing of Tommy in this house. Anything of his, I gave away, threw away, or burned."

I said, "Mm."

"However. I kept a box of things for Traci. I've told her to come get it a hundred times, but has she? No. Regardless, you're free to look."

"I'd like that, Ms. Beller. Thank you."

"On one condition. Tell Traci to come get it. I mean this, Mr. Cole. She can send one of her assistants if she likes. I don't care. But if the damned box is still here come the weekend I'm throwing it out. Will you tell her?"

Georgina Beller meant business. I wondered how many times she'd threatened to throw it out and why Traci hadn't come for her father's things. Maybe the box was the last and only thing they shared.

I said, "Yes, ma'am. I'll tell her."

She flicked a hand toward the far side of the house.

"In the garage. By the dryer. Traci's name is on it. What's next?"

I glanced at Phil.

Phil was perched on the edge of the couch like an uncomfortable, overstuffed teddy bear. He nodded. Encouraging me to continue.

I took out the family and friends list and handed it to her.

"These are people who were close to your husband."

She glanced at the page and handed it back.

"I know. Phil and I made this list."

"Thinking about it now, is there anyone else I should contact?"

"No."

Just like that. No.

I passed the list to Janley. He put on a pair of drugstore reading glasses and murmured as he read.

Georgina grew impatient.

"Phil. They're the same names we gave to Byers."

I said, "Mr. Janley?"

Phil slowly shook his head and handed back the page.

"No, no. You got his friends here, the guys we worked with. I can't think of anyone else."

Georgina pruned her lips. Sour.

"We have no new names to add. Anything else?"

"Yes, ma'am, but I'd prefer if you and I spoke privately."

Georgina glanced at Phil and smirked.

"Here come the marriage and fidelity questions."

Phil lumbered to his feet.

"I'll give you a minute."

Georgina waved him down.

"We don't need a minute. He's going to ask the same questions everyone's asked and my answers haven't changed."

Phil sat and looked even more uncomfortable.

I said, "I'm serious, Ms. Beller. Besides, I might blush."

"So blush. I didn't cheat on him. If he had a girlfriend, I didn't know. A boyfriend, I didn't know. If he was unhappy, I never suspected. I was stupid, Mr. Cole. As far as I knew, Tommy and I were fine. Only he wasn't and I was too stupid to see it. He left and I never saw it coming."

"You believe he abandoned you."

"Didn't he? He left me to pay for this house and raise a child by myself. Alone."

"Were there signs?"

"If there were I never saw them. You see? I was stupid."

She said it simply and without emotion. Then she checked her watch and settled back. Waiting.

I wasn't sure what to say, so I unfolded the list page again.

"Are any of these women a former girlfriend of his?"

"I never knew his former girlfriends. Maybe Phil knows."

Phil squirmed.

"He dated a blonde girl for a while, but this was before you, Georgie. I don't remember her name. Jeez, it was so long ago."

Georgina shrugged.

"Phil doesn't know, either."

I nodded.

"Maybe he stayed in touch with someone?"

"I spent three weeks going through his email with the Byers

detective, who cost a fortune, by the way. We found nothing. Do you know why?"

"There was nothing to find."

She nodded, slowly and with weight.

"Nothing. No flirty emails, no complaints about me or his life, no ugly politics or porn or anything surprising. Nothing real. Which made me think it wasn't."

"You believe he used other email accounts on a device you didn't know about?"

"I believe my daughter deserves to be happy."

Georgina Beller suddenly slapped the arms of her chair, both hands, palms down.

"She should be happy!"

Her hands pounded each word.

"She. Should. Be. Happy."

Her face flushed.

"Look at her. With all her success. The money she's making. He is her curse and she doesn't see it."

Phil, softly again.

"Georgie, c'mon, she's—"

Georgina shoved from the chair, cutting him off.

"He is gone. And this—"

She waved toward me.

"—is unhealthy and tragic. She needs to accept it or she will never be happy. He's gone. Better she spend her money on a psychiatrist than a detective."

Phil glanced away and seemed embarrassed.

Georgina steadied herself. Her eyes cooled, but also seemed sad. I wondered what grade she taught. I wanted to ask, but didn't.

She said, "Will there be anything else?"

"No, ma'am. Thank you."

"By the dryer. Traci's name is on the box. Phil, would you show him, please?"

"Sure, you bet."

Georgina Beller turned toward the dining room.

I said, "You weren't stupid."

She stopped, but did not look back.

"You weren't stupid. Trust isn't stupid."

Georgina Beller stood as still as a reed, then continued through the dining room into the kitchen. The refrigerator opened, then a door, and Georgina appeared in her backyard through the dining room window. She held a bottle of white wine by the neck. She unscrewed the cap and drank.

Phil stood beside me and we watched Georgina drink again.

7

eorgina drank deeper the second time, lowered the bottle, and stared at something I could not see. At a neighboring house, maybe. At a crow gliding past. Phil looked worried.

"She didn't always act like this. Don't judge her by all this anger."

"I'm not judging."

"When Tommy disappeared, we thought he'd turn up. Dead, most likely, but she tried to be positive. She didn't hate him. She didn't think he ran off. All that came later."

"She was scared."

"I blame her sisters. They got it in their heads he ran off and, man, they wouldn't let up."

I said, "Did she really throw out his things?"

He nodded.

"Everything. You won't find a picture of him. Not a cuff link or a fishing rod."

"Must've been tough on Traci."

Phil studied me for a moment.

"Georgie isn't all wrong. I want Traci to get on with her life, too. When she started talking about hiring another detective, I tried to talk her out of it. I thought it was a bad idea."

I had nothing to say so I nodded. The all-purpose nod served me well.

Phil considered Georgina again.

"But Traci was so determined, I don't know, I thought, okay, maybe if she looks for him she'll finally make peace with him being gone."

"I'll do my best."

"I'm sure you will, but c'mon, do you really think you can find him after all this time?"

"If there's a trail. New information would help."

Phil made a grunt.

"Wish I had some, but I'll give you a tip. The only trail you'll find is the trail leading in."

I glanced at him, but Phil was watching Georgina.

I said, "Not leading out?"

"Tommy loved that woman. And those kids? Georgie's wrong on this one and Traci's right. Tommy wouldn't leave them. If he's anywhere, he's there."

"In Rancha?"

The big head swung toward me. His face was grim and more heavily lined. He didn't look like a teddy bear anymore. He looked like a bulldog.

"I'd bet on it. Something happened to him there in Rancha."

According to Byers's timeline, Phil had helped Beller load his van that morning and spoke with him four times during the day. The police had taken Phil's statement for the original MPR and Jess Byers had interviewed him, but he hadn't voiced this suspicion either time.

I said, "Something happened because if nothing happened it means he abandoned them? Or something happened because you actually know something happened?"

Phil drew a breath so deep it went on forever, then his mouth worked as if his face hurt.

"Tommy and I were tighter than any two brothers you know. Between work and hanging out, we spent damn near every day together for twenty-five years. I loved the man."

He looked at me again.

"And not once in all those years did he give two shits about driving home at rush hour, so why would he complain about it to Georgina or Ms. Mason? A client? C'mon."

"You spoke with him that day. Did he mention his concern to you?"

"Never."

"Did you tell this to Ms. Byers or the police?"

He shook his head.

"Never occurred to me until Traci said she was going to hire someone. I started thinking about Tommy and, I'm telling you, something happened. That morning, he was fine, same as always, but that afternoon he was all wound tight. I remember thinking, 'Crap, what's wrong?'"

"Did he say something had happened?"

"He didn't. That's how I know. I asked. He just kept saying everything's fine, but he said it like someone who didn't want to talk about it."

Phil scowled.

"Tommy wasn't fine. I knew he wasn't, but I didn't think much of it, not until now."

"Thanks for telling me."

He made the grunt and glanced at Georgina.

"I'd better see how she's doing. You okay getting the box by yourself?"

"I'll find it."

He started away, but hesitated.

"You know, I lost him, too. If Tommy abandoned them he abandoned me. I don't believe he left me."

I took out a card and handed it to him.

"If you think of anything else."

Phil studied the card. His bulldog face clouded like a thunderhead threatening rain.

He said, "You find something, call me first. Any questions, you call. Anything I can do, call. All right?"

"Sure."

Phil offered his hand and we shook. His hand was thick like the rest of him and felt like iron padded with leather.

The garage was off the kitchen. It was dim as murky water, so I raised the door. Shelves jammed with boxes and containers with labels like CHRISTMAS and 3RD GRADE filled a wall opposite a washer and dryer so large no room was left for a car.

A cardboard box with TRACI written on the side in black marker sat beside the dryer. A green bucket filled with pruning shears, soiled gardening gloves, and a rusty hand rake sat on top of it. The top had been taped, but the tape hung free like a wilted vine.

I moved the bucket and carried the box to the mouth of the garage. Georgina's wedding album sat on top, sealed in a plastic sleeve. Beneath were packs of birthday and Father's Day cards Traci had made, held tight by blue rubber bands. Envelopes and albums were thick with the snapshots and photos Georgina no longer allowed in her home, reminders of a time when their family was whole, Tommy and Traci on a playground slide, Tommy giving Traci a ride on his shoulders. I found no correspondence, diaries, or notebooks; no old cell phones or laptops or guides to creating a new identity. The box held only memories Georgina could no longer abide. I closed the top, put the box in its place, and left without saying good-bye.

8

ome was a redwood A-frame on a winding street off Woodrow
Wilson Drive near the top of Laurel Canyon. The house was
small, but a deck off the back offered a fine view of the canyon
below and the city beyond the ridges. I parked in the carport, let myself into the kitchen, and set the muffins on the counter.

I said, "You guys want anything?"

Humor.

I drank a glass of tap water, rinsed the glass, and heard the cat door
clack. A black cat walked in and looked at me. His head was cocked
to the side from when he was shot with a .22 and his ears were ragged
from too many fights. Most people thought he was scowling. They
were probably right.

I said, "Muffins or sardines? Your call."

He head-bumped my leg.

Dinner for me was three scrambled eggs wrapped in a tortilla with
black beans and chopped tomatoes. Dinner for him was half a can of
wet food, two sardines, and a side of kibble. I put out his food and
fresh water while the eggs cooked, opened a bottle of Longboard beer,
and sat on the floor beside him with my burrito. He growled.

I said, "Take it easy."

I poured a sip of beer into his saucer. He sniffed the foam, growled again, and lapped the saucer clean. Purring.

I called Traci to tell her about the box, but Dina answered.

"Hey. It's Dina. I was about to call you."

"Do you always answer Traci's phone?"

"When she's busy, yes. We need your address. Kevin is sending a contract for your signature."

"A contract for what?"

"An employment contract. Everyone who works for Traci signs a contract. Kevin requires it."

"Even you?"

"Of course. Everyone signs a contract. Even the housekeeper and gardeners."

"Email it. If it looks good I'll e-sign."

"Kevin prefers an actual signature, so we'll have it delivered."

I gave her my address and asked to speak with Traci.

Dina said, "Sorry, she can't. We're shooting. We started as soon as we got back."

"Ask her to call me."

"I'll tell her you called."

"That's not the same as asking her to call."

"We have to make up lost time. Is this upsetting news or good news?"

"Georgina was cooperative. Cooperative is good news, right?"

"Mm."

"She has photos of Traci and her father, but someone needs to get them. Georgina says she'll throw them out if you don't. She means it."

Dina said, "Sounds upsetting. Her mother always upsets her."

"Traci will want the pictures. Also, I asked Traci to phone the people Jess Byers interviewed. Has she?"

"She's been so busy."

"Has she called any of them?"

"I'll tell her you called."

Dina probably wouldn't, so I started making calls. Calling goes quickly when nobody answers. Of the eight relatives and thirteen friends I phoned, only four people answered. None of the four had heard from Tommy Beller. Three of the numbers were bad and fourteen went to voice mail. I left messages, but most would never call back. People never called back, but one still had to try. Detective work was an ugly business.

Jess Byers's interview notes arrived in my inbox while I was leaving messages. An attached file contained twenty-six documents labeled by the subject's name. The interviews had been recorded and transcribed, and the transcriptions totaled two hundred and sixty-seven single-spaced pages. Daunting. Especially when one had a limited supply of printer paper.

Since I'd left messages for the friends and relatives, I printed the transcripts of the five people Beller had seen in Rancha. They weren't as compelling as a David Baldacci novel, but they provided an interesting portrait of Thomas Beller.

Diana Landau and Steadman Collin were Beller's first two service calls and both liked the man. Mr. Collin, a retired salesman, described Beller as "funny." After the Collin job, Beller stopped for lunch at the SurfMutt hamburger stand, where he met a counter attendant named Eric Zalway. Zalway, who'd recently been admitted to UCLA and hoped to be a teacher, described Beller as "a great guy" who told "inspiring stories about his wife's teaching career." Zalway was so impressed he recognized Beller's photograph five years later. So far, Beller sounded like the class president and prom king rolled into one. Everyone loved him.

His third service call was at Lisa Jayne Tyre's residence. Tyre had been in San Diego, so her housekeeper, a woman named Loretta Sienze, met Beller at the house. Sienze had little interaction with the man and barely remembered him.

Samantha Mason was Beller's final service call and the last person known to have seen him.

Mason described a much different Beller than the others, noting he had arrived with a large, yellow SurfMutt soft drink cup. Ms. Mason, who "absolutely loved the double-chili Muttburger with extra onions and pickles," asked what he'd had for lunch. Beller, she said, told her he had a lot of work to do and didn't have time to talk. Samantha Mason was "shocked" by his "surly manner," complaining he had rushed around her house, spent too much time on the phone, and described him as "unfriendly and rude." The progression from "funny" and "a great guy" to "unfriendly and rude" matched pretty well with Phil's description, but I didn't know if this meant anything. Maybe the Muttburger gave him gas. Maybe Ms. Mason annoyed him. Maybe discussing his wife with Eric Zalway was so depressing he had decided to leave her. Or maybe Tommy Beller had simply wanted to beat the traffic.

I wandered into the kitchen for another beer. Something I could not see bothered me like a shadow at the corner of my eye. I tried to see it, but trying made the shadow disappear. I was trying to find it again when Keri Wenn called.

"Sorry, pal. No hits on the VIN."

"Did you check Mexico?"

"Checked. Nothing in the U.S., Canada, or Mexico. I tried."

I signed off and brooded about Beller's morning clients, who liked him so much, and Samantha Mason, who didn't. I flipped through Mason's interview again and the shadow snapped into focus.

"Here he complained he couldn't waste time, but he had plenty of time for the phone. He spent too much time on the phone if you ask me."

I called Jess Byers.

She said, "You get the notes?"

"I did, thanks. I have a timeline question."

"Go for it."

"Your timeline shows two calls between Beller and his wife, one that morning and one in the afternoon, and four calls between Beller and Janley, three that morning and one in the afternoon."

"Just so you know, I'm drinking."

"Did Beller make or receive other calls that day?"

Jessica snorted.

"Dude. Like I'd remember? It's been *FIVE YEARS*."

She'd been drinking, all right.

"Can you check?"

"Wait, hold on, what?"

I heard a voice behind her.

"Check yourself. We sent it."

"Sent what?"

"Scans of his billing statements and stuff. We sent it."

"You sent the interviews."

"They're in the same attachment. If you can't find it, call back, otherwise my martini is getting warm."

"Add ice."

"You're gross."

The scans were in a folder labeled SCANS. Three months of Thomas Beller's cell phone statements were included, up to and including the day he disappeared. As with all phone bills, the statements showed the outgoing or incoming numbers, the times the calls were placed or received, and the duration.

The times on the timeline matched the times on the bill. Janley's last call to Beller began and ended before Beller arrived at the Mason residence. The bill showed no other incoming or outgoing calls, yet Samantha Mason complained he'd spent too much time on the phone. She had likely misremembered or exaggerated, but this was what we in the trade called a discrepancy.

I found Samantha Mason's number in the notes and took a shot. Ms. Mason answered on the third ring.

I identified myself, dropped Byers's name, and told her I'd like to drop around to follow up. She told me she'd be happy to speak with me. She sounded thrilled. I bailed on the call before she asked what I wanted to know. I didn't want to question her over the phone. Reading her facial cues and body language was important. Also, she might hang up.

I wandered into the kitchen and ate a third muffin. The honey mustard pistachio. Effort should be rewarded.

9

The day broke with a crisp golden light filling my loft and a headache from too many carbs. The cat was sitting at the foot of my bed. Small bits of dried leaves and plant matter specked his fur.

I said, "Busy night?"

The cat picked his way closer, testing the air for surprises. He moved carefully and with caution as if his world was filled with menace. When he reached me he purred. I ran my fingers along his back.

I said, "Good cat."

He grabbed my hand, bit me, and sprinted downstairs. This was him saying he wanted breakfast.

I pulled on shorts and running shoes, fed the cat, and let myself out to the deck. I warmed up with twelve sun salutes from the hatha yoga, which was pretty much how I've started every day since I mustered out of the Army. The cat liked to watch, so he followed me out.

The sun salutes flowed into tae kwon do katas. I added kung fu and Muay Thai elements, snapping out punches and kicks back and forth across the deck, increasing my speed and intensity until my thighs and shoulders burned. I finished with a hundred push-ups, two hundred crunches, and a deck splattered with sweat.

I said, "Pretty good, huh?"

The cat yawned and walked inside.

I showered, dressed, and was making a blueberry smoothie when the doorbell rang. The cat jumped sideways, spit, and raced upstairs. He wasn't big on guests.

I peeked through the peephole and saw Kevin. He glanced at his watch, looked annoyed, and pressed the bell again as I opened the door.

I said, "Kevin. Did I know you were coming?"

Kevin held up a manila envelope and managed a grin so tight it looked like a grimace.

"I brought the contract."

I stepped back to let him enter.

"Thanks, but I'm about to leave for Rancha."

"This won't take long."

Kevin swept into the living room. He wore a light gray checked shirt with the sleeves rolled, charcoal slacks, and black Italian loafers. Today's watch appeared to be a Rolex Presidential. The Patek Philippe had the day off. He handed me the envelope and looked around.

"Nice. What do they call little places like this, an A-frame?"

"Yep. That's what they call little places like this."

I slid the contract from the envelope. The document was only three pages, so it didn't take long to read.

I said, "This is a nondisclosure agreement."

Most of my celebrity clients required nondisclosure agreements. NDAs were used to prevent employees from selling or otherwise revealing the celebrity's secrets and personal information.

"It is, yes. For Traci's protection. I'm sure you've signed these before."

Kevin took a pen from his pocket and held it out. I didn't take it.

"I'll sign as soon as my lawyer reviews it. Assuming he gives the okay."

Kevin drew himself taller, annoyed but assured.

"There's nothing confusing about it. I was hoping we could get this settled."

"We will. As soon as my lawyer reviews it."

I had signed a hundred NDAs, but Kevin irritated me. I slipped the contract into the envelope.

The cat growled, low and raspy, and Kevin looked up. The cat was watching from the loft.

Kevin cleared his throat and put away his pen.

"Very well. There's something else I'd like to discuss."

"Sure. What can I do for you?"

"I'd like you to wrap this up. Quickly."

"Wrap up what?"

"This search for her father."

"She hired me yesterday. The search is one day old."

"I'm sure you're a fine detective, but we both know how this will end. I'd like to suggest—for Traci's benefit—you cut to the chase."

"You want me to find him fast."

"Well, that would be ideal, but this is a distraction."

"Her father or me?"

"Take our meetings yesterday. The Palisades and Woodland Hills."

"I remember."

"She didn't sparkle. Investors don't buy muffins. If they buy, they're buying her. A rising star. A promotable commodity. She was distracted."

"You should discuss this with Traci, not me."

He went on as if he hadn't heard.

"Everything she's worked for is peaking. Featured guest spots on national morning television, guest spots on the food channel, investor interest. She is this close—"

He pinched his thumb and forefinger together.

"—but she has to stay focused. Now is not the time for distractions."

The cat made a low guttering sound and raced down the stairs. He skidded to a stop when he reached the living room, arched his back, and crept sideways.

Kevin looked uncomfortable.

"What's wrong with your cat?"

"He has fits."

The cat slipped under the couch, but didn't stop growling. Kevin edged away.

I said, "I don't know what to tell you, Kevin. Learning what happened to her father seems important to her."

Kevin tried to see under the couch but couldn't. He edged farther away.

"Of course it's important to her. Next month marks the tenth anniversary of his disappearance. I get it. But searching for him could go on for weeks, am I right? If you let it."

If I let it.

"You want me to quit?"

"No, absolutely not. She'd only hire someone else."

I didn't like where this was going.

"This is Traci's decision. You should talk to Traci."

"Take two or three days, say, three at the most, and tell her what everyone else has told her. You couldn't find him. He's gone."

I stared. Kevin nodded, hoping I would nod with him, but I didn't. He kept going.

"She'll be disappointed, sure, but she'd be able to focus on what's important. Herself. On being as successful as I know she can."

I said, "It's time to leave, Kevin. Say good-bye."

Kevin didn't look assured anymore. He looked nervous.

He said, "Find the man later if you like. Search all you want after the deals are set. Doesn't this make more sense?"

I took a step toward him.

"Out."

The cat growled louder and Kevin wet his lips.

"Traci's paying you ten thousand dollars, correct? End this now and I'll pay you fifteen."

I stepped close fast, rolled his right hand behind his back, and walked him to the door.

He said, "Hey."

I didn't roll his hand hard, but he gave a little eep. I pulled the door and shoved him out.

He said, "This is in Traci's best interest."

"Leave or I'll beat you to death."

"I'll tell her I was here and why I came, so don't think you can rat me out."

"Man, go."

I closed the door.

Outside, he said, "Asshole."

A few seconds later a car door slammed and he pulled away.

The cat crept from under the couch, flopped onto his side, and licked his anus.

I said, "Good cat."

I took two Tylenol and made the long drive to Rancha.

10

Rancha, California, used to be a prime shooting location in the heyday of studio Westerns. Its dry, rolling hills had been dotted with Old West town sets, false-front saloons, and ranch house facades. Then Westerns fell out of favor and the false fronts and locations were redeveloped as micro-ranches for Angelenos trying to escape the traffic and population crush of Greater Los Angeles. I hoped the escapees found what they sought, but they probably hadn't.

My map app guided me off the freeway and north along a two-lane road past scattered homes, building supply outlets, and convenience stores with signs saying LOTTO and BEER. Many of the homes had horse trailers in their yards, but I saw no horses. Most of the trailers sat in patches of desiccated weeds and seemed sad. They probably missed the horses.

Samantha Mason's home was a sprawling Spanish ranch house with a beautiful California oak in front, a classic tile roof, and an elegant drive curving around the oak. I parked in the drive and climbed from my car as a giant black-and-white Akita dog and a large bi-color German shepherd charged from the house. The Akita had tiny eyes, a head the size of a bear's, and must've weighed a hundred thirty pounds. The shepherd barked with the rapid-fire thunder of a .50-caliber machine gun laying down suppression fire.

I jumped back into my car. The convertible.

The dogs stopped short, the German shepherd bouncing up and down in place, snarling and barking. The Akita simply stopped and watched me in silence.

Samantha Mason called from the door.

"They don't bite."

That's what they all say.

I said, "What lovely dogs."

She hustled up to the car, hipped her way between the dogs, and stuck out her hand. Samantha Mason was a sturdy woman with short, dark hair and light green eyes. She wore Levi's with rolled cuffs and a pale blue short-sleeved shirt. I made her to be in her late sixties, but she might've been younger. When we shook, she gripped my hand like a pipe wrench.

"I like you better than the other one already."

Byers.

"Thanks for seeing me, Ms. Mason."

"Sammie or Sam. Don't start that Ms. or Miss crap. I don't like it. You're not scared of dogs, are you?"

"Only purse dogs."

"C'mon, stop hiding in the car and I'll introduce you."

She stroked the shepherd's head as I got out.

"This is my baby girl, Buffy. Aren't you a sweet baby girl, Buffy?"

The sweet baby girl's tail wagged and she wiggled with joy.

"And this is my good boy, Daniel. He's my little man."

The Akita didn't wiggle or wag. He stood as still as a concrete bear and stared into my eyes.

Samantha Mason said, "See? That wasn't so bad. Let's go make ourselves comfortable."

Buffy raced into the house ahead of us. Daniel walked directly behind me. My little man.

A paver tile entry hall led to a large family room with exposed posts and beams, a long bar, and expensive furniture. The floor and the furniture were littered with dog toys. Buffy jumped onto the couch, pinned a giant toy snake with her paws, and began ripping the snake's white stuffing out. Gutting it.

Samantha Mason said, "You want a pop or a highball?"

"I'm good, thanks."

She dropped onto a reclining chair.

"Sit wherever it fits and tell me how I can help. Wasn't the man declared dead?"

"Yes, ma'am. Dead by decree, but questions remain."

I sat in a leather club chair that probably cost more than all the furniture I owned. Daniel followed me to the chair but didn't sit or lay. He stood facing me and stared. I tried to ignore him.

"His daughter asked me to review the case. She hopes to learn what happened."

"Must be terrible, not knowing, but I told the Byers woman everything I know. The sheriffs, too, back when it happened."

"I brought a transcript of your interview if you'd like to refresh your memory."

I reached into my jacket for the transcript. When I reached, Daniel licked his lips and Buffy leaped to her feet, letting loose a barrage of .50-cal barks.

Samantha Mason slapped her hands and shouted.

"Manners!"

Buffy returned to gutting the snake, but Daniel's anthracite eyes seemed darker.

I said, "These dogs are something."

Samantha Mason nodded.

"Daniel here caught three coyotes the other night and snapped their backs like matchsticks. Just ripped those poor things to pieces. You have a dog?"

"A cat."

"Oh. Well, cats are fine. Can't have one with Daniel."

I lifted out the transcript.

"Anyway, the transcript."

She waved it away.

"Don't need it. He was unfriendly and rude. He basically told me to leave him alone. The way he carried on, I'm surprised he even bothered to show up."

"I'm curious about something you told Ms. Byers."

"Ask away."

"You said he spent too much time on the phone."

"That's right. With all his talk about being in a hurry, there he was, yapping away when he should've been working. I didn't like it."

She spoke with certainty.

I said, "He was on the phone. This is something you remember."

"Yes, and I didn't like it."

She seemed so certain another possibility occurred to me.

"Was this your house phone he used?"

"Lord, no. His phone."

So much for another possibility.

"You saw him using his cell phone?"

She frowned.

"I did. What is unclear about this?"

"Thing is, there's no record he used his phone while he was here."

Samantha Mason shifted and the recliner squeaked.

The shepherd's head came up and swung toward me. The Akita's fur rippled. I should've worn body armor.

Samantha Mason's voice turned cool.

"Then the record is wrong. Do you think I'm making this up?"

"No, ma'am. What happened here is important and only you know what happened. Also, it goes to his frame of mind."

Samantha Mason considered this and nodded. The instant she nodded, Buffy returned to killing the snake and Daniel returned to staring.

She said, "I was annoyed what with his rudeness, but it was hot that day. I went to see how he was doing and brought a bottle of water. I thought it would be a nice thing to do."

"Sure. A nice gesture."

"I expected to find him adding Freon or whatever they do, but there he was, by the tree, yapping away. It made me mad."

Everything about Samantha Mason spelled authentic. Her eyes, body language, and manner were genuine. She might be mistaken, but she believed what she was saying.

I said, "Could he have been checking email or texting?"

"You don't hold a phone to your ear and move your jaw for email. I saw him yapping away and came inside. Mad."

"Did you hear what he was saying?"

"Too far. He was way over by that tree."

She gestured to a tree neither of us could see.

I looked at Daniel. Daniel gazed back. Probably thinking about killing coyotes.

I tried to think of more questions, but only one question came to mind and she couldn't answer it.

"That's about it, Ms. Mason. Thank you."

"That's all you wanted to know? About him using his phone?"

"Yes, ma'am. That's it."

"Well, he used it one other time, too. When he left."

"You saw him on his phone a second time?"

"I was so annoyed I watched him leave. He was on his phone when he drove away. I thought, look, there he is, complaining to someone else. I felt guilty later, you know, when I found out he vanished, but I was angry."

Two calls, neither of which showed on the billing record.

"You've given me a lot to think about, Ms. Mason. Thanks again."

Buffy and Daniel walked me to my car. Samantha Mason waved as I drove away, and I waved back, but I didn't drive far. I pulled over when I reached the main road and called Phil Janley.

"Did Tommy have a work phone?"

Janley hesitated.

"A what?"

"A second cell phone he used for work. So he wouldn't get business calls on his personal cell."

Janley hesitated again and laughed.

"We didn't have the money for second phones. Where'd you get this idea?"

"Samantha Mason saw him using a phone twice after he spoke with you, but those calls don't appear on the billing record."

"She's confused. Tommy didn't have two phones."

"She doesn't seem confused."

Another hesitation.

"You talked to her?"

"I just left her."

"Maybe she saw him talking to me."

"The last time he spoke with you was before he reached her home. The calls she remembers came later."

"I don't know what to tell you. If Tommy had a second phone, I didn't know about it and I would've known. She's mistaken or confused."

"Okay, Phil, thanks."

"You want me to ask Georgie?"

"I'll ask her, but thanks."

I didn't think Ms. Mason was mistaken or confused.

I hung up and wondered if anyone else had seen Thomas Beller on calls that didn't appear on his billing record. I wondered if they remembered and knew who he called.

11

Diana Landau didn't answer, so I left a message. Steadman Collin was happy to talk, but didn't recall Beller using a phone. I saw no point in contacting Tyre's housekeeper, so this left Eric Zalway, who had spent more face time with Beller than the others. I checked the interview list for his number and dialed. A young female answered with an exaggerated, world-weary tone.

"I hope this isn't a robocall."

I said, "I'm not a robot. Promise."

She giggled like a teenager.

"Is this Darin? Darin, is that you?"

"Sorry, not Darin. I'm calling for Eric. Is he available?"

"Sorry. I don't know an Eric."

I read off the number.

She said, "Uh-huh. That's me, but I'm not Eric. Somebody gave you the wrong number."

"How long has this been you?"

"Since summer. How long has this been you?"

"Some days, too long. Some days, not long enough."

She giggled again.

"I hope you find Eric."

"Me, too."

I hung up and thought about it. Eric Zalway had been a senior at UCLA when Byers interviewed him. Five years later, he might be any-where, but he likely had family in the area. In the age of robocalls and spam, most people opted out of listing their numbers, but an internet directory search produced a listing for a Frank and Toni Zalway. I hit the call button and waited.

A quiet male voice answered.

I said, "Mr. Zalway?"

"Yes?"

"Are you related to Eric Zalway?"

Frank Zalway was silent for several seconds.

"My son. Who is this?"

I identified myself and explained I was following up on an interview Eric had given to Jessica Byers regarding a man named Thomas Beller.

Mr. Zalway's voice lightened.

"Oh, sure, the man who disappeared. This was when, almost five years ago?"

"Eric spoke with Ms. Byers five years ago, yes, sir. Mr. Beller disap-peared ten years ago."

"He's still missing?"

"Yes, sir, which is why I'm trying to reach Eric."

"I remember Ms. Byers. Eric was excited when she contacted him. He had no idea the man had disappeared."

"Yes, sir. Anyway, the number I have for Eric isn't good. Could I ask for his current number?"

Frank Zalway took a slow breath.

"Well, I have no number to give. Eric isn't with us anymore."

I knew Eric Zalway was dead the moment he said it.

"I'm sorry."

A voice mumbled behind him. Frank Zalway answered the voice, but the only word I understood was his son's name. Eric. Then he spoke to me.

"Yes, well, be that as it may, is there anything I can help you with?"

"Not really, no, sir. I had some follow-up questions about Mr. Beller."

The voice behind him spoke again.

Mr. Zalway said, "Mm-hm. You might ask his friend, Lori. She might be able to help."

"Who's Lori?"

Zalway spoke again, but to the voice.

"Wasn't that her name, Lori? Laura? Something with an *L*."

The voice mumbled and Zalway returned.

"Lori. You might ask Lori."

"Lori is who?"

"She worked the counter like Eric. She had some sort of interaction with Mr. Beller as well."

After learning Beller arrived at Samantha Mason's home with a SurfMutt cup, Byers contacted the owner, a man named Martin Rast, and obtained the names of three employees who had worked the lunch shift on the day Beller visited Ms. Mason. Byers interviewed all three, but only Eric Zalway remembered.

I said, "Lori worked with Eric at the SurfMutt?"

"At the SurfMutt, yes, but a later shift. It was the later shift, wasn't it? Dinner?"

The voice mumbled and he mumbled back until I interrupted.

I said, "Lori spoke with Mr. Beller?"

"As I recall, she did. She didn't remember him as fondly as Eric, which put Eric off. He felt she wasn't being truthful."

"About what?"

"Seeing Mr. Beller? I don't really know."

"Eric didn't mention Lori in the interview."

"Well, Eric didn't know they'd met until after the interview. Remember, Eric didn't know Mr. Beller was missing until Ms. Byers told him, when was it, five years after the fact? Word spread, I guess, and Lori called. Or did Eric call her? Do you remember?"

The voice mumbled, so I interrupted again.

"So Lori worked the counter that evening and Mr. Beller returned?"

"That's our understanding."

"And she spoke with him?"

"There was some sort of interaction, but I can't say for sure. Eric was vague."

Eric being vague didn't sound good.

"Okay. Do you know Lori's last name?"

"I don't. Eric felt rather cool toward her after they talked, so I guess I misspoke. They weren't actually friends."

I couldn't think of more to ask, so I expressed my condolences and lowered the phone. I wondered why Eric had doubted Lori's story. Maybe Beller had struck up a conversation and asked her to run away with him to Bakersfield. I doubted it, but I wanted to find out.

SurfMutt Burgers & Tacos was a square, white building surrounded by a gravel parking lot large enough for a couple of Kenworth eighteen-wheelers. An asphalt skate park and a basketball court sat across the street. A lawn mower repair shop and an empty brick building with broken windows flanked the hamburger stand, but weren't close. Everything was spread apart and shabby.

A tall sign on the SurfMutt's roof showed a cartoon dog hanging ten with a burger in one paw, a shake in the other, and a tongue-wagging grin on its face. The sign was faded. A long roof soffit like the bill of a cap shaded customers ordering and picking up food at glass windows, but seating choices were limited to your car and three small tables. I parked between two pickup trucks and joined the line at the order window.

Inside, a cook wearing a Dodgers cap backward worked the grill with easy grace while a younger cook in a black hairnet sliced tomatoes. A young woman wearing a yellow SurfMutt T-shirt and SurfMutt cap took orders and filled drink cups. The older cook wrapped burgers and tacos as he made them, scooped fries into bags, and pushed orders through the pickup window. Each time he pushed an order he shouted a number.

"Nine!"

"Ten!"

"Eleven!"

I watched him work until I reached the order window.

The counter attendant wore four rings on her left hand, three rings on her right, and large hoop earrings. A handwritten sign propped inside the glass beside her window read: *T-shirts $18, caps $12.*

She spoke with mechanical precision.

"Welcome to SurfMutt. Take your order?"

"A ChiliMutt, no cheese, extra pickles, and a small iced tea."

"Single or double?"

"Double."

"Double ChiliMutt, no cheese, extra pickles, and a small iced tea. Shaka fries?"

"What's a shaka fry?"

"We dust'm with surf spice. They kinda taste like pineapple."

"No fries."

"No fries. Number sixteen."

I paid. She counted out change, scooped ice into a cup, and filled it with tea.

I said, "Is Martin Rast still the owner?"

The cooks glanced over. The older cook had hard eyes and a homemade tat on his neck. He pushed an order through the pickup window.

"Fourteen!"

The counter attendant said, "Yeah. What's wrong?"

"I'm looking for someone who used to work here. He might be able to help."

The younger cook finished slicing, wiped his knife on a dirty towel, and edged closer to the older cook. The older cook flipped a row of sizzling meat patties with a steel spatula, added more patties to the grill, and passed the spatula to the younger cook. He came to the order window.

"You police?"

I put a card on the counter and turned it to face him.

"Nope. Mr. Rast helped a friend of mine with a matter five years ago. I'm following up."

"Who you looking for?"

"A woman who worked here about ten years ago. Mr. Rast will know."

The cook shot a smirk at his younger partner.

"I been here sixteen years. Try me."

The people waiting at the pickup window gave me blank-eyed stares. The people in line behind me shifted.

The order taker said, "Jaime, c'mon, we got people waiting."

Jaime ignored her and asked again.

"Who you looking for?"

"Did you know Eric Zalway?"

The cook's hard eyes darkened.

"*Sí*. Very well."

"A young woman worked here when Eric worked here. Her first name was Lori or Laura."

The younger cook glanced at me.

The young woman said, "Jaime, I got a line here."

Jaime turned to the grill, scooped two bags of fries, added them to two cartons with burgers, and shoved the cartons through the pickup window.

"Fourteen! Fifteen!"

He muttered something in Spanish to the younger guy, picked up my card, and tipped his head toward the rear.

"Around back. To your right."

The kid checked me again as he flipped burgers.

I walked around the right side of the building and found an open door in the rear. Jaime was waiting in a little storage room, reading my card. He glanced up as I approached.

"Eric was *un buen tío*, you know?"

"A good dude."

"He became a teacher. That was his dream. To teach little kids."

He offered the card back, but I motioned him to keep it.

"Lori or Laura? Do you know her?"

"Does this have to do with the missing man?"

The younger cook peeked at us, then ducked away.

"It might. Eric told his parents someone named Lori or Laura met the missing man here later the same day."

"No shit?"

"She was working the evening shift."

Jaime made an *mm* sound, thinking about it.

"Trouble, that one. Mr. Rast caught her stealing. Fired her ass."

"So you know her."

"Worked here five or six months."

He touched his head.

"Cabeza hueca."

"An airhead."

"Name was Lori Chance when she was here, but she got married. I think she goes by Sanchez."

"Is she still in Rancha?"

"Last I know, she was at the liquor store over here by the builder's supply, the big superstore with the nursery. You can't miss it. If they caught her dipping, too, maybe they know where she is."

I nodded.

"Okay. Thanks."

"My boy, Eric. I trained him. Man, when he left for UCLA I was so proud. He had a future, you know?"

I nodded again.

"How did Eric die?"

His mouth hardened, but his eyes were sad.

"Car. Up in Malibu Canyon."

He made a little diving gesture with his hand, like Eric had gone off the road and over the edge. The ravines were deep up in Malibu Canyon.

"Thanks for the help."

"Hang on."

He walked back to the front and returned with my order.

He said, "Sixteen."

I carried the food to my car and ate in the parking lot. The burger was good, but I didn't enjoy it. The younger cook and the counter attendant snuck glances at me. The men at the tables studied me, too. Everyone at the little hamburger stand watched me drive away.

12

Camille's Discreet Liquor and Waldo's Quik Stop Minimart shared a small, cinder-block building across from one of those giant home improvement superstores. Their glass fronts were papered over with ads and signs and their entrances were at opposite corners of the building. I parked outside the liquor store between an ancient beige Chevelle and a gleaming black Lexus, found Camille's number online, and called. A female voice answered.

"Discreet Liquor."

"Lori, please."

"This is Lori."

I hung up and waited. A wall-mounted air conditioner jutted from the side of the building like a knobby ear. It dripped.

A couple of minutes later, a short man in khaki work clothes came out carrying a six-pack like a bowling ball. He climbed into the Chevelle and raced away like he had a score to settle. As the Chevelle ripped away, two kids in short pants and T-shirts came out of the minimart, eating popsicles. They looked my way and nudged each other. The shorter kid called out.

"Hey. Is that a Ferrari?"

"It's a Corvette."

"Corvettes don't look like that."

"It's an old Corvette."

The taller kid nudged the first.

"It's a '67 Stingray, dummy. Don't you know anything?"

"Eat me. You see how dirty it is? The dirt confused me."

These kids, huh?

Thirty seconds later, a woman in a business suit came out of Camille's with three bottles of wine in a cardboard wine carrier. She slid into the Lexus and I went into Camille's.

The liquor store was cramped and brutally cold. Liquor lined the wall behind the counter and a cooler packed with beer and energy drinks filled the back wall. A woman maybe thirty years old sat behind the counter, bundled in a heavy fleece sweater. A little sign saying SMILE—UR ON CAMERA was tacked to the wall behind her. The woman glanced up when I entered.

I said, "Why is it so cold in here?"

"My fuckhead boss."

Just like that.

I cocked my head, looking at her as if maybe she was familiar. She grinned.

"What?"

"I know you."

She rolled her eyes.

"Bullshit."

"I'm serious. You worked at the SurfMutt, didn't you?"

Her eyes grew wide. Surprised.

"A million years ago."

"Lori, right? Lori Chance?"

Her grin flashed again, surprised but pleased.

"No way! I mean, yeah. It's Sanchez now, and before that, Schneider, but—"

She hesitated, shaking her head.

"I'm sorry. I don't remember you."

I eased off the grin and took out a card.

"You would've if we'd met, but we haven't. I know you from Eric Zalway."

Her smile fell as she read the card.

"A private investigator?"

"Remember Thomas Beller? You spoke with Eric about him a few years ago."

Her eyes came up and now she looked wary. Looking wary meant she was going to lie.

She said, "No, I don't think so."

You see?

"Eric told his parents you did. I'm trying to find Mr. Beller, so I'm hoping you can help."

She glanced at the door as if she thought someone was listening.

"The air-conditioner guy?"

"Right. The man who disappeared. He had lunch at the SurfMutt, which is when Eric met him, and came back for dinner, which is where you come in. Remember?"

"I don't know where he is."

"Maybe you talked to him. Maybe he told you where he was going or his plans for the evening."

She glanced at the door again. The wary eyes made her look nervous.

"He didn't tell me anything. He ate."

"He ate."

"It's a hamburger stand. People go there to eat."

"So you and Mr. Beller didn't talk?"

She shrugged, like the question was stupid.

"I took his order and made change. What's the big deal?"

"Him eating was so impressive you remembered him five years later? He must've eaten a lot of shaka fries."

Now she looked pissed.

"I remembered his van. He parked this big fat-ass van right in front of me."

She spread her hands high and wide like she was framing the image.

"Heating and air. Right in front of me."

"So you and Eric talked about his van?"

"I don't remember. I also don't like you coming in here with these questions. I have work to do."

I said, "Eric was upset after he spoke with you, so I'm guessing you talked about something more memorable than a fat-ass van."

"Eric's dead. How would you know if he was upset?"

"His father told me. He also told me you didn't remember Mr. Beller as fondly as Eric."

Lori rolled her eyes.

"Eric. What a douche."

The door chime cut us off. A thin woman with washed-out hair and a large purse entered, hesitated when she saw us, then lowered her eyes and trudged to the counter. I drifted away, pretending to look at wine. The woman asked for a pack of Newports and three airplane-sized bottles of vodka. She fidgeted as Lori rang her up, stowed the cigs and bottles in her purse, and kept her eyes down as she left. Lori shook her head.

"Same every day, three bottles. She'll drain'm and toss'm before she gets home."

Lori looked tired when she offered her observation.

I said, "Lori."

"Are you still here?"

"Beller had a family. They want to know what happened to him. Can you help?"

Lori seemed to think about it.

"His family hired you?"

"Yep."

"You get paid to find people?"

"Among other things."

She worried her lip and picked up my card.

"Licensed private investigator means you're a detective? You solve whodunits? Mysteries and stuff?"

"Sort of."

She worried the lip some more.

"Maybe you can solve a mystery for me. I've got a three-year-old and two exes who won't give me a dime. I've got bills, no money, and I'm stuck living with my mother, who takes care of my kid so I can sit here praying a drug addict doesn't murder me for what's in this drawer."

She patted the cash drawer as she stared at me.

"What's the solution, Mr. Detective? Whodunit?"

I took out my wallet and placed a hundred-dollar bill on the counter.

"Benjamin Franklin."

Lori reached for the bill, but I pinned it in place.

"What did you tell Eric?"

She hesitated, but only for a moment.

"I asked if the AC guy did anything creepy at lunch."

"Why would you ask if Beller did something creepy?"

"The dude scoped chicks at the skate park for almost two hours right in front of me. It creeped me out, him sitting out front like a big ol' toad watching flies."

I pictured the skate park across from the SurfMutt and a big ol' toad scoping high school girls with Lori behind the order window, watching him scope.

"The skate park across the street?"

"Yeah. Kids used to hang there after school."

A middle-aged man watching teenage girls might be creepy, but watching girls didn't seem outrageous enough to make Beller memorable.

"Did he do more than watch?"

She glanced at the hundred again.

"He picked up a girl. This was later. After dark. But I saw them, right in front of me."

"At the SurfMutt?"

"At the skate park!"

She bugged her eyes for emphasis, the eyes letting me know this was true and actual dirt.

"The other kids had gone. She was on her phone and she started walking. He pulled out and stopped beside her. Then she got in and off they went."

"So he gave her a lift."

Lori smirked and cocked her head.

"You think? I was dying to know, so I called her."

"This was someone you knew?"

"Yeah, a little. Anyway, she didn't call back, so I called a couple of days later and she *still* didn't call back. Then I ran into her over by Barg's—"

"What's Barg's?"

"This shithole dive bar where her mom worked. Her mom was low-rent trash. A convicted criminal. Anyway, I was like, 'Hey, who was the creepy dude who picked you up, was he cool, did he try anything?' Guess what she said?"

Lori plowed ahead without waiting for a response.

"She freaked. You don't freak if all you got was a lift. She totally denied it and called me a liar. I'm like, 'Lie? Calm down, girl!' She's like, 'You shouldn't talk shit, I don't know what you're talking about.' I said, 'Girl, I saw you with my own two eyes!'"

She forked her fingers and touched beneath her eyes. Then she smirked.

"I think they did the nasty. She probably charged him."

I felt tired. I wanted to go home and watch television.

"How old was this girl?"

"I was a senior, so she was a sophomore. Maybe fifteen?"

Fifteen. Great.

"Has she mentioned it since?"

"Not to me. I don't have anything to do with those people. They're trash."

"Okay. I need her name."

She tugged at the hundred. I let her have it and the bill disappeared. She glanced at the door.

"You won't mention me, right? You didn't hear this from me. You've never even met me, right?"

I made a zipping move across my lips.

"Anya Given. I don't know what her last name is now, but then it was Given. She was a loser. A total freak."

Lori rolled her eyes.

"Do you have her phone number?"

"You're kidding, right? I stay away from low-rent trash like her."

"Is she still in Rancha?"

"No idea. I stay away."

The door chimed and an overweight man wearing dark slacks and a white dress shirt entered. He charted a course for the cooler with determined purpose. I lowered my voice.

"One more thing. When you were watching Beller, do you recall if he used his phone?"

"Dude. This was ten years ago. No, somehow the phone thing didn't register. Sorry."

"Okay."

I took out a second card and placed it in front of Lori with the blank side up.

"I might have more questions. Could I have your cell?"

She wrote out her cell and grinned as she handed back the card.

"If you think up enough questions, I'm available for dinner."

I tucked the card into my wallet and went to my car. The sun felt good. I thought about Tommy Beller offering a ride to a fifteen-year-old girl. I wanted to ask Anya Given what had happened and find out why she freaked. I didn't think I'd like the answers, but you never know. I sat in my car in the sun and went to work trying to find her.

13

A directory search produced no listing for Anya or any Given. Searches of the usual social media platforms also gave me nothing. Maybe Anya and her low-rent mother had moved to Beirut. I googled Barg's, hoping to get a line on Anya's mother, but Barg's had been closed for six years. Perfect. Why should anything be easy? Next, I phoned a friend at the Department of Motor Vehicles. If Anya's last name was still Given and she possessed a valid California driver's license, Dickie Timmons would have her information. Dickie was an upper-level manager and True Blue Dodgers fan. I didn't call his office. I phoned his personal cell.

A client I helped out of an ugly situation gave me primo seats in the exclusive Dodgers' Dugout Club at the start of every season. The Dugout Club offered the best seats in the stadium, all-you-could-eat gourmet food, and a chance to mingle with celebrities and retired ballplayers. Seats in the Club were crazy expensive, so Dickie traded information for tickets. This would get him fired if anyone found out, but Dickie bled Dodger blue and the blue ran deep.

I said, "Hey, Dickie, Elvis. Got a minute?"

"Hang on."

These were Dickie's first words every time I called. I had never asked why he wanted me to hang on and didn't know. I hung on.

Dickie returned twenty seconds later.

"If you're calling for the reason I think you're calling, I've got all the minutes you want. What do you need?"

You see?

"Whatever you have on an Anya Given, A-N-Y-A, G-I-V-E-N."

"Middle name, date of birth, DL number?"

"First and last are all I have."

"Give me five and I'll hit you back."

I lowered my phone and waited.

The overweight man in the white shirt left Camille's with a sixer of Miller High Life and drove away in a green Buick SUV. Two minutes later, a black Dodge Challenger parked by the minimart. The driver and his passenger were tall, bony guys with squinty faces and long black hair. The driver squinted at me. His passenger got out and squinted at me, too. Maybe their eyes hurt. The passenger ducked into the minimart. The driver sucked a silver vape stick and exhaled a heavy white cloud of aerosol mist that filled the Challenger like oily fog. I wondered if he'd suffocate. The passenger returned, slid into the fog, and the Challenger backed away. The passenger squinted at me as they left. The driver probably squinted, too, but I couldn't see him through the fog.

Anya Given's DMV file arrived two minutes later. The file contained her current driver's license photo, description, address, phone, and driving history. The photo showed a solemn young woman with a thin face and lifeless sandy hair. Anya Jo Given was twenty-five years old, five-two, a hundred and five pounds, and had never received a traffic citation or reported an accident. Her address and phone were local. This was next-level detective work at its finest.

I called.

Anya's phone rang six times before a ragged male voice answered. The voice sounded older and gruff from cigarettes.

He said, "Yeah?"

"I'm calling for Anya. Is she available?"

I heard breathing. The breathing sounded crackly.

"Who?"

"Anya. I'm trying to reach Anya Given."

"No Anya here. Sorry."

I read off Anya's number.

The voice said, "That's us, but this is a salvage yard. No Anya."

"A salvage yard?"

"Yeah. You got the number wrong."

I thanked him, plugged her address into my map app, and followed the main road up through the center of town. A couple of minutes later I was on smaller roads passing more horse trailers and storage buildings until I arrived at a large metal building the size of an airplane hangar.

I stared at the building with my engine idling. The words R&R SALVAGE were painted on the building in ten-foot letters. Two heavy-duty tow trucks and half a dozen cars sat in a fenced parking area outside a couple of enormous sliding doors. The doors were open. Thirty or forty rusting cars and trucks filled a field behind the building along with a crane, a flatbed trailer truck, and a large hydraulic car crusher. A salvage yard.

I left my car in the parking area and entered the building. The interior looked like an auto body shop, only bigger. Two men in the shadows were laughing while a third sorted bolts in a greasy cardboard box. The bolt sorter glanced up.

I said, "Office?"

I followed his point to a small, windowless office with three metal desks and a swivel fan on a file cabinet. A fleshy woman in tight jeans sat at one of the desks, murmuring into a phone. A large man with jowls and a two-day stubble sat behind another desk, sucking on an unlit cigar and reading something on his cell phone. Stacks of files and folders filled the third desk. The man and the woman looked up when I entered. The woman lowered her voice even more.

I nodded at the man.

"We spoke a few minutes ago. About Anya."

The man put his cell phone aside and leaned back. His chair squeaked.

"She's still not here."

"I'm thinking she used to work here."

The man glanced at the woman. She was watching me as she murmured into the phone.

The man said, "Nope. No Anya now or ever. We're fresh out of Anyas."

The woman finished her conversation and leaned back, maybe thinking I would do something interesting.

I said, "Not now. A couple of years ago. Maybe she used to work here, but left. Possible?"

"Nope."

The woman said, "Who's he looking for?"

"Someone named Anya."

The woman said, "Oh."

I hooked a thumb toward the door.

"Maybe one of the guys here remembers her. Could I ask them?"

The woman said, "No, you may not. Our insurance doesn't permit it."

The man studied her for a moment and yawned.

"Brother, there's your answer. Adios."

Adios.

I considered options as I headed back to town. Putting up wanted posters and questioning random people might work. If people held out, an old-fashioned pistol-whipping might do the trick. Or I could call it a day and head home. Calling it a day seemed the best choice.

Traffic built as I approached the town center, mostly drivers heading home from work or parents with kids running after-school errands. Three teenage girls outside a frozen yogurt shop waited to cross the street. I braked, waved them across, and saw the black Challenger in my mirror four cars back. I probably wouldn't have noticed it, but the

Challenger straddled the centerline. The driver was craning his head, trying to see past the cars ahead of him.

The girls crossed and I crept forward. The Challenger was so far over the centerline an oncoming car blew its horn. The Challenger slid back into its lane, but drifted over the centerline again a few seconds later. Another oncoming car honked and the squint flipped them off. The car behind me turned, leaving the Challenger three cars back. The squint drifted over the line again and our eyes met in the mirror.

The cars in front of me moved, but I stayed on the brake and watched the Challenger in the mirror. The driver realized I was watching him, jerked into the oncoming lane, and floored it up the line. He downshifted, caught rubber, and roared past. The driver and his passenger clocked me and revved the engine like they'd seen too many *Fast and the Furious* movies.

I was thinking up ways to find Anya when I felt a sudden jolt of inspiration and detoured to the liquor store. Lori looked up from her phone when I entered.

I said, "Want to make another hundred?"

She grinned.

"You don't have to pay me to go out with you."

"Not that. I had an idea."

She grinned wider.

"I'm up for anything. Try me."

"You went to high school with Anya?"

"She was two years behind me, but yeah. Everybody here goes to the same school."

"One of your old friends might know how to reach her."

Now she looked wary.

"My friends weren't her friends. Trust me."

"Ask. Get Anya's current contacts, there's another hundred in it."

She shook her head before I finished.

"No. Uh-uh. I'm not asking about Anya or any other Given. I don't want anything to do with those people."

"You don't have to tell them why. Tell them you thought about her the other day and wondered what happened to her "

Lori rolled her eyes.

"I know how to do it. I don't want to."

"I'll make it two hundred."

Lori glanced at the door and crossed her arms. She didn't like it, but she was thinking about it.

"Two hundred?"

"Two hundred."

"Two hundred plus dinner."

"No dinner. I have a girlfriend."

"It's gotta be cash. Don't waste my time with a check."

"It'll be cash."

She finally shrugged.

"I guess I can ask."

I left the liquor store and headed for home. The sun was beginning to sink and the air slid past like a warm caress, but I felt obvious and exposed, as if someone or something was watching me. I checked the mirror. I expected the Challenger to roar up behind me, but nothing threatening appeared. I should've looked more closely. I should have seen what I did not see. I drove faster, but I couldn't outrun the feeling.

14

The Kill Car

The most common car in Los Angeles was the white Toyota Camry sedan, followed closely by the white Honda Civic. Cars like these were as common as roadside pebbles; part of the landscape; anonymous. This was his kill car.

This specific vehicle was eleven years old, well used, and needed a wash, though it wasn't dirty enough to draw attention. It bore no dents, scratches, decals, or memorable characteristics. The car's California license plate and registration stickers appeared in good order, though they were false. Sunscreens on the side windows obscured the driver's face.

The kill car cruised with the flow of traffic, obeyed all traffic laws, and found the yellow Corvette at the liquor store across from the builder's superstore. The man within the kill car suddenly felt exposed. He wanted to punch the gas and race away, but he didn't. He touched his blinker as gently as a kiss, turned to enter the superstore's parking lot, and studied the yellow car across the road. The driver had feared this day for years and now it had arrived.

Another search.

More questions.

The terrible threat he'd be found.

The kill car's driver tried to calm himself, but his heart pounded with the heavy thunder of marching elephants. Sweat soaked his shirt and he trembled like a nervous dog. He turned up the air conditioner, aimed the vents at his face, and closed his eyes.

The man in the yellow car probably wouldn't find any more than the other detectives, but the man was here, he was asking questions, and this made him dangerous.

The kill car's whisper rode the wind from the vents.

"We have to keep an eye on him."

The driver murmured.

"I know. I'm trying to figure out how."

"See who he talks to. Learn what they tell him. Stop him if we have to."

"He went to the SurfMutt."

"Where else?"

"Where they all go. The old clients, probably."

The kill car's tone sharpened.

"'Probably' won't save us. We need to know what he's doing."

The driver's head pounded. The man was a professional investigator named Elvis Cole. They'd seen his yellow Corvette twice, once passing through town and now at the liquor store. They couldn't follow the man; a professional would see them. They also couldn't drift around town like a listless shark, hoping they'd spot him. The driver had an idea and checked the time. Wasn't late. They'd have to make a stop, see if his idea would fly. A lot had changed.

"We won't have to follow him. I know what to do."

"Big talk. You've been asleep for ten years."

The kill car's driver felt a spike of anger. It had been five years since the last detective, not ten, but the driver let it go.

"I can handle it."

Across the street, the detective came out of the liquor store, climbed into his car, and pulled out of the parking lot.

The kill car's whisper turned nasty.

"He's leaving. Where's he going?"

The driver paid little attention. He scrolled through his phone. Shopping for means.

"The freeway? It's late. He's going home."

"We need to know."

"We gotta make a stop. This will work."

"It better. He's dangerous."

"We're dangerous."

"Yes. Yes, we're dangerous."

The kill car growled. The driver let the car drift forward and they left. They had to make two stops. The kill car's driver handled it.

15

Elvis Cole

I picked up takeout from a Mexican place in the valley. Crispy shrimp chalupas and oxtail barbacoa, straight out of Mexico City by way of North Hollywood. The food and I were on our way home when Dina Wade called.

"Hi. This is Dina Wade, Traci Beller's assistant. Will you be home this evening?"

Like I'd forgotten she was Traci's assistant.

"Did you tell her about the photos?"

"Um, not yet. Anyway, will you be home?"

"Unless I starve to death before I arrive. Why?"

"Traci has something for you."

"Another contract?"

"I can't say."

"Kevin already delivered a contract. I'm not signing it."

"Um, may I ask why?"

"I don't like Kevin. Feel free to tell him."

"Um, okay. When will you be home?"

"Soon. Tell her to get the photos."

Thirty minutes later, I was setting out the takeout when the door-bell rang. I peeked to see who it was and opened the door.

Traci Beller flashed the famous Traci Beller dimples.

"I brought you a gift."

She held out a large, beautifully wrapped gift basket.

I said, "Muffins?"

The basket was heavy with more fist-sized muffins. If I ate another I'd need new pants.

I said, "This is generous. Thank you."

I carried the basket to the table. Traci saw the takeout and looked disappointed.

"Oh. You're having dinner. I'm sorry."

"No worries. Chalupas and barbacoa. Would you like to join me?"

She eyed the containers as if she wanted to dive in, but shook her head.

"I can't, but thank you. I really just wanted to apologize. Kevin was so out of line this morning."

"He told you."

"Kevin thinks he knows best and he usually does, but sometimes he acts like I'm a child. Today he was stupid. I'm sorry. I hope you won't quit."

She looked worried, so I tried to put her at ease.

"Because of Kevin? No way. How could I give up free muffins?"

She looked relieved.

"Good. I've been worried sick since he told me."

She hesitated, as if she didn't know what to say next.

"Anyway, I also wanted to tell you I'll be in New York for a couple of days. I'm doing a guest spot on the *Today* show. Isn't it great?"

Her eyes held a nervous expectation, as if I wouldn't think it was great.

I said, "Terrific. Congratulations."

"Kevin set it up. I'm flying out tomorrow morning, I do the spot the following morning, and after the show I'm meeting an investor group. Kevin says they're big in SoHo and the Upper West Side. I'm excited."

"That Kevin is something, isn't he?"

She glanced away.

"You think I should fire him, don't you?"

"Not my business."

"Kevin's been there for me since the beginning. I only had ten thousand followers when he offered to manage my career. He's like family."

"I get it."

She glanced away, uneasy and maybe uncomfortable.

"You have a cool house. It feels like you. Anyway, I should go."

"I was going to call. In fact, I did call."

"You did?"

"Your mother has photos of you and your father. She told me if you don't get them she'll throw them out. I asked Dina to tell you. Twice."

Traci frowned.

"When was this?"

"Last night and half an hour ago."

"She didn't tell me."

"She didn't want to upset you. Like Kevin."

Traci closed her eyes.

"They're driving me crazy."

"Also, I have a question. Do you recall if your father had two cell phones?"

She frowned again.

"Why would he have two?"

"Some people have a personal phone and a second phone they use for work."

"I don't think so, but, honestly, I don't remember."

I told her about the discrepancy between the billing statements and Samantha Mason's recollection.

Traci's eyes widened as I told her.

"You went to see Ms. Mason?"

"And the others. She thought your father spent too much time on his phone. She's still upset about it."

"I'll ask Phil. Phil would know."

"I asked him. Phil says he didn't."

"I'll ask my mom. What do you think it means?"

"It might not mean anything or even be real. Ms. Mason believes what she told me, but people misremember. It happens. We have to check."

She flashed the grin.

"I've dreamed about this day. Someone is *finally* trying to find him."

"There's something else. Remember Eric Zalway? From the Byers report?"

"Of course. What did he say?"

"He's deceased. But a coworker claims your dad returned later that evening and she saw him with someone. If true, this person might provide a legitimate lead."

I didn't tell her the someone was a fifteen-year-old girl who climbed into his van.

Traci stepped back and grinned even wider.

"Hiring you was absolutely the right decision."

"I haven't confirmed this, Traci. It might mean nothing."

Traci stepped closer and touched my arm.

"No. It means everything."

I glanced at her hand and Traci flushed. She stepped back and flushed darker.

She said, "Oh my God. I'm sorry."

"It's okay."

"I'm just—"

She shook her head and backed up even more.

I said, "Breathe and we'll be fine. Want some water?"

Her eyes came up and she studied me.

"I used to go to Rancha all the time. The first time was maybe a week after I got my license. I was sixteen and it was scary. I'd never driven so far on a freeway."

"To see where he disappeared?"

"I don't know. I just wanted to be where he'd been, I guess. I went back a few weeks later and kept going back. I just drove around. I'd drive past Ms. Mason's house and his other clients. I never stopped, but I'd pass real slow."

"A way to be with him."

She fell silent before she continued.

"I never told anyone. My mother would have screamed. And Phil, I thought Phil might tell or want to come, and I wanted to be alone."

Traci hesitated.

"OhmiGod, I sound so weird right now."

"You don't sound weird."

She rolled her eyes.

"Yes, I do."

She glanced away again.

"I never had anyone I could talk to like this, not after Mom wrote him off. I never felt anyone was on my side or understood. Not until now."

I thought she might touch me again, but she didn't.

I said, "You're paying me."

"I know. Which makes me pathetic."

"I'm paid, but I understand. And I'm on your side, but not because you're paying me. Would you like to know why?"

Her smile turned sad.

"You like muffins."

"I didn't know my father. I don't know his name or anything about him. I doubt my mother even knew."

Traci's mouth opened, just a bit, and her eyes searched.

"I am so sorry. Did you try to find him?"

"I spent years trying to find him. I couldn't. Maybe I'll have better luck with yours."

Traci went up on her toes and kissed my cheek.

She said, "I guess we're in it together."

"I guess we are."

"I should go."

I walked her out and stood in the street until her taillights disappeared. The night sky was black and starless. I went inside and studied the basket of muffins and wondered if I could donate them to a homeless shelter.

The cat wasn't home. I missed him, but he was off being a cat. I picked two shrimp from a chalupa, rinsed off the garlic sauce, and put them in his dish.

I opened a Modelo, drank some, and ate the remaining chalupas and most of the barbacoa in the living room. The lights across the canyon glowed like fallen stars and the coyotes were silent. I finished the beer, put the leftovers in the fridge, and went upstairs.

I showered, got into bed, and called Lucy. I told her about Traci Beller driving to Rancha when she was sixteen and the emptiness she must have felt.

Lucy said, "You're talking about you."

Her voice was warm with the lateness of the hour.

I said, "It's different for her."

"How is it different?"

"She knew her father. He raised her and she loved him. He was real. My father wasn't real."

Lucy was silent for a moment.

"How many times did you try to find him?"

"Dozens. Scores. I don't know."

"Loss is loss. If you felt it, it was real."

I didn't respond and Lucy's voice softened even more.

"I wish I could've held you when you were little. I wish I could have helped."

I rubbed my eyes.

"I love you, Lucille."

Loss left a hole and sometimes the hole was so big it couldn't be filled. All we could do was try, but the trying defined us. Trying was everything.

Lucy and I whispered to each other until the hour grew late. The next morning, I kept trying.

16

O n or about the time Traci Beller boarded her flight to New York, I phoned Lori Chance and got her voice mail.

"Call when you get this. I have a question."

Two minutes later I was scrambling eggs with the leftover barbacoa when Lori called. She sounded grumpy.

"You woke me. And no, I haven't found out where stupid Anya lives."

She covered the phone to muffle a shout.

"No chocolate milk! Don't give him chocolate for breakfast! What's wrong with you?!"

She cleared her throat. Phlegm.

"Sorry. My life sucks."

"I need a favor."

"I need a life. Want to trade?"

"Does your high school have a library?"

"So I'm told. I wasn't a library kinda person."

"I want to check their old yearbooks. If I were a former student or parent, it wouldn't be a problem. Since I'm not, high schools frown on unaccompanied men loitering in the stacks."

"I can't do it. I gotta go to work."

"I'm not asking you to do it. I'm asking you to call the school, tell them you're a former student, and ask them to—"

Lori cut me off.

"I know what you want. What does this have to do with Anya?"

"If she was on a team or in a club, one of the other kids might still be friendly with her."

"I already called people. Are you trying to get out of paying me?"

"Did you get the information?"

"Not yet, but I called! People know I asked about her!"

She sounded alarmed.

I said, "Relax. If your friends don't come through, think of this as plan B."

Now she sounded grudging.

"You can have my old yearbook, you want. It's around here somewhere."

"Thanks, but you graduated two years before her. I'd still need to check her junior and senior yearbooks."

"Okay, I get it. You'll have to get a pass at the office, you know. They'll want an ID."

"Give them my name, but don't tell them I'm a private eye working a case. They won't like it."

"I know what to say. What's your time frame?"

I checked the time and eyed the leftovers.

"I'll be there in ninety minutes."

"I should charge you, but I'm holding out for dinner."

"Roll it into the two hundred you haven't earned."

"Live with my mother. See how you like it."

Lori hung up.

I ate the barbacoa and eggs with a tortilla, put out food for the cat, and hit the freeway.

La Rancha High School was a low, flat complex of buildings not far from the skate park. School was in session, so the parking lots and bike racks were filled. Concrete walks connected the buildings and a gym with *La Rancha Scorpions* painted above a fearsome scorpion with huge pincers and a monstrous stinger. Signs at the drive read NO UN-AUTHORIZED ENTRY and VISITORS REPORT TO ADMIN. I parked in the visitors' lot and followed more signs to the administration office.

The office was large, bright, and busy. Neatly dressed adults worked at desks behind a long counter. Half a dozen teenagers sat on plastic chairs facing the counter and most of them didn't look happy. A sign saying VISITORS hung from the ceiling with an arrow pointing at the near end of the counter. I went to the arrow. A tanned woman with glossy lips smiled from her desk. Her nameplate read MS. WALLER.

She said, "May I help you?"

"I hope so. I'd like to see the school's yearbook collection."

Ms. Waller smiled wider and came to the counter.

"You must be Mr. Cole."

She reached across the counter and we shook.

"I take it you spoke with Lori."

Ms. Waller clung to my hand.

"I think this is so sweet. I really do."

I nodded and pried my hand away. A vague response seemed the best response.

"Thank you."

Ms. Waller stepped from behind the counter and took my hand again.

She said, "I don't know Lori, but I can promise you she is over the moon. When are you two getting married?"

Married.

I managed to slip her grip.

"It's a complicated decision."

"Aren't they all? Here. I'll walk you to the library."

Ms. Waller led me out of the office and along a wide, empty hall. Class was in session.

She said, "Now, as I understand it, you want class photos from the years she was here."

"Class photos, groups and clubs, whatever I can find. It might take a while."

"Take as long as you like."

We passed through a glass door into a hall lined with lockers and closed doors.

"I love your idea. A photo montage of her growing from a baby into the woman you'll spend the rest of your life with. You are just the most romantic thing!"

I said, "Mm."

"And you'll show this at the wedding?"

"Whatever Lori wants."

"Smart. From what she told me, I think she's counting on it."

We left the building, entered the next building, and reached the library.

"Here we go."

The library was a large room lined with bookcases and study cubicles. Six or eight tables and floor-to-ceiling stacks filled the center. Three girls huddled at one table, whispering, and two boys slouched at another. Detention. A balding man sat in a swivel chair behind a desk. Ms. Waller introduced me.

"Mr. Cole, this is our librarian, Mr. Toman. Michael, Mr. Cole wants to see some yearbooks. Will you help him, please?"

Toman's chair squeaked as he stood.

"You bet."

Ms. Waller gripped my hand again, wished me a lifetime of happiness, and left me with Mr. Toman.

Toman said, "Which years would you like?"

I told him. Toman went away and returned a few seconds later with four thick volumes with embossed black and red covers. I carried the yearbooks to a study cubical and started with Anya Given's freshman year.

An index at the back of the yearbook made finding each student's photo easy. The index told me Anya appeared on pages eighteen and thirty-nine. Her freshman class photo was on page eighteen. Anya's light brown hair was pulled back and she was smiling. Page thirty-nine showed Anya with three boys and another girl in a group photo of the Frosh Photography Club. The students were identified beneath the photo. I copied the names Trevor Blake, Ricky Santos, Dante Hurwitz, and Carol Topping.

Anya appeared in her sophomore yearbook only once. Her class picture showed Anya with longer, darker hair, and an angry scatter of pimples marring her chin. Her lips were a thin line. The index listed only the single class photo, but I checked the photography club group shot anyway. Blake, Santos, and Topping were still part of the club, but Hurwitz and Anya were missing.

Anya's name didn't appear in either her junior or senior indexes, but I checked the class photo pages and club photos anyway. I didn't find her and wondered if Anya had changed schools.

A loud bell rang. The two boys lurched to their feet as if they'd been tasered and hurried out. The three girls left, too.

I returned the yearbooks to Mr. Toman, avoided Ms. Waller on the way out, and left through a flash mob of students scrambling to their next class.

It was midmorning and I had the names of four people who might help me reach Anya.

Working in a high school parking lot wasn't ideal, so I drove to the SurfMutt and parked where Lori Chance claimed Tommy Beller scoped Anya. I got out of my car and sat at a shaded table. It beat sitting in the sun.

The closed sign was in the window, but Jaime and his assistant were in their little kitchen, prepping for service. Jaime saw me and opened the order window.

"Yo! We ain't open."

"Okay if I sit here while I make a few calls?"

His head bobbed once.

"Yeah. Find the thief?"

Meaning Lori.

His assistant glanced from Jaime to me.

"I did. Thanks for the help."

Jaime wiped his hands and closed the window. The younger cook side-eyed me until Jaime barked an order. The younger cook went back to chopping and I went to work finding the Frosh Photography Club.

17

ars and trucks passed in both directions, but not enough to call it traffic. The skate park was deserted, but a short Latin kid shot baskets behind the sagging chain-link fence while two kids sat cross-legged, watching him. He would bounce the ball twice, fire off a jumper, and sprint for the rebound. Bounce, bounce, shoot. Bounce, bounce, shoot. The old rim had no net, but the kid stripped the hoop every time. A machine.

A light gray car dropped off the female counter attendant as I searched online for Trevor Blake. She smiled when she saw me.

Trevor's Facebook page told me he was stationed in Rota, Spain, with the U.S. Navy. Scratch Trevor. I found Ricky Santos by way of his younger brother, Dennis, who provided Ricky's number. Ricky worked as a Mercedes-Benz salesman in Van Nuys and was willing to talk, but had to call me back in five. I didn't expect him to call me back, but he called in four. Ricky didn't remember Anya Given, but he offered a great deal on a certified pre-owned Mercedes. I passed.

SurfMutt customers began arriving while Ricky made his pitch. Most waited in their cars for the SurfMutt to open, but the more ambitious formed a line at the order window. I was googling Dante Hurwitz when the counter attendant flipped the sign and the SurfMutt opened for business.

I reached Dante Hurwitz through his mother. Hurwitz, who now sold lawn mowers and gardening equipment in Oxnard, didn't remember Anya any better than Ricky Santos.

I was searching for Carol Topping when the black Challenger appeared on the road coming from town. The Challenger slowed as it passed and the squints clocked me. The driver revved his engine, hit the gas, and roared away. Maybe they had a crush on me.

Carol Topping was listed. I was about to tap the call button when Jaime set an order carton and drink on the table.

"Double ChiliMutt, no cheese, extra pickles, and an iced tea. Got a shaka fries here, too, let you try'm. On the house."

"Man, thanks. You didn't have to do this."

Jaime was already heading back to his kitchen.

"Try'm."

I tried them.

The shaka fries had a pleasant salty-sweet taste, but the sweetness wasn't cloying. The hint of pineapple grew on me. Also, the fries were crisp and perfectly cooked. I caught Jaime's eye and raised a hand with my thumb and pinky extended and three middle fingers folded in the classic shaka sign. *All is good, brah.* Jaime tipped his head and continued slinging orders. An older green pickup with two men inside arrived and parked opposite me. The two kids watching the shooter across the street stood and the three started playing.

I called Carol Topping after I finished the fries. Topping remembered Anya, though the two had not been close.

Topping said, "I'm pretty sure she dropped out. She ditched a lot."

"Ditched meaning she cut classes?"

"She was always sick or something. I don't know. She just stopped being around."

I could hear the shrug in her voice.

"Did she transfer to another school?"

"They might've moved. They moved a lot. Her mom was kinda sketchy."

Sketchy.

"Moved out of town?"

"I'm not positive they moved. I'm just saying. Her mom worked all these jobs, but they were kinda poor."

"The sketchy mom."

"Uh-huh."

"What about her dad?"

"I kinda remember she didn't have a dad. It was just her and her mom."

"Would you have an old phone number for her or an address?"

"No, I don't. Sorry."

The green pickup finally opened and the men climbed out. They were weathered guys in their forties who looked like oil rig rough-necks. The driver was a thick, blocky guy and bigger than his passenger, but not by much. He wore an unbuttoned, flower-print Hawaiian shirt over a dingy white T-shirt and his friend wore a faded Voodoo Ranger IPA T-shirt. Both men finished the look with jeans, work boots, and drugstore sunglasses. The Voodoo Ranger took a seat on the table next to mine. The Hawaiian shirt circled my car, checking it out. I watched him as I continued with Carol.

"Okay. Last thing. Do you remember who she used to hang out with?"

"Like, her friends?"

"Yeah. Other than the kids in the photo club."

"Wow. I dunno. I didn't see her much after she left the club, what with being sick or whatever."

"How was she sick?"

"Just—"

She hesitated, figuring out how to describe it.

"—acting out? Cutting class? She might've had problems at home or whatever. I really don't know. It's not like we were close."

The Hawaiian shirt finished inspecting and nodded at me. I nodded back.

"I understand. Listen, thanks for the help, Carol, okay?"

"Okay."

I lowered my phone and spoke to Mr. Hawaiian.

"How's it going?"

"Nice ride you got here."

"Thanks."

He glanced at my car.

"Seen you around town and got to thinking. If you're looking to sell I'll give you a price."

"Thanks, but it's not for sale."

Voodoo Ranger said, "You sure?"

I studied him. The T-shirt probably made him feel like an actual ranger.

"Positive."

He said, "You gotta be looking to sell. You're sure as hell looking for something."

I glanced from the Voodoo to the Hawaiian shirt and back to the Voodoo.

"Am I?"

The shirt ignored me and spoke to his friend.

"He's looking for the right buyer, is what. What else could he be looking for?"

The man on the table slid to his feet.

"Something to steal, a place to rob, someone he shouldn't be looking for. I could go on."

I glanced at the SurfMutt and saw Jaime watching.

I said, "You guys are subtle. Why do you think I'm looking for something?"

The shirt went on with his friend as if I hadn't spoken.

"Yeah, you're right. Plenty of stuff he shouldn't be looking for."

The shirt turned to me and took a step closer.

"Anyway, I like your car. Be awful if something happened to it."

The Hawaiian shirt was on my right and the Voodoo was on my left. They were crowding me and I didn't like it. I stood.

"Here's a tip. Step away."

Then Jaime shoved between us and crowded the Hawaiian shirt.

"There a problem?"

He speared the Voodoo with a glare and Mr. Hawaiian stepped back. Jaime's knife was down along his thigh. He slapped the blade on his leg, making sure they saw it.

"I said you got a problem?"

The driver spread his hands and took another step back.

"Whoa, brother. Easy now. I was admiring the man's car."

"Looked like you was in his face. Were they in your face?"

I said, "Definitely in my face."

Jaime stepped toward the Voodoo.

"Why you in his face, *puto?*"

The Voodoo swung into the truck.

"Lighten up, man. Dude took it wrong."

Hawaiian Shirt opened the driver's-side door and smiled again as he slid behind the wheel.

"Think about my offer. I'll be around."

I watched them drive away and saw no plates on the truck.

Jaime said, "What the fuck happened here?"

"I was threatened. You know those guys?"

"Never seen'm before."

The knife slapped his thigh.

"Why they threaten you? The missing man?"

"Maybe."

The knife slapped again. He looked at the knife as if he hadn't known he was holding it and wiped the blade with the cloth.

"You be careful, bro."

Jaime started away, but hesitated.

"How you like the fries? They good, right?"

"The best."

"You see?"

Jaime returned to his kitchen and I climbed into my car. I was thinking about the men in the green truck when my phone buzzed. Lori. She sounded excited.

"I did it! I got the dirt on Anya! I know how to find her."

"I'm listening."

"For which you're paying me two hundred in cash?"

"Two hundred in cash. What's the dirt?"

She told me.

18

She lives with her mom and, get this, she and her mom work to-gether, too. Talk about having no life. I'd kill myself."

"Where do they live?"

"I don't know. They lived in this scuzzy mobile home place when I knew her."

"I need an address, Lori."

"I didn't get an address. I couldn't say, 'Hey, what's the address?' Be casual, you said. I was casual."

"Casual isn't worth two hundred dollars."

"I found out where they work. She delivers flowers or something for this place in Calabasas."

"Did you casually find out which florist?"

"Yes, and I can do without the attitude, thank you."

"Do you want the two hundred or not?"

"Harrison James Floral Boutique. It's in Calabasas. And her moth-er's name is Sadie, which I already knew."

"Sadie Given?"

She hesitated.

"I think it's Given."

"How about Anya? Is her last name still Given?"

"I don't know. Ask her."

"Is this a for-sure thing or a maybe thing?"

"It's for sure. My friend saw her at Harrison James, like, two weeks ago. She actually spoke with her."

"Okay. Are you at work today?"

"I work every day. I don't have a life, either, by the way. Hint."

"I'll swing by later."

"With the cash?"

"Yes, with the cash."

"Don't show up with a check. And if you don't show up, I swear to God I'll find you."

"I'll see you later."

"Want to buy me dinner?"

"No."

Lori was wearing me out.

I googled Harrison James Floral Boutique and called the number.

I didn't want to speak with Anya Given or ask about a man she might not remember on the phone. I also didn't want to warn her I was coming. I wanted to find out if Lori's information was correct.

A male voice answered.

"Harrison James."

"Oh, hi, this is Jeff. I'm calling for Anya Given, please. Is she available?"

The voice hesitated.

"Um, she might be making deliveries. Let me check."

The voice put me on hold. I hung up and left for Calabasas.

19

The Kill Car

The hamburger stand was a black hole, drawing the universe into itself. Trapped by its attraction, anyone and everyone connected to his disappearance returned. The yellow Corvette returned. A cartoon puppy's face on a map marked the car's location.

The driver had bought the GPS pet tracker at a pet store in Woodland Hills. The model he chose was the size of a fat quarter and rated for large, active dogs. It used information from cell towers and satellites to pinpoint a pet's location on an app and had cost sixty-nine dollars. The driver paid cash, downloaded the app, and dropped the tracker behind the Corvette's front seat four hours later. Walked up to the car in the detective's carport, dropped the disk behind the driver's seat, and walked away. He'd been terrified.

Now, the next day, the kill car drifted past the SurfMutt behind a lumbering flatbed truck. Hunched low behind the wheel with the sunscreens up, the kill car's driver saw the detective seated at a table near the yellow car.

The driver was pleased.

"I told you so, didn't I? The app even stores the routes he takes. We can see where he is, where he's been, and how long he stayed. We don't have to follow him. It's like we're with him."

The kill car hissed, dry as a desert breeze.

"Did your app tell us he's eating?"

The driver felt irritated.

"It's something to work with."

"Does it tell us why he went to the school? Or who he spoke with?"

The app had tracked the car's route from Laurel Canyon to the high school, where the car remained for thirty-two minutes. The length of time concerned him.

"We wouldn't have known he went to the school. Now we know."

"Which helps us how? We need to know why."

The driver shifted, uneasy. His face split with a nervous grin.

"Let's go ask."

The kill car hissed.

"Do it. Let's do it."

The kill car passed the SurfMutt and the shitty basketball court and skate park, and wandered to the high school.

The driver studied the school, uncertain and worried, and the hiss came again.

"We have to ask to know. There's no other way."

The driver checked the app. The yellow car was still at the SurfMutt.

The driver said, "Shut up. It's my ass they want."

"I knew you wouldn't do it."

"Shut up."

The kill car circled back to the hamburger stand and approached from the opposite direction. The yellow car remained and more vehicles crowded the little parking lot. The detective still sat at the table, but now people were speaking with him. The kill car's driver felt a sick tingle.

The kill car passed the hamburger stand and pulled over at a collectibles and novelty store eighty yards away. A tattered FOR LEASE sign was tacked to the door.

The kill car's driver could not see the yellow car, but he would see when it left.

They waited.

Eighteen minutes later, the dusty yellow car turned out of the parking lot and drove away in the opposite direction. The kill car's driver watched it go.

The driver said, "Start your engine."

The kill car purred to life.

The driver said, "We have to ask to know. Isn't this what you said?"

The kill car hissed.

"There's no other way."

"No."

The kill car's blinker came on and they drove to the SurfMutt.

20

Elvis Cole

Harrison James Floral Boutique occupied its own island in a sprawl-ing, upscale mall built to serve the affluent expat Angelinos pop-ulating Calabasas and nearby Hidden Hills. Two pale blue electric SUV delivery vans were parked by a loading door in the rear and a jungle of lush plants and flowering vines surrounded the entrance. Customers milled in the jungle, while clerks wearing aprons spritzed the greenery with portable misters.

I parked near the entrance, ambled inside, and tried to look like a customer.

None of the employees looked like Anya Given. A woman using a phone behind a counter looked managerial, so I smiled. The woman smiled back and raised a finger, the finger saying she'd be with me in a moment. She hung up a few seconds later and smiled again.

"Sorry about that. How may I help you?"

"One of your delivery people, a woman named Anya Given, went above and beyond at my wife's office last week. I wanted to thank her. Would you mind?"

The woman smiled wider.

"Of course not. Let me get her."

The woman picked up her phone, touched a line number, and asked whoever answered to have Anya come to the front.

"She'll be right up."

"Thanks."

Anya Given stepped from a hall behind a large display of orchids ten seconds later. She was slight, though not as thin as she looked in her DL photo, and the blemishes had faded. The long-sleeved white shirt she wore was buttoned at the wrists and large enough to be a smock. The counter woman caught her attention and pointed at me. I smiled when Anya saw me and met her in the center of the floor.

She said, "I'm Anya. You wanted to see me?"

Florists were arranging flowers at the end of a hall behind us, while other employees carried plastic buckets of lilies and long-stemmed pink roses from somewhere in back. I led Anya away to speak privately and gave her my card.

"I know you're working, so I won't take much of your time."

A tiny vertical line appeared between her eyebrows.

"I don't understand. A private investigator?"

"I'm looking for a man who disappeared ten years ago. Someone saw you with him at a hamburger stand called the SurfMutt in Rancha."

She glanced at my card again.

"Uh-huh."

I took out my phone and showed her the photo of Thomas Beller.

"His name was Beller. Thomas Beller."

She stared at the photo.

"He was driving a white panel van like this."

I swiped to a photo of the Bel-Jan van.

Anya did not move or react. I swiped back to Beller's photo and showed her again.

"You were at the skate park. This was after dark, so he probably offered to give you a lift. Remember?"

Anya seemed smaller, as if the shirt had grown. She shook her head.

"No."

I tried to encourage her.

"Ten years is a long time, so think about it. You and he were seen talking. He may have mentioned his plans."

Anya swayed as if she felt faint and turned toward the hall.

"Mom."

She said it again, louder, and sounded afraid.

"Mom."

A woman in her forties appeared. She was a taller, heavier version of Anya, with deep lines at the corners of her eyes and mouth. Their resemblance was obvious.

Sadie Given said, "May I help you, sir?"

I gave her the charm.

"I hope so. I was asking Anya about someone she met."

Anya showed her mother the card and Sadie stiffened, her eyes turning as hard as a chisel. The charm only went so far.

"This is a place of business. Who is it you think my daughter met?"

"A man named Thomas Beller. I'm trying to find him."

Anya touched her mother's arm, but Sadie didn't react.

"Mom?"

I raised my phone again to show Beller's photo, but Sadie didn't look at it.

"He isn't here. Please stop bothering my daughter."

"Anya isn't in trouble. I hoped she might be able to help."

Anya touched her mother again. She sounded confused.

"Mom?"

Sadie glared at Anya, but only for a second. Then her eyes softened.

"It's okay, baby. Do you know what this man's talking about?"

Anya shook her head.

"No, ma'am."

Sadie turned back to me.

"I'm sorry, but there's your answer. She doesn't know what you're talking about."

I held out the photo again.

"You don't remember this man or his van?"

Anya glanced at her mother.

"No."

Sadie shrugged.

"There you go. She never met him. She doesn't know who you're talking about."

"Anya was seen getting into his van."

Sadie's left eye ticked.

"Who saw her do this?"

"People who were present."

The left eye ticked again and Sadie glanced at Anya.

"Well? Did you talk to the man and go for a ride with him?"

Anya was twenty-five years old, but sounded five when she answered.

"No, ma'am. I didn't. I've never met him or seen him before."

Sadie touched her daughter and smiled, but spoke to me.

"Show us his picture again."

I held out the picture.

Sadie said, "Look at it real good, baby. Are you sure?"

Anya didn't look at the picture. She watched her mother.

"I'm sure."

"You never met this man?"

"No."

"You didn't go for a ride with him?"

"No."

"It's all right if you did. Just tell—"

Sadie glanced at my card.

"—Mr. Cole."

Anya never looked at me or the photo or anything but her mother.

"I didn't."

Sadie studied the photo. She stared at Beller's image as if inspecting each individual pixel.

"Whoever says they saw something doesn't know shit. I'd say they're mistaken, but they're probably just vile. And this was supposed to be when, ten years ago?"

"Ten years next month."

Sadie considered her daughter.

"Anya would've been fifteen. Who in hell remembers what they did when they were fifteen? I can't. Where do people come off?"

A man with tight-cropped hair appeared in the hall.

"I need roses, please. And the lilies."

Sadie said, "I'm coming."

The man eyed me.

"Do we have guests?"

"I'm coming, Mo."

Mo smirked and disappeared.

Sadie touched Anya's arm.

"Go with Mo. Start the roses. I'll get the lilies."

Anya glanced from her mother to me.

Sadie said, "Mo's waiting."

Anya hurried away and Sadie faced me.

"Is there anything else?"

"No. Sorry to bother you."

"Can you find your way out?"

"Thanks for speaking with me."

"You have a good day."

I found my way to my car. Anya had shriveled like a dying balloon when she saw Beller's photo. It was obvious she remembered him. I was still wondering why she hadn't admitted it when Sadie Given appeared in the shop's front window. She held a container of large white lilies and stared at me across the flowers.

I started my car and pulled away.

Sadie watched me go. She stood very still, then lowered the lilies as if placing them on a grave.

21

I drove to the far side of the mall and parked again.

Anya had recognized Tommy Beller. His photograph had rocked her enough to call her mother, who also seemed to recognize him. Lori believed Beller picked Anya up because he was a lech, but I kept coming back to Beller's second cell phone. If Beller made calls on a second phone, those calls might have been to Anya or Sadie.

I checked the time. Georgina Beller would be at work, but I called anyway and left a message.

"This is Elvis Cole. Please call when it's convenient. I have a quick question."

I killed the call and thought about Anya's reaction. She had looked to her mother for cues each time I asked about Beller as if afraid she would say the wrong thing and Sadie had directed her answers. Maybe the problem was Sadie. Maybe Anya would be more cooperative if her mother wasn't present.

I moved my car closer to Harrison James. A bald man and a slender woman were loading flower arrangements into one of the blue vans. When the van was filled, the woman climbed in and pulled away and the man disappeared into the building. I bought an iced mocha from a coffee kiosk and sat at an outdoor table to wait.

Twenty minutes later, Georgina Beller called and started in right away.

"Did you tell her to take those damned pictures?"

"I did."

"Well, she hasn't. I won't tell her again and I'm not going to beg. I've had it."

"She flew to New York this morning. She's going to be on the *To-day* show."

"Kevin told me. He also told me this find-her-father madness has already hurt her career as I knew it would. She lost the Palisades."

"Does Kevin tell you everything?"

"He cares. Now she's in New York and she'd better not be distracted when she's on national TV. You be careful what you say to her."

I was tired of listening to it.

"Did Thomas have more than one cell phone?"

She was silent for several seconds.

"I don't understand."

I told her Samantha Mason saw Beller use a phone at times other than the call times on his billing record.

"Some people have two phones, one for personal use and one for work. I asked Phil and Phil said he didn't."

She was silent again.

"And you expected me to know."

"I had to ask."

Her silence went on for so long I thought I'd dropped the call.

I said, "Ms. Beller?"

Her voice was dull when she answered.

"It wouldn't surprise me. He kept many things to himself."

Georgina hung up.

I lowered my phone and wondered what she meant.

I was still thinking about it when the bald man reappeared and moved the remaining van to the loading door. Anya joined him and they loaded the van with flowers. They made five trips, in and out, then Anya climbed in behind the wheel and pulled away, heading toward the nearest exit.

I drove fast for a different exit and followed her.

22

Anya made deliveries to five office buildings on Ventura Boulevard and six along Topanga Canyon Boulevard in Woodland Hills. The deliveries went quickly, but offered no chance to approach her.

I was thinking I could shoot out her tires when her blinker flashed and she turned into a Ralphs parking lot. I made the same turn two cars behind her and parked three rows away. Anya entered the market as I parked.

I didn't want to come off like a stalker, so approaching her in the market with other shoppers around seemed the way to go. Also, I could pretend our meeting was accidental. Accidentally bumping into someone she didn't want to see would be less threatening than being accosted by a stalker who followed her.

I started in the produce section and found her halfway down the chips and snacks aisle, studying bags of chips as if she couldn't decide between chili-lime potato chips and tortilla chips. An older woman in purple pants was at the far end of the aisle with a cart filled with groceries. A younger man with two small children was at the near end. Perfect. Families meant security.

I started down the aisle, expecting her to notice me, but she didn't. I slowed and cleared my throat, but she was focused on the chips. I slowed even more and cleared my throat louder.

Anya reached for a bag and studied the ingredients.

I stopped eight feet away to give her space and did my best to look casual. I tried to sound like Mr. Rogers.

I said, "Ms. Given."

Anya Given lurched as if she'd been tasered and the bag of chips skittered across the aisle. Her startle response was so dramatic I stepped backward.

"Sorry. I didn't mean to startle you. I shop here, too. I didn't expect to see you."

The older woman glanced our way.

Anya Given stared like a frightened child caught in the headlights of an onrushing car. Her face was dead white.

The intensity of her reaction felt over-the-top wrong.

I gave her an easygoing, nonthreatening smile.

"Can we start again? My name's Elvis. Like the singer."

I edged closer and offered my hand.

"I'd still like to speak with you if we could."

She didn't take my hand. I'm not sure she saw it. When she spoke her voice was faint.

"I didn't do anything."

The older woman glanced at us again and pushed her cart closer. Suspicious.

I hooked a thumb toward the front of the market.

"May I buy you a coffee? There's the coffee bar here. We could sit."

"I didn't do anything."

"I don't think you did anything. I just want to know if Mr. Beller mentioned where he was going."

Anya glanced past me as if she was looking for a way to escape.

"I don't know who you're talking about. I never met him."

Her eyes were wider now and her breathing was shallow and fast. Anya Given looked terrified.

I said, "You don't have to be scared of me, Anya. I'm only trying to find the man."

"Why?"

"His daughter hired me."

I gestured at the chips she'd dropped.

"Let me get these for you."

I edged toward the bag of chips the way acrophobes inch toward a cliff, as if a misstep would send them plummeting to their death. I picked up the bag and held it toward her.

"Here. The breakfast of champions."

Anya Given didn't see the bag. I thought she might be seeing a memory. Her expression left me empty.

I made my voice even softer.

"Did something bad happen between you and Mr. Beller?"

The wide eyes focused and grew pink.

"Nothing happened."

"You won't get in trouble. It might help to tell me."

"Nothing happened."

"Good. I'm glad nothing happened."

Her eyes fluttered and her voice was suddenly loud.

"I don't know what you're talking about. Get away from me."

The older woman pushed her cart toward us.

"Is this man bothering you?"

Anya said it again. Louder.

"Get away from me."

The woman shouted.

"Goon! Leave her alone! I'm getting security!"

The woman left her cart and hurried up the aisle.

"Security! Security!"

Anya was still loud.

"I don't know him. Go away!"

People were peeking around the ends of the aisle. I backed away.

"I'm going. I'm leaving."

"Go away!"

Anya shoved past and ran up the aisle. I didn't chase her, but I left the store quickly and saw Anya reach her van. She fumbled opening the door, backed from her spot too fast, and clipped a woman's cart. The woman flipped her off, but Anya didn't see it. She raced away in a panic. Anya wasn't running away from me. She was escaping.

My phone buzzed with an incoming call.

Lori.

23

Lori sounded angry.

"Are you going to pay me or not?"

She wanted the two hundred dollars.

"I'm in Woodland Hills. Are you at work?"

"*Yes*. Freezing my ass off and waiting for you."

"Bundle up. I'm fifteen minutes away."

I entered the liquor store fourteen minutes later.

A bone-thin old man was at the counter, counting out coins to pay for a six-dollar bottle of wine. He smelled like damp socks. Lori was watching him count when I entered. She glanced up, looking sullen.

Four crumpled singles lay on the counter and now the old man fished nickels and pennies from a clear plastic bag until the bag was empty.

He sighed.

"Hell. Looks like I'm short."

Lori said, "How short?"

His brow furrowed with hope.

"Sixteen cents?"

Lori raked the coins into a pile.

"Close enough."

The old man snatched up the wine and shot me a wink as he left.

Lori put the four singles and change into the cash drawer, then arched her eyebrows. Cold.

"Are you short, too?"

I put a hundred and five twenties on the counter, but Lori didn't seem happier.

I said, "Cash. What's the problem?"

Lori tucked the money under her fleece, came from behind the counter, and went to the door.

I said, "What's going on?"

She turned the OPEN sign to read CLOSED, locked the deadbolt, and spun toward me.

"Asshole! Tell me you didn't rat me out! Tell me you did *not* mention my name! We had a deal!"

I didn't know what she was talking about.

"I didn't mention you."

Lori stalked toward me. Furious.

"*LIAR!* You're going to get me killed."

Lori Chance was so frightened she trembled.

"Lori, I didn't. Tell me what happened."

"Two mean-ass shitkickers came! They knew you were here! They scared the shit out of me!"

"Were they driving an older green truck?"

Lori looked surprised.

"It was brown. Why'd you think it was green?"

"When were they here?"

"An hour ago! They asked what you wanted. I was *scared!*"

She punched me in the chest and shouted again.

"Asshole! Who did you tell?"

I felt a small, sharp pain behind my right eye.

"A cook at the SurfMutt told me you worked here. Frank Zalway gave me your name. People knew I was looking for you."

Lori sighed and hung her head.

"I knew this would happen. I'm screwed."

I softened my voice. Mr. Calm and Concerned.

"Are you okay?"

She rolled her eyes.

"No, stupid, I'm scared. These dudes were *big*."

"Tell me what happened."

"They wanted to know why you were here."

"Okay. So what did you tell them?"

"The truth. Kinda. I told them you're looking for some missing guy and I didn't know what the fuck you were talking about, or them, or why you thought I'd know about some missing guy because I don't. I did *not* mention Anya. That girl's name did *not* pass my lips."

"That's it?"

"They kinda knew I'd seen him. They mostly wanted to know what you knew."

"You've never seen them before?"

She crossed her arms, sullen again.

"No, else I would've said."

"So they showed up, asked why I was here, and left."

"No, they showed up, scared the shit out of me, and delivered a message. Smart people mind their own business."

They sounded like the men in the green truck.

I nodded toward the SMILE—UR ON CAMERA sign behind the counter.

"Show me. I want to see them."

Lori rolled her eyes.

"Get real. My fuckhead boss won't spring for a camera."

"Maybe Waldo's has a camera."

"Please. He owns Waldo's, too."

"Okay, so let's do this the old-fashioned way. What did they look like?"

"They were big. The one guy, he was huge. The other was smaller, but still honking big. They had the whole shitkicker vibe going on."

"Jeans and work boots?"

"Yeah."

"The shorter guy, was he wearing a Hawaiian shirt with flowers?"

"What the fuck? Yeah."

"Two men in a green pickup fronted me. The shirt man was one of them."

Lori shook her head.

"Their truck was brown. I saw it when they left."

The Challenger, a green truck, and now shitkickers in a brown truck. I'd fallen into a Southern Noir action movie.

I went to the door and studied the parking lot. My car was the only vehicle.

"Was anything written on the side? Like, *Sal's Plumbing* or *A-1 Construction*?"

"No. And no, I didn't get the license plate. I just wanted to make sure they left."

My car was parked in the same spot as yesterday. The Challenger had parked pretty close.

"A black Dodge Challenger pulled up when I was here. The driver was a tall, thin guy with long hair. A second guy was with him. Did you see them?"

"I didn't. Why?"

"It showed up a couple of times later. They might be working with your truck men."

Lori slumped into her fleece, looking miserable.

"I shouldn't have told you. I shouldn't've called stupid Eric. I knew this would happen."

This was the third or fourth time she'd used the phrase, her knowing this would happen.

"You knew what would happen?"

She sighed again and went behind the counter.

"I didn't tell you everything."

The pain behind my eye grew sharper.

"Tell me now."

"The night after I asked Anya about the van guy, I was in my mom's driveway, which is where I park, and these women jumped me. Right in my mom's driveway."

I said, "Women?"

She nodded, more to herself than me.

"Full-grown, heifer-class women. They kicked the shit out of me. I didn't know them. I'd never seen them before. But the one woman, she said if I spread shit about certain people, they'd be back. I knew who they meant."

"Anya."

"Who else? Duh."

"Was one of them Sadie?"

"No, but they were trash like her, only bigger, like burly biker chicks."

"Is this what you told Eric?"

"I didn't mention Anya. I told him the van man picked up a girl. I was feeling him out to see if he knew, but I never mentioned her. I was scared it would get back to them."

Lori gave a forlorn sigh.

"I guess it got back to them."

I checked the lot again. Anyone driving past could see my car.

"Maybe you should call it a day."

"I've got a kid. I don't work, I don't get paid."

I checked the lot again. The builder's superstore across the street had acres of parking.

"What time do you close?"

"Not soon enough."

"You have a car or someone picks you up?"

"A car. The piece of crap in back."

I nodded.

"Don't worry about the men coming back. I'll be close."

I didn't go directly to the builder's supply. I turned toward the freeway, climbed the ramp for Los Angeles, and left the freeway at the first exit. I bought two bottles of water at a gas station, used the restroom, and thought about Anya and Sadie as I drove back to Rancha.

I wondered why full-grown, heifer-class women had delivered a message of silence ten years ago, and now, ten years later, big men had delivered the same message. I wondered what they were hiding.

No cars were at Camille's when I reached the builder's supply. I picked a spot facing Lori's store and called a man named Joe Pike.

24

Pike and I co-owned the agency, but he wasn't a licensed investigator and his name wasn't on the door. Pike was more like a silent partner. He answered on the third ring.

"Pike."

"I'm on a missing person job in Rancha. It's getting complicated."

"I'm there in two-point-five."

Pike didn't hesitate or ask for an explanation. The World's Greatest Friend.

"Don't you want to know who we're working for?"

"Why?"

"Traci Beller. The Baker Next Door."

Pike said, "Uh."

"Yeah, me, too. Listen, I'm not at battle stations, so don't kill yourself getting here, but the thug count is rising."

"On your six in two-point-five. Say where in Rancha."

I wasn't sure how to answer. If Lori closed the store I intended to follow her home. If the brown truck returned I wanted to meet the shitkickers.

I said, "I'm at a liquor store called Camille's, but I might move. Text when you're close and I'll let you know."

Pike hung up and I settled in to watch Lori's store. Vehicles passed.

No black Challengers appeared, but brown trucks and green pickup trucks were as common as mice. None of them stopped and none of the greens was the truck from the SurfMutt. I thought about the trucks and how their timelines overlapped.

The green truck had found me at the SurfMutt before I met Anya and Sadie. The brown truck, containing the Hawaiian shirt dude from the green truck plus a different, jumbo-sized partner, had leaned on Lori a couple of hours later while I was following Anya. I didn't know how these people were connected, but I kept seeing Sadie as she watched me from the florist shop. Anya had been terrified, but Sadie had been hard and determined, staring at me as if I was a problem she was willing and ready to deal with.

The more I thought about Sadie the more I wondered about something Lori mentioned. I called her.

"Camille's Liquor."

"It's me. Got a question for you."

"Yes, I'll go out with you."

"Why did you say Sadie Given was a criminal?"

"'Cause she was. Real low-rent trash. Everybody knew."

"Poor doesn't equal criminal."

"Our parents talked about her being in prison. This friend of mine, her little sister wasn't even allowed to play with Anya at school. Forget playdates at whatever shithole where they lived."

"She did time as an adult?"

"That's what I heard."

"For what?"

I heard the shrug in her voice.

"I don't know. Dealing drugs, stealing, low-rent-trash stuff I'm sure. Now I have a question for you. What did you mean, I'll be close?"

"What it usually means. I'm close."

"Like, you're-watching-the-store close?"

"Yes."

"In case those men come back?"

"Them or whoever."

"Like, you're protecting me?"

"I'm the reason they came."

"This is kinda hot, you watching out for me. I'm getting turned on."

"Bye."

I hung up and moved my car to a new location. An hour later, the eastern sky was deepening when Lori called again.

She said, "Man, I'm dying in here."

"What's wrong?"

"I'm bored. Are you still close?"

"As close as two coats of paint."

"What?"

"As pennies in a tightwad's fist."

She hesitated.

"Oh. I get it."

"As close as two pimples on a fly's behind."

"You're bored."

"Humor is a gift. I can do this all day."

"When does it get funny?"

Ouch.

"I've been thinking about what you said, that I should call it a day. I'd close now if you took me to dinner."

"Dinner's out."

"*Why?* I'm cute. I'm fun. I'm available."

"I have a girlfriend."

"You suck."

Lori hung up.

Twenty-six minutes later, the sun was kissing a copper horizon when the Challenger appeared.

25

I sat taller when I saw the low black car. The Challenger approached from the direction of town and did not slow. The squint was behind the wheel and alone. He stared at Camille's as he passed.

I didn't like the squint showing up and wondered if his passing meant something. I wanted to chase him down, but told myself to wait. I didn't want to leave Lori.

I was still thinking about it when the Challenger appeared from the opposite direction. The squint slowed, studied her store as he passed, then hit the gas and blasted away. I tried to read the license plate, but couldn't. I called Lori.

She said, "Change your mind about dinner?"

"The Challenger passed your store twice. I don't like it."

"Maybe he's looking for you."

"Maybe."

"What about the assholes in the truck?"

"Nothing so far."

"So far? Thanks."

"Just keeping you in the loop."

"If you're my bodyguard, you could guard my body better here in the store with me."

"You don't quit, do you?"

"Your girlfriend lucked out. Bitch."

She hung up.

I lowered my phone and sighed.

Eight minutes later, the Challenger returned and glided into Lori's parking lot.

I fired my engine, but the Challenger didn't stop. It made a lazy circle past Camille's, turned from the parking lot, and headed toward town. I tried again to read the license plate, but couldn't.

I wanted to stay with Lori, but the squint might be working himself up for something bad. Also, he could identify the big men and explain their connection to Beller. I called Lori as I headed for the exit.

She said, "Now what?"

"The Challenger just left your parking lot. I'm following him."

"Are you serious?"

Lori appeared at her door as I turned after the Challenger.

"Ten seconds ago. He checked your store, maybe to see if you were working."

"You're freaking me out."

"You should leave. If the truck guys sent him, they might come back."

"Fuck this. I'm going home."

"Go. Text me when you're safe."

The Challenger wouldn't be far ahead.

I powered up the road, swung around two cars, a box truck, and a van, and spotted the squint three cars ahead. I settled into the flow and followed.

Twilight was fast becoming darkness. Headlights and taillights dotted the gloom. We passed the SurfMutt and skate park and a roadhouse already bustling with early-evening drinkers. The Challenger slow-rolled past the roadhouse as if the squint was stopping, but he didn't. I let a fourth car get between us.

The main road split before we reached town. We followed a smaller road past more bars and a couple of tiny restaurants. The squint slowed at the bars, but didn't stop. I wondered if he was looking for me. Three of the cars between us turned, leaving a single car. I dropped farther back.

My phone buzzed with an incoming text. Pike.

Close. Where u

I hit the callback button so we could speak.

"No idea. I'm following a guy in a black Challenger in the middle of nowhere and I don't know where he's going."

Pike said, "Need help?"

"Go to Camille's. See a woman named Lori and follow her home. Otherwise, wait. I'll shout if I need you for this."

"Rog."

The bars gave way to a shabby stretch of small local businesses dotting both sides of the road. None were lit inside or out, no parked cars sat nearby, and the buildings were as lifeless as an abandoned movie facade.

A quarter mile ahead, the Challenger's taillights flared and his headlights swung left as he turned. His lights went off.

I killed my headlights and pulled over.

His interior light came on and went off.

I waited three minutes. Nothing happened, so I rolled forward and stopped across the street.

The Challenger sat beside what looked like a small, abandoned drugstore or hair salon, cloaked in shadows as dark as a puddle of ink. The building appeared shabby even in the darkness with litter and weeds dotting a gravel yard. Two small windows on either side of a narrow door glowed dimly through grimy yellowed shades, layered dust, and cobwebs.

I shut my engine and heard nothing. The Challenger was the only vehicle present. Maybe this was the squint's home. Maybe he had a wife and kids and they were huddled at the TV, watching game shows, but probably not. You never knew until you knew. Maybe the squint would see me sitting across the street and shoot me with a double-barrel shotgun.

I pin-dropped the location on my phone, slipped from my car, and walked to the Challenger. Quiet. The night air was cold. The stars were sharp. I went to the little building's door, listened, and returned to the Challenger. I photographed the license plate, but I wanted the driver's registration for his name and official address.

I heard a soft crunch behind me.

A tall, wide man the size of a mountain stepped from the shadows, his voice a deep rumble coming from a face I couldn't see.

"You shoulda listened."

The big man was between me and my car and the pistol beneath my seat. I glanced at his hands but couldn't tell if he carried a weapon. He was big, but I'd be okay if he wasn't armed. Sure.

I said, "Guys like me don't listen. It's part of our charm."

Then the door opened and another large man appeared, not as large as the first but still big.

"It makes you stupid, messing in people's business."

The second voice was familiar. Light from the door revealed his Hawaiian shirt. The squint stepped out behind him and drifted sideways, trying to flank me.

I moved to the side, angling around the big man.

"Stupid is what you're doing. The police are coming."

The shirt and the squint moved with me and the big man stepped closer. His voice rumbled again.

"There's nothing here, boy. Whatever you want, it ain't here."

"Where's Thomas Beller?"

"He don't want to be found."

"His daughter wants him found. She misses him."

The shirt said, "Tell her to get over it."

I kept moving and saw the big man's hands were empty.

I said, "This won't end the way you think."

The big man said, "It'll end like I think and you're going. How you go is up to you."

The squint said, "Here they come."

Headlights swept the house and the green truck skidded to a stop, spraying gravel like shrapnel.

I charged the big man head-on and the big man reacted the way big, unschooled men react. He set himself to meet the charge and dropped his shoulder. I slipped outside, shoved his arm inside, crushed his nose with a palm strike, and hooked a hard right punch to his ear. The big man stumbled as the shirt man slammed into me, throwing wild lefts and rights like a beer-drunk bar brawler. I stepped close, thumbed his eyes, and pushed past the squint.

The big man found his feet as I reached my car. He hit me from behind, throwing crazy wild punches like his friend. A shot caught me in the head and another in the back. People ran toward me, but I only caught glimpses. The big man hit me again and someone grabbed my legs.

I dove across the driver's-side door, reaching for my gun beneath the seat, when something hard kicked me into the steering wheel. Someone grabbed my legs and dragged me from the car. I fell and fought from the ground, kicking and scrambling like a crab, but shapes like towering tombstones surrounded me. I tried to crawl under my car, but the shadows dragged me back. Kicks and punches hammered down like falling rain, falling and falling until the world faded.

I faded.

I disappeared.

Like Thomas Beller, I vanished.

26

Joe Pike

The parking lot was empty when Pike arrived at Camille's Discreet Liquor. He parked his red Jeep Cherokee, went to the door, and found a CLOSED sign. The lights were on inside, but nobody was present. Pike knocked, thinking the woman might be in a back room. He knocked three times hard, got no response, and walked next door to Waldo's.

The clerk behind the counter was a heavy young guy with a milk-white face wearing a T-shirt saying MOVIES SUCK. The kid glanced up when Pike walked in and shriveled like he'd seen his death. Pike didn't approach the counter.

"Relax. I'm looking for Lori. Next door."

The kid raised his hands.

"Who?"

Pike had been a combat Marine, a uniformed patrol officer, and a professional soldier. A lifetime of training had left him lean and hard. Mil-spec shades masked his eyes and a sleeveless gray sweatshirt revealed long, corded muscles with blood-red arrows tattooed on his delts. They pointed forward. At the kid.

Pike said, "Lori. She works next door. I'm supposed to meet her, but the store's closed. Do you know if she's coming back?"

"Uh-uh."

"Did you see her leave?"

"Uh-uh."

"Put your hands down."

The kid's hands were still up when Pike left and crossed the parking lot. He noted the builder's supply superstore across the road and the light flow of passing vehicles. The purple twilight sky was giving way to deep royal blue and black. Pike studied Camille's and Waldo's, their incandescent signs bright in the dimming light. Flood lamps for lighting the parking lot were mounted above the signs and lamps at the corners of the roof lit the sides of the building. Pike checked the rear. Overgrown brush and nut trees were thick behind the building. A narrow gravel alley separated the building from the brush with more lamps angled to light the alley. An ancient Saturn compact car sat behind Waldo's.

Pike returned to his Jeep and messaged Cole.

camille's closed

lori gone

advise

Cole didn't respond.

Pike turned the Jeep around, parked facing the street, and settled in to wait. At eight o'clock, the kid at Waldo's stuck his head out, saw Pike, quickly locked the door, and left in the Saturn. The Jeep's red hood, polished to a high sheen, glittered with the building's signage and from passing headlights. Pike wondered where Cole was and what he was doing, but mostly Pike thought about nothing. He floated within himself. Being.

Pike sent another message.

advise

Pike watched the road. He watched the builder's supply superstore.

Fewer vehicles passed as the minutes ticked away, meaningless lights going nowhere. Pike held his phone, as still as a pond on a windless day, in his Jeep but elsewhere. An emerald glade in a deep forest, a green world Pike had known since before the Marines and the badge and his years fighting other people's fights. Pike had found the place and held it dear; a place free of his father's brutal rage, the pain of seeing his mother beaten, the shame of his inability to protect her or himself. That was then. The green world offered calm in a world of chaos and terror.

Calm.

Stay calm.

Pike slid from the Jeep into the chill night air and walked to the edge of the parking lot. He sent another message.

I'm here.

He thought and added more.

Camille's.

Pike returned to the Jeep, but didn't get in. He leaned against the grille, crossed his arms, and watched the road.

I'm here.

27

The Kill Car

The kill car glided through a hollow night so clean the air glittered. The cargo rode in back. The driver had never carried cargo, but a mad compulsion told him to take the thing. He was ravenous.

"I'm starving. Let's get something."

They found an open McDonald's near Calabasas. The driver bought two large orders of fries and a small Diet Coke at the drive-thru and ate right there at McDonald's with the cargo in back.

A death wish. *Probably.* A desire to be caught. *Maybe.* He'd lost his mind. *No doubt about it.*

Buzzing with a strange new energy, the driver entered Mickey D's, used the facilities, and returned to the kill car. He was tempted to peek at the cargo. The idea of popping the trunk, just a crack, and seeing it there in a public place excited him, but a harsh voice whispered: *Get in, go, get out of here.*

Opening the door, the voice warned: *This day has been coming for ten years, run.*

Slipping behind the wheel, the voice thundered: *GO NOW! RUN BEFORE THEY CATCH YOU! RUN!*

The kill car whispered.

"You're hearing voices."

"The least of my problems."

The driver opened the tracker app and checked the yellow car's location history. He'd been so distracted by the cargo he'd forgotten the detective.

The yellow car had moved from the SurfMutt to the big mall in Calabasas, then followed a path through Woodland Hills, where it made a brief stop. The mall stop and the short stop on a commercial street in Woodland Hills weren't concerning. The detective had probably eaten or been killing time.

From Woodland Hills the yellow car moved to a location across from the big builder's supply, where it spent thirty-six minutes, after which the car moved closer to the builder's supply. It had spent one hour and forty-eight minutes at the builder's supply before moving to its present location. The driver wondered why the detective had spent almost two and a half hours at and across from the builder's supply.

The kill car's whisper was critical.

"We should have followed him. We need to know who he sees."

The driver felt defensive.

"We learned something. The cargo helped."

"Enough to explain two and a half hours?"

The driver rubbed his eyes and studied the app.

The yellow car had moved from the builder's supply to its current location on the far side of town. It had been at this location for, as of now, twenty-one minutes and counting.

The kill car hissed.

"What's he doing? Who's he talking to? We have to know these things."

The driver nodded.

They drove up from Calabasas past the SurfMutt and along quiet dark roads. The yellow car's unchanging location suggested the gathering of information, evidence, and clues. The kill car's driver hated this detective and the lonely location out in what appeared to be nowhere and not knowing what they would find when they arrived or what they would do. The driver sucked the last of his Diet Coke loudly through a soggy paper straw.

He said, "I hate this. What in hell could be out here?"

"The detective."

They were less than a mile away.

"All right, fine. We find him and then what? He's at some house, what do we do, knock?"

"Get the address. We'll look it up, see who lives there. Come back."

Half a mile.

They were the only car on the road and the driver didn't like it. He wished the shitty little road was jammed with bumper-to-bumper traffic. Thousands of cars to hide them like a forest hides a tree.

"This sucks, being out here all alone. We stand out."

"Nobody remembers us."

"*He* might see us. Then what?"

"He goes."

A quarter mile. An eighth. The kill car slowed. The driver peered ahead, seeing a pale speck in the distance.

"Is that him?

The speck became the yellow car, parked off the road. The driver's heart pounded and a greasy sweat dampened his face.

The kill car slowed, bathing the yellow car with light as it eased to a stop. A body lay crumpled at the edge of the road.

A voice thundered.

RUN!

The driver wanted to run, but lights weren't approaching and the darkness was a comfort. He studied the body.

"Is it him?"

The kill car whispered.

"Go see."

The other voice thundered.

IT'S A TRAP! THEY'LL CATCH YOU! THEY'LL FIND THE CARGO!

The driver studied the house across the street and glanced at the
body again.

"Looks dead."

"Great. Now's our chance."

The driver studied the house again. Its front door was open. Beyond the door was impenetrable darkness.

"Someone might be inside. They might be watching us."

The kill car whispered.

"Nobody's watching. Search him. Do it fast before someone comes."

The kill car pulled ahead of the Corvette and shut its lights. The
driver took a small metal flashlight with a red lens from the glove box,
pulled on a pair of black nitrile gloves, and hurried to the yellow car.

A 9x12 manila envelope was wedged between the console and the
passenger's seat. The driver took it without checking the contents. A
pistol wrapped in a shoulder holster was beneath the driver's seat. He
left the gun and recovered the tracker. He wanted to leave the little
device, but feared someone would find it. The Corvette's registration
and proof of insurance were in the cluttered glove box. The driver took
the registration, left the proof of insurance, and hurried to the body.

Blood and cuts on the dead man's face gleamed in the crimson light.

"Damn, it's him."

"Good. Hurry."

"Who do you think killed him?"

"Don't care. Hurry."

The driver checked the detective's pants and pockets for notes and
notebooks, found nothing, and rolled the body to take the wallet. The
dead man moaned.

The kill car's driver lurched to his feet, ready to run. He checked
the road for approaching cars, then stepped closer and stood over the
man. He studied the bloody face.

Alive.

The man's eyes moved beneath his lids, dancing and darting as if
seeking a way out.

The driver could not look away. The eyes danced and blood leaked from the nose and mouth and head. The driver watched a pulse in the detective's neck and his chest rising and falling and felt an urge to crush the head, bust it open, make it look like a watermelon crushed by a bowling ball. The driver saw the head break apart and grew aroused. He saw himself killing the man and grew harder. He flashed red light across the gravel yard, searching for a heavy object.

The kill car whispered.

"Lights."

The driver saw twin pinpricks of light approaching. He ran to the kill car and pulled away fast. Laughing. The driver was elated. Nobody had seen them or ever would see them and the detective was messed up bad. Good. Asshole.

The kill car drifted toward the freeway, searching for a well-lighted place. A furniture outlet store offered an empty parking lot dotted by towering lamps. The kill car stopped within a cone of light.

The driver emptied the envelope and found pages from an old report and interview transcripts with handwritten notes scrawled in the margins. The transcripts were of interviews with people who'd known nothing. This was good, but the handwritten notes left the driver worried. They were short, terse, and contained names the driver didn't recognize. New names might mean new information and new information could be dangerous. The driver slipped the pages into the envelope. He had to dump the cargo and protect himself.

The kill car whispered.

"This is fun."

28

Joe Pike

ike's phone buzzed with an incoming call. The caller ID showed an unknown number, but this meant nothing. During his time as a contractor, the men Pike worked with changed numbers as often as socks. They were all unknown.

Pike answered.

"Yes?"

A woman.

"I'm calling from Desert Pacific Hospital in Agoura Hills for a Mr. Joe Pike."

"This is Pike."

"I'm calling in regards to a Mr. Elvis Cole."

Pike closed his eyes. He opened them.

"Yes?"

"A card was found in his wallet asking for you to be contacted in an emergency."

Pike started the Jeep.

"What's his condition?"

"Mr. Cole has been admitted and is being evaluated."

Pike put the call on speaker and map-apped directions to the hospital.

"Evaluated for what?"

"Head trauma is the best I can tell you at this time. He was unconscious when he arrived."

Pike jammed the gas and powered away from Camille's, following the thin blue line toward the hospital. It wasn't far.

"What happened?"

"The sheriffs told us he was assaulted. Multiple assailants, they said."

Pike glanced at his watch, a heavy steel Rolex he bought on his first combat deployment. One-fourteen a.m. Zero-one-fourteen hours.

Pike hit the freeway and screamed up the ramp. He pictured a black Challenger.

"Do the police have a suspect?"

"Sir, I don't know. I can give you a number for the Malibu sheriff's substation, if you'd like."

"That's okay. I'll find out."

"Would you like me to give Mr. Cole a message if I can?"

The exit ramp was dead ahead. Pike hit it hard, the Jeep drifting through the curve.

"Yes. Tell him—"

Signs streaked past, a horn sounded, lights blurred. Everything was blurry.

"I'm coming."

Pike saw the hospital.

29

Desert Pacific Hospital was a three-story complex set at the base of the foothills, surrounded by parking lots and palm trees in a soft violet glow. The air was crisp and unnaturally clear. An arrow pointed toward the main entrance, but a vertical sign on the far end of the hospital read EMERGENCY.

Pike entered the ER through double glass doors. A deserted admissions counter sat on the far side of a spacious waiting area. Two haggard women in their forties and a tall man in a wrinkled gray business suit were the only occupants. The women sat together, their faces drawn and worried. The man sat across the room, trying not to fall asleep. He had taken off his tie and draped it over his leg.

Pike went to the counter.

A security guard wearing a short-sleeved uniform stepped from an office. A name tag on his chest gave his name. LYLE.

Lyle said, "Help you?"

He was in his early thirties with a slight paunch. Armed. A tattoo of a snarling bulldog was on his forearm with three block letters written beneath the bulldog. MOM.

Pike said, "The hospital called. A friend of mine was admitted. Elvis Cole."

A middle-aged female admissions nurse pushed through a swinging door as Pike was speaking.

She said, "Are you Mr. Pike?"

"Yes."

She smiled and offered her hand.

"I'm the one who called. Connie Vargas."

Pike recognized her voice.

"May I see him?"

"I'll need your ID."

Pike handed over his driver's license. The guard stepped away, but didn't leave the area. Pike guessed he had nothing else to do.

Connie Vargas scanned Pike's DL, handed it back, and moved to a computer station. She tapped at the keyboard.

"The doctor ordered a CT. Let me see if Mr. Cole's back from imaging. Does he have family in the area?"

"No. Is he conscious?"

"I couldn't say. How about a spouse or legal partner?"

Pike shook his head.

"Anyone besides you I should notify?"

Pike figured the hospital wanted someone to bill. He opened his wallet again.

"I'll cover the cost."

Vargas frowned.

"It isn't necessary. Mr. Cole's insurance cards were in his wallet."

She finished tapping and stepped from the keyboard.

"They haven't updated his chart. I'll check his status and be right back."

Vargas disappeared through the swinging door and Pike turned to Lyle. The security cop was watching him without expression. Pike thought he looked bored.

"Were you here when they brought him in?"

Lyle hooked his thumbs in his gun belt.

"Yeah. Didn't look good, man. Sorry."

Vargas had told him Elvis was unconscious.

"Head trauma?"

"He was thumped pretty good."

Pike considered this.

"Who brought him in, paramedics?"

"Yeah."

"The police came in with them?"

"The deps who found him, yeah. They were just cruisin' along and found him. A couple of sheriffs."

The coppers would've tagged along to make notes for their report and take a statement, if Elvis made a statement. Pike had done this when he was a uniformed officer. Lyle, being bored, would've talked up the cops.

"Ms. Vargas mentioned multiple assailants."

"Yeah. Three or four, they said. Your friend must've told them, them or the medics."

"My friend drop any names?"

"Of the guys who did it? Nah. The one dep, he said your friend couldn't or wouldn't name the guys. He figured they fought over a woman."

Pike studied the guard. Lyle grew uncomfortable and shifted his weight.

Pike said, "So Elvis was awake and answering questions."

Lyle shrugged.

"When I saw him, he was kinda in and out, but I didn't go in back. I have to stay out here."

"Why'd the dep say this was about a woman?"

"Stuff your friend said, something about a brown truck and a woman named Lucy."

"Lucy lives in Louisiana. This wasn't about Lucy."

Lyle shifted and shrugged again.

"I don't know what to tell you. A head injury like this, you don't make a lot of sense."

The swinging door opened and Vargas appeared. She held the door open.

"He's asleep. I can't let you disturb him, but I'll let you see him if you'd like. From the hall."

Pike followed Ms. Vargas through a large room with a central nurses' station and the usual medical equipment. Beds divided by blue curtains lined the wall, though most of the curtains were open and the beds were empty. A male doctor in a white coat was suturing a cut on a middle-aged woman's forehead in one bay. A fully clothed Latin male lay on his side in another bay, holding his stomach and groaning. Vargas led Pike into a hall with glass-walled rooms, a white floor, and pale beige walls. Then she stopped and repeated herself.

"He's asleep. We can't go in."

Pike moved to the glass. He stood on the clean white floor in the silent hospital hall and stared at his friend.

Elvis Cole lay beneath a thin yellow blanket with his head elevated. Wires climbed from beneath the blanket to a vital signs monitor on a wheeled chrome stand. Cole's eyes were closed. His left cheek was swollen with a large, greenish-purple contusion, split at its base by a sutured cut. A second contusion covered Cole's temple at his hairline. Cole's mouth was swollen and discolored where another sutured cut was crusted with blood. A bright blue cold wrap covered the top of his head like a knit cap. Pike was silent for several seconds before he spoke.

"Is his skull fractured?"

Connie Vargas answered softly and repeated herself.

"The CT wasn't on his chart. I'm sorry. I don't know."

Pike removed his dark glasses and stepped closer to the window.

Ms. Vargas said, "You can't go in."

Pike stopped, so close his breath fogged the glass.

He studied Cole's eyes for movement beneath the lids and his feet for movement beneath the blanket. Pike had seen traumatic brain injuries many times. He knew ocular biomarkers like patterned eye movements and twitching of the hands and feet could indicate brain damage. Cole was still. Pike told himself this was good.

Ms. Vargas said, "We should go."

Cole's right hand was hidden by the blanket, but his left was exposed. Cole's index, middle, and ring knuckles were bruised and both the index and middle knuckles were split. Pike knew his friend to be a skillful fighter and Ranger Ready all the way. Cole had fought hard and landed blows.

"Mr. Pike?"

Pike checked the vital signs monitor. Heart rate was steady at fifty-eight beats per minute, blood pressure one-fourteen over seventy, and oxygen saturation was a solid ninety-nine. All good. But the vitals meant little if a hemorrhage developed in his brain. Pike glanced at Cole's hand. The split knuckles.

Pike whispered.

"It's not over until we win."

Ms. Vargas said, "Excuse me?"

Pike put on his sunglasses and faced her.

"He had his wallet when he arrived."

"The officers had it. That's how we knew to call you. The card in his wallet."

"Was there cash or credit cards in his wallet?"

She stiffened.

"Yes. And all of it will be returned. The duty nurse logged his belongings and stored his things in a security box. His wallet, a watch, a ring, and a cell phone. And no, you can't have them. The card doesn't say we're to give you his things."

"Keys?"

She hesitated, but only for a second.

"I don't recall keys."

"A pistol?"

Connie Vargas stared.

Pike turned away.

"I'll be back."

Pike left through the swinging door to the lobby. The two women and the man in the gray suit still waited. Lyle the security guard stood at the entrance, thumbs still on his belt, staring into the deserted parking lot.

Pike stepped up beside him. Lyle startled and glanced around to see if anyone saw him jump.

"Shit. I didn't hear you."

"The deps say where they found him?"

"Yeah. Over in Old Town. On the road going out to the old movie sets."

Pike's head moved from side to side. Once.

"What's Old Town?"

"Those days, you had little shops and bars along the road. Half those places are gone and the rest are abandoned. They call what's left Old Town."

Pike said, "Old Town."

Lyle nodded.

Pike took out his phone and opened a map app.

"Show me where it is."

Lyle showed him.

"This road here. See this little stretch? Found him right about here. Nobody else around."

"Did someone call it in?"

"Nope. Deps were out prowling around and happened to see him."

Pike wanted to go.

"Okay. Thanks."

Lyle had a distant look on his face, like he was seeing himself out prowling around with the deps.

"Good thing they found him, huh? He might've been there all night. He might've died."

Pike turned away. He stepped into the cool, lonely night and followed his map.

30

His headlights found Cole's Corvette across from one of the old abandoned shops Lyle described. Pike saw no other vehicles and no movement. The police had departed the scene.

Pike parked behind Cole's car, turned on his flashers, and slipped from the Jeep. He lit up the building with a handheld mini-Maglite and cleared the area left to right, clocking ten-degree increments. A small square building; dark; maybe a former house later used as a souvenir shop; gravel parking area in front; graffiti, litter, weeds. The front door stood open.

Pike killed the light and listened. A ticking from the Jeep was the only sound. The stars and a few distant homes were the only lights. A desolate, lonely place.

Elvis had said he was following a guy in a black Challenger. One person. The cops told Lyle Elvis was beaten by multiple assailants. Maybe the others were here when Elvis arrived. Maybe they arrived later. Pike didn't care. He only cared about finding them.

Pike hooked his sunglasses on the neck of his sweatshirt and flashed the building again, the light cutting the darkness like a lightsaber. He checked his watch. Oh-two-thirty-eight hours. Pike wanted to finish quickly. He didn't like leaving Elvis unguarded.

The shadowy shape of the Corvette crouched in the shadows like a cat bunched to spring. An image of Elvis sprawled beside it appeared, but Pike pushed it away. L.A. police would've called for an impound truck and waited for the tow. Here, the local sheriff's substation provided services and probably didn't have the manpower.

Pike lit the car and found two dark smudges and a thin streak on the driver's-side door. Their reddish-brown tint told him the marks were blood. He found more spatter on the tarmac a few feet from the door and a sprinkle of drops leading into the yard. Scraped earth and upturned gravel told him the fight began in front of the house. Elvis had made it to his car, but the men caught him from behind. Pike studied the tiny droplets and wondered which had fallen from Elvis and which from his assailants. He wondered how many men Elvis fought. Three, if they were good. A better guess was four or five. One or more might have needed medical attention.

Pike returned to the Corvette and flashed the interior. A dark smear streaked the driver's seat and another smudged the center console. Connie Vargas said they'd found no keys in Elvis's pockets, but the ignition was empty.

Pike opened the door and searched around and under the seats. Elvis usually stashed his pistol under his seat or behind the passenger seat, but Pike found nothing. He checked the glove box. No gun.

Pike turned off the light and sat in the open convertible in the dark. He leaned back and considered the stars. The red, green, and blinking white light of a small airplane passed overhead. Pike watched the lights disappear, then gripped the Corvette's steering wheel, both hands, ten and two. He held tight.

Pike pushed up out of the Corvette and locked his Jeep. The old Corvette was easy to start. Pike hot-wired the ignition and had it rumbling in less than a minute. He checked the time again. Three-oh-nine. Zero-three-zero-nine hours. He knew the police would likely return to tow the vehicle, but Pike didn't care. He put the Vette in gear and imagined Elvis fighting faceless men. Pike gave no thought to their purpose or reason. They were shadows. He wondered if they were still awake, laughing and high-fiving each other, riding a thrill-high from kicking someone's ass. Pike saw them pumping their fists. It didn't matter to Pike how skilled or dangerous they were, or how many their number. These men had no idea what was coming.

Pike checked the time. Zero-three-ten.

Pike pumped the clutch and hit the gas. The Corvette fishtailed off the shoulder, clawing its way onto the road. He clutched again and slammed the shifter. The Corvette roared, tearing a hole through the night.

PART TWO

31

Elvis Cole

woke beneath a night sky filled with flashing blue lights as a floating sofa carried me toward an ambulance. A county sheriff's car drifted past, the sofa dipped, and a surfing dog rode a crashing wave over my head.

I said, "Dogs don't surf."

An upside-down EMS tech peered at me.

She said, "He's awake."

I said, "I'm what?"

I threw up into my mouth and passed out.

I woke again in a hall so bright I clenched my eyes.

A male voice spoke behind me.

"What's your name, sir?"

The answer didn't present itself, so I guessed.

"Los Angeles."

The light faded and I faded with it.

I woke in a bed surrounded by pale blue curtains in a room with a glass wall and Joe Pike on the far side of the glass. I called out to him and swung out of the bed.

"Joe! Did you feed the cat?"

Joe faded. I faded. We were gone.

I woke in a bed surrounded by pale blue curtains in a room with a glass wall and a sandy-haired woman wearing a white lab coat. She smiled.

"Hello there. Do you know where you are?"

"How many choices do I get?"

"Let's go with your best guess."

"A hospital."

"Very good. Can you tell me your name?"

"Elvis Cole."

I noticed Joe Pike in the hall behind the glass and raised my hand. The woman turned to see why I waved.

"Your friend. Remember his name?"

"Joe Pike."

"Excellent. I'm Dr. Sherman. How about your date of birth?"

The side of my head felt cold. I reached up and touched something heavy.

"Am I wearing a dunce cap?"

"It's a cold wrap to suppress the swelling. Now tell me when you were born."

I told her.

"Good. Open your eyes real wide and look at my finger."

She held up her left index finger. I watched the finger as she shined a light at my eyes. The glare made me cringe.

"Bright."

She put the light away.

"Your pupils are dilated. They showed a slight anisocoria when you arrived, but they're normalizing. This is good. Do you know what anisocoria means?"

"Different size pupils."

"Very good. Have you had a concussion before?"

"Yes."

She jotted a note on a chart.

"Recently?"

I tried to remember, but forgot her question.

"I feel sick."

I threw up in my mouth again and passed out.

I woke in a bed surrounded by pale blue curtains and monitors on stands in a room with a glass wall. Joe Pike stood on the other side of the glass in exactly the same place. A light-haired man wearing a tan sport coat over a white shirt and red tie was speaking with Dr. Sherman, but they weren't standing with Pike. The man looked like a cop. Then he felt the weight of my eyes and turned. Cop.

I faded.

I woke in a bed surrounded by pale blue curtains and monitors on stands in a room with a glass wall and Joe Pike standing over me.

I glanced past him to the glass. The hall was empty.

I said, "Good thing Lucy isn't here."

Pike's voice was low.

"What happened?"

"I was following someone."

"I know. Who did this?"

I remembered my car, grabbed Pike's arm, and tried to sit up. My head spun.

"My car. My gun's in the car. A kid could find it."

Pike's voice was calm.

"The police bagged your gun when they found you. It's safe."

Pike leaned closer. He whispered.

"Tell me who did this."

I saw shadowed faces, but the faces swirled into a large manila envelope and I felt frightened again.

"Did the cops find my file?"

Pike glanced toward the door.

"In your car?"

"Between the seat and the console. A manila envelope. Do the cops have it?"

"I don't know. I have your car. I didn't see a file."

I closed my eyes. Thoughts collided in a mad rush. Traci Beller pinballed into Lori Sanchez slammed into Lucy. My head throbbed.

I said, "She's screwed."

Pike said, "Who?"

"Traci."

I opened my eyes. The lights behind him were nuclear bright.

"How long have you been here?"

Pike leaned closer and whispered again.

"You followed a Challenger. You're working a missing man. Tell me who did this."

I was sleepy. My eyes closed.

"Did what?"

Pike placed his hand on my chest.

"No matter. Rest."

"Everything matters."

I faded.

I woke in a bed surrounded by pale blue curtains and monitors on stands in a room with a glass wall and the cop in the tan sport coat standing over me. He held up a badge.

"Feel up to a few questions?"

"No."

I faded.

32

woke in the same room, but the lights didn't bother me. My head hurt less and I didn't feel queasy. Joe Pike stood at the foot of my bed with his arms crossed. He looked like the *Colossus of Rhodes*.

I said, "How long have I been here?"

"Not long. Seems longer because they wake you."

I shifted to sit up. The side of my head felt tight and my back hurt. The glass hall was empty.

"Is the cop gone?"

"He'll be back."

I couldn't remember if Pike knew about Traci Beller and Sadie and the men in the truck. I remembered telling him, but the memory was vague and seemed fractured.

"Did I tell you about Traci Beller?"

"Client. You said she's screwed. You followed a black Challenger. Before the Challenger, you watched a liquor store."

I remembered the file and my head hurt worse.

"My file wasn't in the car?"

"No."

"The cops have it?"

"I don't know."

The ache in my head grew to a steady throb. I wanted to protect

Traci Beller. I hadn't planned to tell her about Lori and Anya and the things I suspected until I knew the true story, but if the cops had my file they'd roll in like blundering bulls. Traci would be blindsided, her secrets would no longer be hers, and the answers she wanted might never be found.

Pike said, "Elvis."

I opened my eyes.

"I fell asleep."

"No worries. Rest."

I pushed myself taller and told him about Traci and her father and Lori and what Lori saw at the skate park. I told him about the Challenger showing up again and again and the men in the trucks. Pike listened, shades masking his eyes, his face grim.

"When did the Challenger show up?"

"The first day. At the liquor store."

"And the truck guys?"

"After I spoke with Anya and Sadie. I was still on Anya when they muscled Lori."

I flashed on big men towering over Lori and felt a stab of panic.

"I've gotta warn her. Where's my phone?"

"Finish telling me."

"Sadie must've called them. Or Anya. The truck guys knew I was looking for Beller and knew Lori saw Beller with Anya. They told her to keep her mouth shut."

"You think they know what happened to him."

"Yes. Anya panicked when she saw his picture. She literally bolted. And Sadie looked like she wanted to stab me."

Pike checked the hall and leaned close again. His voice was soft.

"The men who did this. Where can I find them?"

"I don't know."

"A name. The Challenger."

I was tired. I wanted to close my eyes, but didn't.

"Sadie and Anya might be at work. The men, I don't know who they are or how they're connected or where to find them."

Pike stepped back and patted my arm.

"We don't have to find them. I'll drive around in your car. They'll think I'm you and turn up."

I stared. Pike stared back, his face flat and expressionless, eyes hidden. Joe Pike was my closest and oldest friend, but I couldn't tell if he was joking. Pike never smiled.

I said, "You made a joke."

"Yes."

A riot.

Dr. Sherman rapped on the glass and came to the bed.

"Well, good news. The second scan confirms no intracranial bleeding. How do you feel?"

"Like a man who doesn't remember being scanned."

She checked my eyes for the hundredth time.

"Any dizziness? Headache?"

"A headache, but it's not bad. No dizziness."

She touched her ear.

"How's your hearing?"

I raised my voice.

"*What?*"

Dr. Sherman sighed.

"Do you know how many times I've heard this joke?"

"First time you've heard it from me."

She smiled. Warm.

"Let's hope the last. Can you stand for me?"

I swung my feet over the side, felt myself tilt, and gripped the bed. The doctor stood ready to catch me, but the floor didn't flip. Being out of the bed and upright helped. I felt pretty good.

"Think you can make it to the bathroom?"

I walked to the bathroom without throwing up and checked myself in the mirror. My left eye was purple and swollen. The right side of my mouth was thick and the stitches in my lip were black with crusted blood. A purple knot decorated my forehead and a green lump rode my right cheek. The contusion above my ear looked like a hairy clam.

I said, "And the role of Elvis Cole will be played by Quasimodo."

"Doing okay?"

"I look like a troll."

"Besides that."

I walked back to bed and climbed in.

"Couldn't be better."

"In that case, I'll cut you free, but plan on taking it easy. A concussion is serious business."

She clicked off instructions like she'd recited them a thousand times.

"No sports, jogging, or biking for at least two weeks. Lay around, take naps, and let your brain rest. The headaches and nausea will pass fairly quickly, but if they worsen or your speech slurs, get your butt to a hospital. I'm talking nine-one-one right away. Got it?"

"Yes, ma'am."

"We'll give you a handout with instructions before you leave and something to help the nausea."

She glanced at Pike.

"Will Mr. Pike drive you home?"

Pike said, "Yes."

The cop appeared in the hall with a battered gray briefcase. The doctor caught my glance and lowered her voice.

"He'd like a word, but if you don't feel up to it, I'll tell him no. My hospital. My rules."

The cop was watching.

I didn't want to answer questions about Thomas and Traci Beller. I wanted to warn Lori and find Anya and Sadie, but assault victims who didn't cooperate became suspects. If the cop asked about Thomas

Beller, my only chance to protect Traci was to deny it and lie. Lies were my business. I should print it on my cards.

"Sure, Doc. Happy to talk with him."

She touched my arm.

"I'll start the paperwork. Stay out of fights, Mr. Cole."

The doctor left. The cop and his briefcase entered.

33

The cop had an easy manner, a fleshy face with large, goldfish eyes, and looked to be in his early fifties. He flashed a badge as he introduced himself.

"Dan Carmack. I'm a detective with the sheriff's department."

"You were here before."

"That's right. You were kinda woozy."

"Still am."

Carmack chuckled. It was the kind of chuckle cops make when they're trying to establish rapport.

He said, "Been there myself. Had my bell rung playing ball. Scrambled me cross-eyed, but I was good as new in a couple of days. You'll see."

Carmack set the briefcase on a table at the foot of the bed.

"Anyway, it's my job to find the people who did this to you."

I said, "Great. They should go to prison."

Elvis Cole, Cooperative Victim.

Carmack popped the latches, but didn't open the case. He glanced at Pike.

"How about you give us a minute?"

Pike settled against the wall and crossed his arms again. He looked like Gort from *The Day the Earth Stood Still*. Solid and impossible to move.

I cleared my throat.

"The doctor said my memory might be off for a few days. Mr. Pike is helping me. I'd rather he stay."

Carmack wasn't happy about it but he didn't object.

"Mr. Pike and I met."

Carmack opened the briefcase. I expected him to lead with the file, but he held up my keys.

"We sent a truck to get your car, but your associate here beat us to it."

Carmack set the keys on the table and dipped into the case.

"The deps who found you checked your vehicle. Found something interesting."

I braced for the file, but Carmack held up a clear plastic evidence bag containing my pistol.

"A Dan Wesson .38-caliber revolver in a leather Bianchi shoulder rig. I like these old wheel guns. Nice piece."

Carmack made a small, thoughtful smile.

"I ran your papers. It's properly registered, it hasn't been recently fired, and your carry permit is valid and up-to-date. We have no reason to believe the weapon played a part in last night's event or any other, so here you go."

Carmack placed the pistol on the table with the keys.

I said, "Thanks."

Carmack glanced at Pike.

"Sure."

He painted me with the thoughtful smile again and reached into the case.

"Then there's this."

I saw the large manila envelope and the throb in my head became a bass hum. Carmack held out the envelope and I realized the envelope wasn't mine. It contained my wallet, watch, phone, and the ring Lucy gave me.

He said, "The hospital had these, but I took the liberty. You're a private investigator."

I emptied the contents before I answered. I wanted to check my messages, but ignored the phone.

"Yes, sir. Licensed and bonded."

"Uh-huh. Here on a job?"

I said, "The job?"

I slid Lucy's ring onto my finger. My knuckles were swollen and the ring wouldn't fit.

Carmack said, "Being a PI. Investigating."

Detectives often asked questions when they knew the answers to see if a subject would lie. If Carmack read the file he was testing me, but if he had the file testing me made no sense. I decided to go with a lie. Lying early was always better than lying later. If he called me out, pivoting to a more believable lie would be easier now than after I'd wrapped myself in a lie cocoon.

I strapped on my watch and noticed the face was cracked.

I said, "Nope, not working. Came to look around for a weekend spot, but after this, forget it."

Carmack didn't react.

"Well, that's too bad. Let's get on with it then. Tell me what happened."

"I was jumped. Three or four guys. Maybe five. My memory's kinda jumbled."

"You remember the men who attacked you?"

"Not so much. Shapes, mostly. Glimpses. It was dark."

Carmack glanced at Pike.

"Meaning, you can't identify them?"

"Never saw them before."

Carmack didn't believe me.

"Had you arranged to meet them?"

"No. Like I said, I've never seen them before."

Carmack glanced from me to Pike and back to me.

"A beef at a bar? Involving a woman? These guys got pissed and followed you?"

"I don't recall a bar."

Carmack's eyes turned flat. Maybe I had hit the lie limit and he was about to drop the Traci card, but he didn't. He took out a small green notebook with a silver spiral, opened it, and studied a page.

"The deps heard you mention a woman named Lucy. Were you with a woman named Lucy?"

Pike shifted. We felt it at the same time and knew Carmack didn't have a Traci card. He hadn't seen my file.

I said, "Lucy's my girlfriend. She's in Louisiana and I wasn't at a bar. If I knew their names I'd tell you. I don't."

His mouth tightened.

"They just showed up and beat you half to death."

"Yes."

"And these three or four or five assailants all showed up in a little brown truck?"

Carmack cocked his head, the head saying he might not know the whole truth but he knew I was lying.

I didn't answer, so he kept going.

"Dep heard you mumbling about men in a brown truck. You were talking about big guys, all squeezed into a truck like little fish?"

I wondered what else the deps heard. I tried to think of something to say, but the throb grew worse.

"There were two or three vehicles. A car and a couple of trucks."

Carmack's eyebrows arched. The arch was smug.

"Ah. And the car was, what, a Challenger?"

"I don't know."

"You may have mentioned a Challenger."

"I did?"

A smile split his face like a slit fish belly.

"Let's get back to the three or four or five gentlemen who happened by and left you for dead. What were you doing in Old Town?"

"I had to pee. I stopped to take a leak."

"At an abandoned shack in the dark."

"I wouldn't have stopped where people could see me."

"And the men who jumped you, were they peeing with you?"

Pike said, "Take it easy."

Carmack looked and Pike said it again.

"Take it easy."

I interrupted.

"They saw my car and stopped. The one guy said he wanted to buy it. I told him I wasn't interested. The next thing I knew someone threw a punch."

The goldfish eyes floated back to me and Carmack folded the pad.

"Because you wouldn't sell your car."

My head hurt, my face hurt, and I didn't like lying to him. Carmack seemed like a good cop trying to do the right thing. I felt jammed up and embarrassed.

"Because they were drunk assholes and if I could've reached my gun we'd be having a different conversation."

Carmack nodded, but not to me.

"Yeah, I guess we would."

Carmack's eyes went to Pike again, lingered, and returned.

"I ran his paper, too."

Carmack placed his little notebook in the briefcase and closed it.

"You, you have a pretty fair rep as a dick. Him, he's an out-and-out killer."

Carmack latched the case, the two snaps making a single sound.

"Don't do crime in my area."

"I don't do crime."

"Don't go looking for revenge or try to finish whatever bullshit business you were up to last night."

I didn't respond.

Carmack and his briefcase went to the door.

"Go home. My deps are gonna be watching for you, and they sure as hell better not find you here. Do we understand each other?"

"You're running me out of town."

"Both of you."

Carmack stepped into the hall and disappeared.

Pike said, "I don't think he bought your story."

I stared at Pike, thinking about the file.

"It had to be them."

"Who?"

"The file. Last night was about Thomas Beller. They didn't care about my gun or money, but they must've checked the envelope. They took it to see what I know."

Pike pushed from the wall.

"Let's get you home."

34

P ike left to find a nurse. I phoned Lori while I waited and got her
voice mail.

"It's me. Don't go to work today. If you're at work when you get
this, leave. These people are dangerous, Lori. Call me. I'll explain."

Pike returned a few minutes later, but getting released from the
hospital was like tunneling out of Alcatraz with a spoon. Everything
took forever.

I said, "Maybe we should run for it."

Pike said, "One of us would fall."

You see? A riot.

I checked my messages and found three texts from Traci and one
text from Dina.

TRACI:

Hey! Did u c me? They were so nice!!! It went
really really well! Kevin says I hit it out of the
park! The producer wants me BACK!! YAY!! Off
to meet investors—UGH!! Flying back tonight!
Have u detected anything??? haha

Ha ha.

TRACI:

Hey! At the gate! I hope I sleep on the plane!
UGH!! Did u find anything?? I'm dying to
know!!!

TRACI:

Hey! I'm home!! Hello??? Where R u?? U must
be busy but PUHLEEEZE!?!?

Reading her texts wore me out. Maybe it was the exclamation points.

Dina's text echoed Traci's, but without the exclamation points.

DINA:

Hi, this is Dina, Traci Beller's assistant.
Traci's trying to reach you. Please respond.

The text blurred. I blinked, trying to make the words and letters focus, but blinking didn't help. I wanted to respond, but didn't know what to tell them. I listened to Lucy's message. She had left a voice mail in her whispery, bedtime voice, hoping I had a good day and saying she loved me. I listened to her message twice and was halfway through it again when a male nurse arrived.

The nurse went over my discharge instructions. He had me sign a document saying my discharge instructions had been reviewed and left a printed copy for me to take home. It was eight pages long. A woman from the "administration team" walked me through the hospital's billing policy on a tablet computer and had me initial fourteen paragraphs I could not read. Pike watched me from the corner, silent as a sphinx.

A short, pretty nurse's aide swept into the room with a wide smile and cheery brown eyes.

"Hi, Mr. Cole, I'm Lila. I hear you're leaving us."

"As soon as possible."

"Do you need to go potty?"

"I'm good."

"The doctor wants me to check for blood in your urine, so you need to wee-wee and I have to see it."

Pike said, "Wee-wee and let's go."

Lila swept into the bathroom and returned with a large plastic drawstring bag.

"Here are your clothes and shoes. Would you like help getting dressed?"

"I'll manage. Thanks."

"Go make wee-wee and I'll come see. Use the cup."

I urinated into a clear plastic cup. Lila seemed delighted. I brushed my teeth with a hospital-issue toothbrush, washed my face with liquid soap that didn't lather, and dried myself with paper towels. The left knee of my pants was ripped and the top two buttons on my shirt were missing. Both the shirt and pants were specked with dark spots and streaks. I wanted the blood to be their blood, but it was mine.

I dressed and sat on the toilet to put on my shoes. It went okay until I stood. The room wobbled and tipped. I sat fast and braced against the wall. The room slowly righted like a ship rolled by a swell. I rode it out and stood again. Better.

Lila beamed when she saw me.

"Wonderful! You look great, Mr. Cole!"

"Lila, the world needs more people like you."

"Aren't you sweet! I'll get an orderly and we'll get you on your way."

Lila rushed away.

Pike was still in the corner, watching.

I said, "I'm fine."

Pike said, "Mm."

"I'm fine."

Pike told me he'd meet me at the entrance and left to get his

Jeep. He took my pistol. An orderly named Warren appeared with a wheelchair.

Warren said, "You ready?"

I sat. The next thing I knew Warren was gripping my shoulder.

"Mr. Cole?"

I looked around, but nothing made sense.

"You fell asleep. You damn near slid off the chair."

"I'm fine."

"I don't want to lose you, man. It'd be my ass."

I was in a wheelchair in a long beige hall and everything smelled cold. The world shook itself like a great shaggy dog, rolling until the floor was on the ceiling then rolling back, but only once, just the once. I was fine.

35

Joe Pike

Pike sat at the hospital's entrance, pondering the woman and her daughter and the Challenger and the trucks. Pike didn't believe Sadie or Anya would return to work, but a quick check made sense. If Anya or Sadie were present, Pike would return after he took Elvis home. Pike would start with the Givens and finish the mission. Pike's mission was the men who did this to Elvis.

Sliding glass doors opened and an orderly wheeled Cole into bright morning light. Pike noted how Cole winced and raised a hand to shield his eyes. Still sensitive.

Cole stood and walked to the Jeep without assistance, but he moved like a tightrope walker on a windy day.

Cole opened the passenger's door and paused.

"Where's my car?"

"At your house. Rick and Denny picked it up."

Pike owned a gun shop in Culver City. Rick and Denny worked for him.

Cole climbed aboard, squirming to make himself comfortable. He had trouble buckling up, so Pike reached across and did it for him.

Cole said, "Let's hit the florist first. If we luck into Anya or Sadie, we'll own this thing."

Pike started the engine and headed for the freeway, watching for black Challengers and brown or green pickup trucks. The early-hour sun blazed in front of them. Cole shielded his eyes again.

Pike pointed at the glove box.

"Shades."

Cole found an old pair of Oakleys with metallic-blue lenses. The traffic flowed well. Pike glanced at Cole. His eyes were closed.

"Elvis."

Cole's eyes opened. He seemed confused, then sat up and seemed fine. It was like his brain had double-clutched.

Pike said, "You good?"

"I fell asleep."

Pike was blown off a roof in Al Bayda, Libya, back in his contract days. Pike and his team had been hired to provide security for a group of British journalists who were meeting a local mullah at what they claimed was a secure location. Pike knew the three-story site was bullshit when he saw the narrow streets teeming with watchful locals, but the journalists wouldn't listen. So Pike was on the roof, clocking their surroundings, when a Soviet 82-mike-mike mortar round hit the building. The pressure wave slapped him off the roof and Pike hit the street flat on his back. Three stories. Pike had double-clutched for a week.

They reached the mall. Pike spotted the florist and stopped on the far side of the parking lot. Elvis was asleep.

"Elvis."

"I'm awake."

"We're there. How do I recognize these people?"

Cole tapped his phone and brought up a bad DMV photo of a skinny girl with hollow cheeks and pimples.

"This is Anya. Sadie looks like her, only older, bigger, and thicker. Five three, one-thirty. Dark brown hair with some gray, pulled back. Anya's still thin, but her skin is better."

Pike left Cole in the Jeep and entered the flower shop.

A tall, thin woman wearing a Harrison James apron immediately offered to help. She flashed big teeth and touched his arm when she offered. A toucher. Pike told her he'd like to look around first and moved away. None of the women he saw looked like any version of Anya's photo, but much of the shop was behind closed doors. One or both women might be in a back room or in the restroom or off making a delivery. Pike didn't like not knowing. The toucher was watching him, so he approached her.

"Excuse me. Is Sadie here?"

The toucher flashed the teeth and touched him again.

"Sadie? Why no, she isn't. May I help you?"

"Sadie usually helps me. Will she be in later?"

"Not today. She's out sick."

"Okay. Thanks."

Pike started away, but turned back.

"I hope Anya doesn't catch it."

The toucher grimaced.

"They're *both* sick. I hope it isn't the new Covid. They might be out for *days*."

Pike returned to his Jeep.

"Runners."

Cole looked up from his phone. His eyes looked heavy and his face was pale.

"She won't go."

Pike didn't know who Cole was talking about.

"Lucy?"

"Lori. I told her what happened, but she won't leave. Let's go to Camille's."

Pike decided Lori would keep. He fired up the Jeep and headed toward the freeway.

"I'm taking you home."

"Lori doesn't get it. She doesn't want to lose hours, but those guys could hurt her."

"I'll drop you off. I'll come back."

"But we're *here*."

Pike twisted the rearview so Cole could see himself.

"Your eyes look like pinwheels. We're going home."

Cole turned away and shook his head.

They reached the freeway and climbed the ramp to Los Angeles. Pike checked the mirror for trucks and Challengers, but he wasn't afraid they'd be followed. He was hoping.

They rode in silence for several minutes before Cole spoke again.

"You made Rick and Denny drive all the way out here in the middle of the night to pick up my car?"

Pike wasn't sure what to say.

"Yes."

Cole shook his head and dozed off a few minutes later.

Pike left the freeway in Studio City and turned south toward the hills. Cole woke at the bottom of the exit ramp but didn't speak until they reached Mulholland Drive at the crest of the hill.

He said, "Thank you."

Pike nodded.

They reached the A-frame a few minutes later. Cole's Corvette was in the carport. The top was up and the car's pale yellow skin gleamed. Cole studied the car as if it belonged to someone else.

"They washed my car?"

"Someone has to."

Cole laughed and let them into the house through the carport. Pike followed him through the kitchen into the living room. Cole slumped onto the couch, looking bone-deep exhausted.

Pike said, "How you doing?"

"I need a shower. I want to get out of these clothes."

Cole looked down at himself.

"They ruined my shirt."

Pike wondered what to do with Cole's pistol and finally set it on the dining table.

"I'll see Lori. She saw the truck? She spoke with the men?"

"Yeah."

"Call her. Tell her I'm coming."

Pike wanted to get going. If the Givens were running, the men might run. Pike had to run faster. He checked the time.

"Grace will check on you in a couple of hours."

Grace Gonzales and her husband lived next door.

Cole frowned, annoyed.

"No way. Why'd you tell Grace?"

"The doc said someone should check on you."

"I can check myself."

"It's set up. If you tell Grace not to come, she'll come anyway."

Pike went into the kitchen, took two bottles of water back to the living room, and handed a bottle to Cole. He opened the other for himself.

Pike felt uneasy about leaving.

"Need anything before I go?"

Cole took a breath.

"Did you tell Lucy?"

"Not my call."

"Okay. Thanks."

Cole struggled to his feet.

Pike said, "Want something to eat?"

Cole went to the stairs.

"I gotta clean up, is all. Go. Call if you need me."

Pike watched his friend mount the stairs, one careful step after another, as if his footing couldn't be trusted.

Pike wasn't sure what to do. He needed to go but didn't want to leave. Then he heard water running up in the loft. Elvis had turned on the shower.

Pike listened to running water.

He said, "I'll feed the cat."

Pike put out fresh food and water for the cat and let himself out.

36

Elvis Cole

Cold water beat into my back like freezing rain. I washed as best I could, taking care around the sutures, and watched bloody water circle the drain. I stayed in the cold until I was numb, then shut off the water, toweled myself, and went into the bedroom. The cat was on my bed.

I said, "I got my ass kicked."

The cat yawned.

I pulled on a fresh T-shirt and a clean pair of shorts, and sat with the cat. The lump throbbed, my back was stiff, and my hands hurt. The cat rubbed his face on my arm.

I said, "You're the best."

I sat with him for a while, then carried the ruined clothes down to the kitchen and threw them away.

I drank a glass of tap water, rinsed the glass, and fell asleep standing at the sink. I caught myself, filled a plastic bag with ice, and wandered back to the living room. The house felt strange. A cabinet door was ajar, but only a bit. The glass bowl on the narrow desk behind the dining table was usually on the right side of the desk. Now it sat on the left. I might have moved it, but didn't remember. Not remembering bothered me.

I was holding the ice on the lump when I remembered to call Lori. I called her cell and got her voice mail again. I told her Pike was coming, then called Pike to tell him I'd told her. He hung up without saying anything. Dependable.

Keeping my eyes open was difficult. I thought about Thomas Beller and Anya and Sadie and wondered what had happened. I thought I knew, but thinking you know and knowing weren't the same. Thinking without proof was only suspicion. *How to Be a Detective*, page one.

I pictured the big men reading my file. I'd made no meaningful notes except for a few names and one- or two-word comments. The Zalways and the SurfMutt. The salvage yard. Harrison James. The truck men knew I'd seen Lori, and Thomas Beller's clients were old news. My file would tell them nothing they didn't already know. I wondered what they thought of my penmanship.

I wanted to hear Lucy's voice. I held the phone in my lap and played her message on speaker. Hearing her made me smile. My split lip hurt, but I smiled anyway. Tough.

Her message ended and Lucy was gone. My head sagged. I dreamed, but not of Lucy. Shadows moved within my house. Traci Beller ran across a brushy desert. I tried to reach her, but shadowy tendrils wrapped my legs. Traci was screaming. I tried to save her. I tried to reach her in time, but I couldn't. She screamed.

37

Joe Pike

Pike left the freeway near Rancha and drove to Camille's. He doubted Lori Sanchez could offer anything new, but she'd stood face-to-face with the men from the brown truck. This made her valuable.

Two boys and a dog were sitting outside the minimart when Pike arrived, the boys sucking slushy drinks through bright pink straws. Pike parked at Camille's door and climbed from the Jeep. The taller boy saw him and jumped to his feet, the slushy cup flying.

"Holy crap! Run!"

The boys disappeared around the far end of the building. The dog stayed, licking slush from the curb as Pike entered the liquor store.

Camille's was meat-locker cold. A woman bundled in fleece behind the counter straightened when she saw him.

"You gotta be him."

"Joe."

Her lips flickered with a smile.

"Of course you are."

Pike moved through the store to the rear, clearing the premises. Lori stood as he passed.

"I can't believe this. Is Elvis okay?"

"No."

A door behind the cooler opened to a small room. Stacks of cased beer and soda. A small desk and chair. A toilet. The back door.

Lori called from the front.

"That's it? Just no? Is he going to be okay?"

"Yes."

Pike checked the door. Secure.

Lori's voice called again.

"Hey! What are you doing back there?"

Pike returned to the front.

"Have the truck guys come back?"

Lori rolled her eyes. Elvis had warned him about the eye-rolling.

"No, and don't start about I should leave. I can't afford to lose this job."

Pike checked the parking lot.

"You can pick them out of a line. You're a threat."

Lori's face scrunched and she crossed her arms. Angry.

"This is bullshit! That fucking Anya Given and her trash mother! That douche Eric and his big-mouth father! I minded my own business all this time and now I'm *fucked*. I don't deserve this!"

Pike said, "No."

He didn't know what else to say.

"I don't get it! I'm a good mom. I bust my ass at this shitty job. I don't have a life. It isn't fair!"

She seemed to be finished, so Pike asked the next question.

"How about the Challenger?"

Pike believed the Challenger was key. The Challenger had dogged Elvis since the beginning and led Elvis into the ambush. This meant he could reach the big men through the Challenger.

Lori made a half-hearted shrug.

"They came back last night. I didn't see them, but Elvis saw them. He was across the street."

"He was. Watching out for you."

Lori darkened, but didn't reply.

Pike said, "These are dangerous people. They could hurt you."

She slapped the counter with both hands.

"I *know*! They scared the shit out of me and you're making it worse."

"Sorry."

"I can't leave. I got a kid to feed. I get canned, it might take weeks to find another job. Months!"

Pike studied the cars rolling past and decided to let it go.

"I need your help to find these people."

Lori snorted.

"I helped Elvis find Anya and now I'm fucked."

Pike faced her.

"When I find them, I'll unfuck you."

Lori blinked twice and burst out laughing. Pike didn't see the humor.

He said, "Elvis saw the Challenger at least three times, but the first time he saw it was the day he met you. Here."

"Maybe they followed him."

"Not Elvis. These people couldn't follow Elvis."

Lori nibbled a lip, brooding, then came around the counter, locked the door, and put up the closed sign.

She studied him for a moment, thoughtful.

"Yeah. I've been thinking about it, too. It's weird."

Her mouth tightened into a bud.

"I'll bet that nasty little shit Jaime told them he was here."

"The cook?"

Elvis had spoken well about Jaime.

"Elvis was at the SurfMutt before he came here. It's like, what, a six-minute drive to get here? And the stupid Challenger showed up while Elvis was here? It was Jaime. Jaime knew Elvis was coming, so the little shit must've told them."

Lori seemed convinced and confident in her conclusion. Pike wasn't, but he decided to question Jaime.

"Okay. Thanks."

"Jaime got me fired once, so I know what I'm talking about. He's a shit."

Pike nodded, wondering if the big men would roll up after he left, the two trucks, green and brown, or the Challenger again. He thought she should leave but knew she wouldn't.

He said, "Can you shoot?"

"What are you talking about?"

Pike lifted his sweatshirt, letting her see the Python.

"Can you shoot?"

Lori made a tired smile.

"Thanks, but I'd end up shooting myself."

Pike covered the gun. He wanted to leave her with something.

"Then play it like this. If they come, run out the back. Don't try to lock the door or call anyone. Don't wait to see what they do. Run hard until you're with other people."

The eyes rolled.

"Okay. I'll run like I've got a rocket up my butt."

He went to the counter and wrote his cell number on a receipt slip.

"First call is nine-one-one, but not until you're safe. Second call is me."

She glanced at his number.

"You're serious."

Pike dipped his head and went to the door.

"You're right. It isn't fair."

Lori glanced at his number again and tucked it into her pants.

"If you want to go out sometime, I'm available."

Pike left the freezing store and went to his Jeep.

38

Pike reached the SurfMutt five and a half minutes after leaving the liquor store. Lori was spot-on with the drive time.

Cars and work trucks crowded the parking area, dust from a recent arrival swirling in the air. A dozen people were queued up to order, while a handful more waited near the pickup window. Pike parked at the skate park and unclipped the Python. The smell of hot grease and burning meat was strong.

Pike crossed the street and stopped near the queue. Two employees were in the SurfMutt, a sweating male wearing an apron and Dodgers cap and a younger female with multiple rings on her fingers. The male waved a spatula at the woman like he was angry and the woman didn't like it. She shouted so loudly Pike and the people in line heard her.

"I'm going as fast as I can, you asshole!"

The male pushed cartons of burgers and fries through the pickup window.

"Six! Seven!"

He spun to the grill like a man on fire, snapping at the woman.

"Call the little prick. Get his ass in here."

"I called! How many messages you wanna leave?"

"*More*, Donna! 'Til you get'm!"

Donna snatched up a phone and turned away.

Pike figured the male was Jaime. He stepped through the crowd to the pickup window and called the name.

"Jaime."

Jaime glanced over, his dark eyes angry.

Pike said, "Elvis Cole sent me."

The anger vanished. Jaime hurried to the window, wiping his hands as he shrugged at the line.

"I'm gettin' slammed here, bro. Whatchu need?"

Pike decided Jaime didn't know what happened.

"Answers."

Donna was back at her station, shouting another order.

"Two double ChiliMutts, no tomato, no onion. Two shaka fries add jalapeño."

Jaime glanced at the line.

"Gotta wait, bro. Fuckin' helper left me hanging."

Donna's voice rang again.

"Two beef tacos, two chicken tacos, one KahunaMutt taco!"

Pike didn't care about the line or the helper.

"Elvis got hurt, so let's talk."

Jaime stared, the line forgotten.

"Whatchu mean, hurt?"

"Jumped. Remember the guys in the truck?"

Jaime turned toward the grill.

"Around back. The door. We'll talk while I sling."

Pike found the door as Jaime pushed cartons through the pickup window.

"Eight! Nine! Ten!"

Jaime spun to the grill, glanced at Pike, and built more burgers and tacos while Donna filled cups and scooped fries.

"He gonna be okay?"

"He'll make it. Seen the green truck again?"

"Nah. It was them?"

Jaime pushed more cartons.

"Eleven! Twelve!"

Pike said, "A brown truck? A big dude. Huge."

Jaime dealt fresh patties and scooped fried meat onto tortillas, talking as he worked. He waved the spatula at the parking lot.

"Trucks all the time, but not those *culeros*. They didn't want him here. Got up in his face."

He glanced at Pike as he worked.

"You work with him, friends, what?"

"Both."

Another order rang out. Pike waited until Donna finished before he continued.

"Know anyone drives a black Challenger?"

"Thirteen! Fourteen! Knew a cat had a black Firebird. Had the big bird on the hood."

"A Challenger dogged Elvis when he saw Lori Sanchez."

"Yeah. The liquor store over here, by the builder's supply."

"Camille's. You told him where she works. Elvis drove over and the Challenger showed up. Right after he spoke with you."

Jaime stopped. He stood very still as Pike continued.

"The same Challenger led Elvis into an ambush last night, part of the crew who jumped him."

Jaime turned toward Pike as Donna called an order.

"One SurfMutt, no cheese, one double, no cheese, no—"

Jaime cut her off.

"Hold the order."

Donna blinked.

"Hold? You see this line?"

"No orders."

Jaime wet his lips.

"What the hell, *ese*? You saying something here?"

Pike watched the spatula. Jaime held it at his side and gripped it like a hatchet.

"Someone told the Challenger where to find him."

"I don't know anyone drives a Challenger. I sure as hell didn't tell anyone Elvis asked about an old employee. Who'd give a shit?"

Donna suddenly spoke.

"Arturo's friend has a car like that."

Jaime scowled.

"'Turo?"

"Uh-huh. I think."

Pike said, "Who's Arturo?"

Jaime's scowl deepened.

"The lame-ass helper who left me hanging. He was here when Elvis asked about Lori."

Pike went to Donna.

"Arturo's friend has a black Challenger?"

"It was wide and black. Aren't they wide?"

She didn't know. A wide black car could be anything.

"The friend, do you know his name?"

Donna made a shrug like a cringe. Apologetic.

"They passed me this time, in the car? I said, who was your stupid friend, you guys were going too fast? He just laughed, told me watch I don't get hit."

Jaime slapped the counter with the spatula.

"Damnit!"

He tossed the spatula aside and snatched up the phone.

"Little prick ain't been answering, but I'll find him. I'll kill him, he had anything to do with this."

Pike touched the phone, the touch saying stop.

"Where does he live?"

A male voice shouted from the pickup window.

"What the hell, Jaime? Where's my food?"

Pike said, "Get his food. I'll find the kid."

Jaime stared at Pike, then the customer.

"Comin' right up."

Jaime flipped the open sign to closed, shut the order window, and handed the spatula to Donna.

"Finish the orders. I'm gonna go."

Donna's eyes filled with terror. She shook her head.

"Wait. You want me to cook?"

"Yeah. Cook."

Jaime pulled off his apron and turned to Pike.

"He lives with his *'lita*. I'll take you out there."

Pike didn't know Jaime and didn't want company.

"An address is fine."

"They don't have an address. Nobody has an address out where they live. I gotta show you."

They took the Jeep. Pike drove.

39

Jaime directed him along roads lined by telephone poles with sagging lines dotted with crows. The crows watched them pass.

Pike said, "Who lives with Arturo besides his grandmother?"

"Just them. His 'lita, Ms. Melendez, she's nice. Got the arthritis bad, though."

"A girlfriend? The grandma's boyfriend? Brothers and sisters?"

Pike wanted information. The more you knew going in, the better your chances coming out.

Jaime shrugged, like how should he know?

"Nobody, far as I know. I've been out here, what, two or three times? All I know is what they say."

They passed a sign. Landfill.

Jaime sat forward, peering ahead.

"Right up here. Pass the tank and go left."

They passed a rusted propane tank as large as a landlocked submarine. Pike went left.

"How close?"

"Coming up. Go left again."

Small buildings half-hidden by oak trees appeared.

"What kind of car does he drive?"

"Rides a bike. He don't have a car."

"What color?"

"Shit, I don't know. Red? Black? Who gives a shit?"

Jaime sat taller and pointed.

"There. That one."

Arturo and his grandmother lived in a small, square stucco box six-point-two miles northeast of the SurfMutt. Other boxes were scattered nearby and all the boxes looked the same. White. Flat rock roofs. Gray dish antennas all aimed at the same point in space. A two-tone, tan-on-brown Chevy pickup was parked in the yard by the bright blue front door. Pike didn't see a bike, but the bike could be inside or behind the house. Cars and trucks sat at the nearby homes, but none were black Challengers.

Pike said, "Whose truck?"

"Ms. Melendez. I'll bet the little prick ain't even home."

Pike slid out, clipped the Python at his waist, and covered it with the sweatshirt. Jaime stared like Pike was nuts.

"Bro! You doan need no piece!"

Pike went to the door. Jaime hurried after him and got there first. Jaime reached to ring the bell, but Pike stopped him.

"Listen."

"She's an old lady."

Pike listened for movement and voices, and heard nothing. He nodded, the nod telling Jaime, go on, ring.

Jaime pressed the button. A screeching metal buzz inside was so loud Jaime made a joke.

"If he was sleeping, this sonofabitch sure woke his ass."

Pike heard a board creak and a slow rhythmic tap tap tap. A woman spoke behind the door.

"Who's there?"

Jaime said, "Jaime Gomez. From the SurfMutt."

A short, wide woman opened the door. Marisol Melendez had

wispy gray hair, arthritic hands, and a brown wood cane. Her eyes flicked from Jaime to Pike to Jaime. She smiled, but Pike thought her smile was worried.

"Mr. Gomez. *Buenos días.* So good to see you."

Jaime ducked his head. Respectful.

"*Buenos días.* I'd like to see Arturo, *por favor.*"

The woman shifted, steadying herself with the cane.

"He isn't at work?"

A small living room was visible behind her. Empty.

Jaime said, "No. He didn't come to work this morning and he hasn't returned my calls. I been looking for him. You know where he is?"

Her eyebrows bunched like nervous caterpillars. She shifted. Tap.

"He didn't come home. Wasn't he at work last night?"

"Yes. Until we closed."

"He didn't come home. He wasn't here this morning, but I assumed he went to work. I'm so embarrassed."

"Arturo should be embarrassed. Not you, *madrecita.*"

Shift. Tap. She leaned on the cane with both hands, the worry bubbling beneath her skin.

"This isn't like him. He calls. I don't know where he is."

Shift. Tap.

Pike said, "Maybe he was with friends last night."

Her eyes grew blurry.

"Are you police?"

"Jaime's friend. I offered to drive."

Jaime nodded.

"He's a friend, *madrecita.* I need Arturo at work. If you know who he was with, I'll pick him up."

"I expected him home. He didn't say anything about friends."

The woman was afraid and growing more afraid. Pike felt bad for her, but he wanted Arturo. He held out his phone, showing a black Challenger.

"Does one of his friends drive a car like this?"

She glanced at the picture. Tap.

"Yes."

"Tall guy, thin. Straight black hair like a curtain."

She glanced at Jaime and Pike saw a flash of anger in her eyes.

"Yes. I don't like this one. I told Arturo, stay away from these boys, but he don't listen."

Pike held the phone closer.

"A car like this."

"This car. The boy, he was here, he spun the car in circles here in my yard. I could see him laughing, making the dust. I had to wash my truck."

Pike put away his phone.

Jaime said, "Who is this, 'lita?"

"I never knew. I told Arturo, don't have friends like this, so he never been back. How do you know this boy? Are they in trouble?"

Jaime took her hand. Offering comfort.

"From the restaurant. I thought Arturo might be with him, but I don't know. He might be with a girl. Maybe they eloped, ha?"

Ms. Melendez laughed.

"Stupid girl!"

Jaime squeezed her hand.

"Arturo will be home soon. Have him call me."

"Will he lose his job?"

Jaime glanced at Pike.

"Give us a minute."

Pike went to the Jeep and climbed in behind the wheel. He studied Ms. Melendez's home and her two-tone truck and the surrounding homes and vehicles. A dull red Toyota Highlander outside the far house, a two-door Chevy sedan and Yamaha trail bike at the house to the right, a house with three pink flamingo lawn decorations on the far left. Pike fixed the scene in his mind and memorized their relative locations.

Jamie finished with Ms. Melendez and walked to the Jeep with his head down. He didn't look at Pike or say anything when he got in.

Pike said, "You were good with her."

"I used to be that kid. Fuckin' idiot."

They drove back in silence.

The SurfMutt was closed when they arrived. Donna had locked up and gone.

Pike stopped by the tables and Jaime got out.

Pike said, "Thanks."

Jaime closed the door and walked to the SurfMutt without looking back.

Pike pulled away and went hunting for the Challenger.

40

Elvis Cole

Explosions rocked my A-frame like cannon fire.

SNAP SNAP SNAP.

"Wake up."

I opened my eyes and saw Grace Gonzales inches away.

I said, "This is silly."

"Look at me. Here."

She tapped her forehead.

Grace was a professional stuntwoman. Her husband was a stunt coordinator and their three grown sons made livings by crashing cars, jumping motorcycles over trains, and falling off buildings. Concussions probably ran in their family.

Grace studied my eyes. She probably knew more about concussions than the doctor.

"Any numbness or slurred speech? Tingly feelings where you shouldn't tingle?"

"Only when you're close."

Grace stepped back and shook her head.

"You look like you got your ass kicked."

"I fell off the deck."

The lumps felt tight, but didn't throb. The headache was gone and I felt pretty good. I stood to test myself and felt normal.

Grace said, "We made Mexican lasagna last night. I'll bring some when I come back."

Grace and her husband were my nearest neighbors. We could see each other from our decks.

"You don't have to come back. I'm fine."

Grace hesitated. I knew she wanted to ask what happened, but she didn't.

"Hydrate. Rest. I'll be back."

I drank another glass of water, peed, and opened the sliding glass door. The sky was a lovely crystal blue and no brighter than usual. I walked to the far end of the deck and back, then took a slow, deep breath to see what would happen. My upper back hurt and a sharp pain lanced my lower right ribs, but I'd broken ribs before and felt worse. Toughness was a virtue.

I went inside, checked my messages, and found the same three texts from Traci, the text from Dina, and the voice message from Lucy. Nothing new. I was listening to Lucy's message when Joe Pike called.

"Elvis Cole Detective Agency. Our dicks are tough."

"Grace says you're doing okay."

"Does everyone talk about me behind my back?"

"A kid named Arturo Melendez works with Jaime. He's tight with the guy who drives the Challenger."

I remembered Jaime shouting.

"The assistant cook?"

"Yes. He could've heard Jaime tell you about Lori and flagged the squints."

"You get their names?"

"He hasn't been seen since last night."

"Another runner."

I flashed to the fight, a truck roaring out of the dark, shapes piling out, running toward me.

"Was he with them last night?"

"I'll know when I find him."

Pike hung up.

I returned to the couch and felt depressed.

Anya and Sadie, gone. Our first new lead, Melendez, gone. The big men and the squints were probably gone, too.

I pictured them barreling down the highway in a crazy psychedelic bus like in Tom Wolfe's book about Ken Kesey and his Merry Pranksters. Anya and Sadie were driving, Anya looking small and frail, Sadie looking hard and fierce, every inch the woman who'd sent thugs to frighten Lori. I thought about how Lori described her, an actual card-carrying convicted criminal, and wondered if it was true. If it was true, something in her record might help find her, so I called a friend named Lou Poitras. Lou was an LAPD captain and one of my closest friends.

Poitras said, "Lemme guess. You've been arrested and need a bondsman."

"I need the sheet and DCR on a female named Sadie Given, no s at the end. Can you get it?"

Pulling a record of arrests and prosecutions from a civilian aggregate site was easy, but the information provided by civilian sites was limited. And filing a formal request with the California DOJ and Department of Corrections took forever.

Lou said, "I can get it. The question is, do you want to get me fired?"

"No, I want you to be careful."

LAPD personnel weren't allowed to check criminal histories or DMV records without cause. Case and badge numbers had to be provided and computer activity was reviewed. If a supervisor questioned the request, the requesting officer had to provide a legitimate reason.

Lou said, "Sounds like something's in your mouth. Are you eating?"

The swollen lip.

"Dentist. I'm still numb. C'mon, Lou, it's important."

"Is this person currently incarcerated?"

"No, but I'm told she did time."

"So what's your interest here?"

"Background. Her history and criminal affiliations are relevant to a case."

"I'll see what I can do."

"Thanks, Lou."

"You oughta sue your dentist."

I tossed the phone aside and checked myself in the downstairs bathroom mirror. The mirror sent me back to the kitchen for more ice, but the ice didn't help my frustration. I was sidelined and didn't like it. I wanted to work the case.

Losing my file wasn't like losing a lottery ticket. The file could be replaced, so I pulled out my laptop and went to work re-creating it.

I printed the lost sections of Jess Byers's report, took the pages to the couch, and added the notes I'd made on the original. Recalling them was easy. Even concussed.

> *Samantha Mason—Beller on phone twice?*
> *Frank Zalway—Eric deceased—worked w Laura or Lori—saw*
> *   Beller?*
> *SurfMutt—Jaime—Lori Chance worked w Eric—fired*
> *Lori Sanchez—Camille's Liq—Beller back 4 din?—Anya Given—*
> *   ride w Beller?—15? Whoa!*
> *Anya—DMV address & phone—salvage yard?*
> *Anya and Sadie Given—Harrison James*

The original file had included a few addresses and phone numbers, but I needed to look them up. I yawned and decided to look them up later.

The big man must've read it. He and Sadie had probably read it together. I wondered if the awesomeness of my detection left them frightened or relieved. It probably made them yawn.

I yawned.

I stretched out on the couch and wondered what they knew about Thomas Beller. I wondered what they had done and where they were and what they were doing.

I yawned again and fell asleep while I was yawning.

41

Grace woke me with a tray of Mexican lasagna. Grace's Mexican lasagna was layered with corn tortillas, refried beans, asadero and cotija cheese, and chopped beef slow-cooked with chilies in home-made salsa roja. Hers was one of the world's great Mexican lasagnas and my all-time favorite.

I sat up wide-awake and starving.

"You're beautiful."

I ate half the tray standing in the kitchen, put the rest away for later, and checked my messages. Nothing new. I examined my face. The lump was still a hairy clam and my lip was still swollen and split. The healing power of even the best lasagna was limited.

I let myself out and sat on the deck. A hawk glided past in a gentle descent. Three crows glided past in the opposite direction, rolled onto their backs, and dropped away like sparkling black diamonds. Showing off for the hawk. The sun was nice. I felt myself nodding, so I went inside, turned on the television, and turned it off. I watched the black screen until I fell asleep. This was me, accepting the inevitable.

Grace came again, but I was awake when she arrived. She looked surprised.

"You're awake."

"Your lasagna. I am healed."

She laughed, went away, and I napped again. Maybe I wasn't concussed. Maybe this was sleeping sickness.

Something woke me, but it wasn't Grace. The cat was on my chest. Purring. I scratched his head.

"Hey, buddy."

He hopped off and trotted straight to the kitchen.

I gave him fresh food, used the toilet, and returned to the couch. The canyon was cut with shadows. The eastern horizon was a deep blue tinged with purple.

I checked my phone and found a new text.

TRACI:
Since you haven't answered, I'm coming to see
what's wrong.

I was staring at the text when a car pulled up out front.

I made it to the peephole as Traci Beller and her Uncle Phil reached my door. I didn't have enough time to punch eyeholes into a grocery bag, pull the bag over my head, and pretend I was the Unknown Detective. I opened the door before Traci rang the bell.

"I'm practicing for Halloween. Great makeup, huh?"

They stopped, caught in a moment between expectation and shock. Traci reached to touch my arm, but didn't.

"Oh my God. What happened?"

"Fell off my bike. It's fine. C'mon in."

They stepped past me, but stopped in the entry, Traci staring at me and Phil looking suspicious.

He said, "Doesn't look fine. You must've fallen a damn long way."

I didn't want to explain about the big men and the squints and the rest of it. Explaining would only offer disturbing speculations based on assumptions and innuendo, and they'd have questions I couldn't answer.

I said, "Far enough. Idiot came flying down the trail too fast and piled into me."

Traci said, "That's awful. You could've been killed."

Phil frowned and glanced at Traci.

"Well, sorry to barge in, but Traci was wondering if you'd made any progress."

Traci looked embarrassed.

"You didn't answer my texts."

"I know. Sorry. I didn't have anything new to report and then this happened."

I tried to make an apologetic shrug, but shrugging hurt. Traci looked even more embarrassed.

"I'm so sorry. I just thought, you know, after you found someone who saw him, you might've found someone who spoke to him, like that boy, Eric."

Like Anya.

"I'm on it, Traci. I won't let you down."

Phil said, "Honey, let's let Mr. Cole get back to healing. Give us a minute, okay?"

Traci said good-bye and started away. I stopped her.

"Hey. I'm glad the TV appearance went well. Congratulations."

She flashed the Traci Beller grin.

"Did you see me?"

"I didn't. Forgot to record it."

"They put up a link. I'll send it."

Phil waited until Traci reached the car before he spoke.

"I called the lady who kept our books. She doesn't remember Tommy having an extra cell. She even checked her old address book. The only two numbers she had were the same numbers we all had, his home and the cell."

"You wanted a moment to tell me about the phone?"

He hesitated.

"I didn't tell her about the phone. It makes him look bad and it might not even be true."

Phil considered me for a moment.

"I know what an ass-kicking looks like. You had your ass kicked."

"Occupational hazard."

"Because of Tommy?"

He glanced toward Traci.

"C'mon, man, I won't tell her. Is this because of Tommy?"

"Because I'm asking about him."

Phil's jowly face grew intense.

"What happened to him?"

"I don't know. Maybe nothing. That's the truth."

Phil gestured at my face.

"The boy who did this knows."

"Did I say boy, as in singular?"

Phil's face split with a tight grin.

"Sorry. I meant men, as in a whole damn gang."

The grin vanished.

"What happened out there?"

"People started following me. They got tired of following and decided to be more assertive."

"You don't know who?"

"Jumped me in the dark. If I knew who, I'd have them arrested."

Phil nodded and pooched his lips, thinking.

"Is Tommy dead?"

The lump hurt. I was getting a headache.

"I don't know."

"He still alive? Is Tommy living out in Rancha?"

I was sorry I'd opened the door.

"Phil, I don't know."

"People did this, they're scared. Scared means they're hiding something and you were getting close."

"To what?"

"To whatever they're hiding."

The lump throbbed. I stifled a yawn.

"I guess."

"Or whoever."

"Phil, I have to make some calls. The minute I know anything for sure, I'll tell Traci."

"Should I keep digging around for a second phone or let it go?"

"Keep digging."

Phil nodded.

"Rest. You look like hell."

He turned to leave.

I said, "Phil?"

Phil stopped.

He said, "What's that?"

"Tell Traci not to send more muffins."

I closed the door and went back to sleep.

42

Joe Pike

Pike returned to the Melendez home, but didn't drive to the door. He parked near the main road, approached on foot from the south, and studied Ms. Melendez's house and the neighboring homes through a pair of Zeiss binoculars from three hundred yards away.

Ms. Melendez's two-tone truck had not moved. Pike saw no bicycles, other vehicles, or people at her home. The red Highlander was where he remembered it. A young woman sprayed two small children with a hose near the Yamaha dirt bike. The children were laughing but Pike could not hear them. Nothing else moved. He checked for dogs. A dog would be a problem. He memorized the relative locations of the houses and vehicles from this location, then backed away and circled behind the house.

From his new position, Pike saw the back of the house. He noted a windowed door beneath a metal awning, a small half-sized window to the left of the door, and two full-sized windows to the right. The windows were shut, but their drapes were open. The remains of a rusted-out metal tub once used as a backyard pool or water trough was ten yards from the door. Pike wasn't able to see the two-tone truck or the front of the house, but he could see the woman and her children and three of the five neighboring homes. Satisfied he knew the layout, Pike withdrew and jogged to his Jeep.

Most of the criminals Pike arrested during his three years as a Los Angeles police officer had returned home when being pursued. Car thieves who'd fled on foot when five-oh had them boxed, armed robbery suspects on the run from shootouts with Glock-wielding shop owners, and gang rat savages BOLOed for shooting into a crowd of women and children at a bus stop. Wanted and on the run, they ran to a place where they felt safe, which usually meant a girlfriend or their mother. Home. And they almost always waited until dark. If Arturo felt the police were after him, he would probably show up after sundown. This gave Pike the rest of the day to search for the Challenger.

Pike parked near the freeway and made a list of sixteen independent garages, transmission repair shops, and brake and alignment specialists within twelve miles of Rancha. He then drove from shop to shop, asking mechanics and service managers if they knew anyone with a black, late-model Challenger who might be willing to sell. Pike had tried to come up with a better pretense, but nothing came to mind.

Pike phoned Camille's at twenty after four. Lori answered, sounding bored.

"Discreet Liquor."

"Pike. You okay?"

"I'm bored. Hang on."

She finished with a customer and returned.

"They haven't been back. You got me all worked up for nothing."

Pike wasn't sure what to say. She went on before he could think of something.

"I've been watching out this damn window all day, too scared to go pee. They're not coming back and I'm tired of waiting for them. This place is dead. I haven't had a dozen customers."

Pike said, "Okay."

"That's all you got? Okay?"

"If you see them, run. Run and call me."

"Oh. My. God."

The phone went dead.

A murky sun hovered above the western horizon when Pike left the last shop. Of the sixteen service centers and garages, only two recalled servicing a black Challenger, but both promised to check their records and get back to him. Pike knew they wouldn't.

The sky was a serious purple when Pike left his Jeep, once again approached the Melendez home on foot, and settled in the brushy field to wait. The two-tone truck remained in its place. The front door was closed, the window drapes open. The purple overhead deepened to black and the black crept west. A light SUV arrived and parked at the far house. A woman entered. A darker pickup arrived, stopping at the house to the right. A man lifted something bulky from the truck's bed and carried it into the house. People returning from work.

The star field and moonlight painted the landscape in silver and gray. The stark white boxes in the distance glowed, their windows tiny golden rectangles and squares.

Pike watched.

A small humped car arrived, following its headlights to the house beyond the Melendez home. A couple got out, entered the house, and its windows filled with gold.

Pike watched.

Time didn't pass. Nothing passed. Pike ate trail mix and a sour-dough roll. He was.

Headlights approached.

A black-and-white SUV arrived, sweeping the two-tone truck with light as it parked. Pike checked the vehicle with his spotting scope and saw a six-pointed star on its side. Sheriffs. Two uniformed deputies climbed out and went to Ms. Melendez's door. The door opened and Ms. Melendez appeared. They spoke for a moment before the deputies entered her home. Pike knew the police went to a home for only two reasons: to ask questions or deliver information. This time of night, they were delivering.

Pike circled behind the house and crept to the back door. He heard nothing inside, so he rounded the corner of the house to a living room window. He stayed well back, beyond the glow from the window.

Ms. Melendez was on the couch, pressing a clutch of tissues to her eyes. An older dep sat beside her and the second dep sat in a chair nearby. Pike crept closer to hear.

The older dep's voice was kind.

"Do you have someone you can call? It'd be good to have someone with you."

"I can't believe this. My little Arturo."

The younger dep said, "Maybe a friend or one of your neighbors?"

"Who would kill him? Who? How could someone kill him like this?"

The older dep took her hand.

"Detectives will come see you tomorrow. They'll find who did it. We'll find them."

The younger dep stood.

"I'll see if one of your neighbors can come over."

Ms. Melendez waved the tissues.

"Don't. I don't want to see nobody."

"Someone should check on you, see how you're doing. Make sure you're all right."

She waved the tissues again, annoyed.

"My niece checks. I'll call her. She's always checking."

Pike backed away and waited behind the rusted tub until the deputies drove away. When their SUV disappeared, he circled back for his spotting scope, returned to his Jeep, and phoned Cole.

"Arturo's dead. The sheriffs just left his grandmother."

"Wow. His pals with the Challenger do it?"

"All I know is he was murdered."

"I'll see what I can find out. What are you going to do?"

"Think of something else."

Pike ended the call and considered Ms. Melendez. He liked the old woman. Pike wondered if he should let Jaime know, but decided against it. The police would question the people who worked with Arturo and Jaime might tell them Pike had called with the news.

Pike's thoughts returned to something one of the deps told Ms. Melendez, how someone should check on her, see how she's doing.

People did this. When they were worried or wanted to know how someone was doing, they checked. Pike wondered if someone had checked on Elvis.

The hospital was quiet when Pike arrived. He parked near the ER entrance and entered the waiting room. The man in the gray suit and the two tired women from the night before had been replaced by a thin young woman with a bad cough and a three-year-old in her lap. The woman's cough was deep and dry. COUGH . . . COUGH . . . COUGH. It sounded bad.

The desk was deserted, so Pike rapped on the counter.

A heavyset woman stepped from the security office.

"May I help you?"

"The security officer last night was a Mr. Lyle. Is he on duty tonight?"

Lyle emerged from the same office and came to the counter. He was wearing a short-sleeved plaid shirt and cowboy boots.

"Hell yeah I am. Soon as I change."

The woman went back into the office. Lyle watched her disappear and turned to Pike.

"How's your friend?"

"Home. Got out this morning."

"Hey, that's real good. What can I do you for?"

"Did anyone come around last night, asking about him?"

Lyle looked vague.

"Asking what?"

"If he was here, how he was doing? Might've been this morning."

"The sheriff asked."

"Not the sheriff. Might've asked about him by name, but maybe not."

"If someone asked up at the front or called, I wouldn't know."

"I understand."

Lyle looked vague again, so Pike let him think.

"A woman. Yeah, a woman came in. Wasn't me she asked, but I was here. Charleen had the desk."

Pike said, "Good."

"Good what?"

Pike took a slow breath. The breath flowed out. He clocked the black ball camera domes above the desk and in the ceiling, the cameras covering the entrance and the waiting room. Hospitals had more surveillance cameras than banks.

Lyle said, "What?"

"What time did she come in?"

"Around seven, something like that. You want to ask Charleen, she won't be here until oh-four-hundred."

"I don't want to ask Charleen."

Pike touched the monitor on the desk.

"I want to see the woman. Around seven. Something like that."

Lyle glanced toward the office.

"My boss. She'd kill me."

"I can wait."

Lyle glanced again and lowered his voice.

"The woman, she involved with what happened?"

Pike nodded. Once.

"The guys who beat up your friend?"

Pike nodded. Once.

"No shit? Tell the police."

Pike didn't respond. He didn't move. He stared at Lyle and Lyle's eyes turned smoky.

"I help, you can't tell anyone. I'd lose my job."

"I won't tell."

"Not ever. I mean it."

"I always mean it."

Lyle studied the waiting room.

"She takes off at midnight. She goes, we'll look."

At midnight, they looked.

PART THREE

43

Elvis Cole

Morning filled my bed with a lovely amber light. The lump was still tender and my side was stiff, but I felt rested, hungry, and good to go. Sitting up hurt. The cat was curled at the foot of my bed, surrounded by downy, gray feathers and a tiny clawed foot.

I said, "You're killing me."

I got up to pee and checked my face. The lump was still a clam, but maybe smaller, and my lip was less swollen. The bruising was still purple, but I ignored it. A positive outlook was important.

I cleaned the cat's mess, pulled on a pair of shorts, and went onto the deck. I tried a few stretches. My side hurt and downward-facing dog made the lump throb. I knocked off ten dips and ten push-ups in a burst of optimism. My ribs screamed, but my head didn't explode. Progress.

I was filling a bag with ice when Pike called.

I said, "Elvis Cole tip of the day: Don't do dips with broken ribs."

"Check the picture. Know the woman?"

"What picture?"

My phone buzzed with an incoming message.

A high-angle photo showed Sadie Given at a counter in what looked like a bank or business. The image was sharp, clear, and in color. I smiled. My lip hurt, but screw it.

"Damn. You got her."

"This is Sadie?"

"Yes. Where is she?"

"Dunno. This is where she was, at the ER desk in the hospital. She wanted to know if you were going to make it."

I expanded the image. The overhead lighting made her eyes hollow and the lines in her face deeper than I remembered. She looked worried.

"When was this taken?"

"Yesterday morning, a little after seven."

I was still in the hospital. Pike was with me and the cop was in the hall.

"Maybe she came to finish what her friends started."

"She wanted to know your status. Told them she heard you were dead or died on the way in, was it true? That kind of thing."

"Trying to figure out their next move. If I'm dead, maybe they stay and ride it out. If I'm going to make it, they're thinking I'll go to the cops, so they run."

"The hospital wouldn't confirm or deny, so she left. This was her ride."

A second photo arrived.

The new image showed a brown Chevy pickup in the hospital's parking area. The truck was turning away from the camera. The driver wasn't visible, but Sadie was the passenger.

"You get the plate?"

"A partial."

The next image showed the first four numerals of a license plate. The numerals were pixelated, but the first three were readable. 6UJ. The fourth one could've been B, E, or D.

I caught myself breathing faster and told myself to calm down. It was early, but Dickie Timmons had a bad commute. He went in early to beat the traffic.

I said, "Where are you now?"

"Home. Cleaned up. Ate."

"I'll call Dickie and get back to you."

I called. Dickie told me to hang on, followed by the usual pause.

"Okay, I'm back. Whatcha need?"

"You up for an add-on?"

"What's add-on mean, no tickets?"

"It's a single plate, Dickie. What the hell?"

"Okay, all right, take it easy. What?"

"Registration for a two-door Chevrolet pickup, brown, first three numerals Six, Uniform, Juliet. The fourth could be Bravo, Echo, or Delta. I'd guess Bravo."

"Guessing doesn't help. I'll run all three. You got the year?"

"No. Limit the owner address to L.A. and Ventura County zip codes."

"That's it? Just the one?"

"Just the one."

"Back soon."

Soon felt like forever. The big man was in my sights and I wanted to bring him down. I paced and rolled my shoulders and walked in circles on the deck until I got fed up with circling and called John Chen. Chen was a criminalist with LAPD's Forensic Science Division and was the greediest person I knew. John was also a profound paranoid. He answered with a whisper.

"Can't talk. She's watching me."

You see?

"They're not watching you, John. You're paranoid."

"Not my boss. The new lab tech. The bitch is *smokin'*! I think she wants me!"

John never missed a chance to display his misogyny.

"Watch her back. I need a favor."

"Upside potential?"

John and I had helped each other in the past and helping me had led to face time on the local news. John coveted fame almost as much as money and hot lab techs.

"None, but this is easy. Are you at your desk?"

"Yeah. Watching this sexed-up bitch."

You see?

"Murder vic by the name of Arturo Melendez out by Rancha. I need the deets."

"That's the sheriff, not us."

LAPD's Criminalistics Lab handled crime scenes within LAPD's service area, but the Sheriff's Department's Scientific Services Bureau covered crimes outside the area. They were two different agencies, but both worked out of the Hertzberg-Davis Forensic Science Center at Cal State L.A.

I said, "You work next door to each other, John. Walk across the hall."

He lowered his voice still more.

"They don't like us. We're better."

"Get the deets, John. Please."

"Was the dude rich? Tied to a celeb?"

"He flipped burgers."

"Yawn. I'll get back to you."

I was eating leftover Mexican lasagna when my phone dinged. I grabbed it, thinking Dickie or John had responded, but Sadie Given's records had arrived. The combined CDOJ and DCR documents totaled forty-seven pages. I was printing her record when my phone dinged again.

Dickie.

The DMV search produced a surprisingly short list. Including the B, E, and D combinations, the number of two-door, brown Chevrolet pickups registered in L.A. and Ventura Counties totaled twelve vehicles. Each registration began with the license number followed by the owner's name and address.

The owner names meant nothing, but the third address stopped me. I called Pike.

"The owner is a Charley Lloyd Reed. The address on the registration is the address Anya used for her driver's license."

"The salvage yard."

"Yeah. R&R Salvage. The staff claimed they'd never heard of her. Charley and Sadie probably know I was there. They'll avoid it."

"Maybe the staff wasn't lying."

"How could they not know her?"

"Maybe Charley owns it and let Anya use the address because he's with Sadie and Anya's their kid."

"You should be the detective and I should be the sidekick."

"The what?"

"It's a term of endearment."

I gave him the address and the truck's full plate and carried my laptop to the couch. Pike had me thinking about the salvage yard, so I ran a business license search for R&R Salvage and found Charley L. Reed and Christopher P. Reed named as the co-owners. I called Pike to tell him.

"You were right. Charley owns the salvage yard with someone named Christopher P. Reed."

"Brothers."

"Christopher P. is probably the other big man."

Pike didn't respond.

"Anyway, thought I'd call, let you know you were right."

Pike hung up.

You had to love him.

I gathered Sadie's records and went through them.

Juvenile records weren't included in her jacket, but her adult arrests were listed in order with each entry including the usual booking information (date, place, charges against, etc.), the ultimate disposition of the charge (dismissed, reduced, or convicted), and case notes by arresting officers, prosecutors, and judges. Between the ages of eighteen

and twenty-five, Sadie had been arrested twice for shoplifting, once
for petty theft, once for assault, and three times for drug possession.
Each of the seven arrests was marked DISPO DISMISSED, which meant
the presiding judge had given her a break, or DEJ DISMISSED, which
meant the judge diverted her to counseling. Notes included by two
judges and three prosecutors referenced Sadie's status as the single
mother of a minor child.

The various breaks and diversions hadn't helped. Sadie was arrested an eighth time when she and her friends were busted for joyrid-
ing while they were smoking meth. Sadie was charged with Unlawful
Taking of a Vehicle, being Under the Influence of a Controlled Substance (Meth), and simple possession of methamphetamine. The judge
had run out of patience. Sadie, then twenty-six, was sentenced to
sixteen months at the Century Regional Detention Facility. The state
assumed custody of her minor daughter and placed the child in a fos-
ter home. Anya had been nine years old.

Reading this left me sad for Anya and even a little sad for Sadie. I
poured a fresh cup of coffee and continued reading.

I noted the date of Anya's removal.

Sixteen years ago.

I noted something else.

Sadie's parole and probation records comprised the bulk of the
forty-seven pages. Prison counselors and parole officials painted a picture of a young woman getting herself together. Sadie behaved well,
took classes, and attended every counseling session and rehabilitation
class offered by Century Regional. After serving eleven months, Sadie
petitioned for parole and her petition was granted. Sadie returned to
Rancha. She began a work-release job at a commercial stable, attended
substance abuse meetings and counseling sessions, and found a second
job at a grocery store. She stayed out of trouble and regained custody
of Anya the following year.

I was reading the last of several glowing reports by her former parole officer when I found the address.

Parole officers often dropped in on parolees at their places of residence, so parolee addresses were part of the parole record. The address was old, but it had been Sadie's address of record for almost four years. She and Anya had lived there when Beller disappeared.

An edgy energy made me want to move, but not walk in circles on my deck. I wanted to find them.

The cat watched me from the loft and licked his lips. Maybe he sensed the hunt.

I said, "Me, too."

I left to find them.

44

Turning my head to check for traffic caused a stitch in my ribs, but I wasn't impaired, dizzy, nauseous, or confused. I put on my sunglasses, hit the freeway, and was rolling across Tarzana when John Chen called.

"Deceased male, Latin, age nineteen, Arturo Melendez. He your guy?"

"Yes."

"They found him hanging from a tree out in Thousand Oaks with a black extension cord."

This surprised me.

"Suicide?"

"Not even. Died elsewhere and somebody strung him up. Lividity suggests he spent a couple of hours on his right side before being dumped."

"Cops have a suspect or witness?"

"Nothing about it in the intakes, but it looks like a gang thing. Get this."

John lowered his voice even more.

"His dick was missing."

"His penis?"

"Yeah, yeah. Somebody cut his dick and balls off. That's why they think it's a gang thing. Melendez messed with the wrong dude's woman, so the dude sent a message. Hard-core, right?"

"Thanks, John. Appreciate the help."

The map app led past a newish home development south of Rancha with freshly paved streets to older roads lined with dried brush, dead foxtails, and more abandoned horse trailers. I passed the trailers, rounded a stand of gnarled oaks and walnut trees, and found myself at the entrance to a mobile home park. The map app told me I'd arrived.

I stopped and sat idling at the entrance.

Seven metal mailboxes stood in a neat line on 4x4 posts. Addresses were painted on the mailbox doors. The paint was faded, but legible. Sadie's old address was on the second box from the left.

The mobile home park looked old. Single-wide homes faced each other at odd angles across a wide common ground, three on the left side facing three on the right, with the seventh at the far end. The homes were faded, but neat, and the grounds were well kept. Gray gravel served as parking spots below front doors with small porches reached by wood steps. Cars were parked at three of the homes. No black Challengers or brown Chevy pickups were present.

I pulled off the road, slipped on my gun, and covered it with a light blue jacket. The blue went well with the bruises.

Sadie's mobile home was the second on the left. Curtains were drawn across the windows and the parking pad was empty. Three steps climbed to a small porch and the door. The mobile home park seemed deserted, so I went to the steps. A heavy layer of dust covered the handrail and the steps. Nobody had touched the rail or climbed the steps in a long time.

I climbed to the door and heard nothing inside. I knocked. I knocked again and tried the knob. Locked.

A woman's voice rang out behind me.

"It's empty!"

An older woman wearing baggy white shorts and a baggy white shirt stood at the door of the mobile home across from Sadie's. The

woman looked to be in her eighties and shielded her eyes from the sun
with an upraised hand.

I said, "Nobody lives here?"

"That's what empty means. Not in a while. You want to rent it?"

"I'm looking for Sadie Given."

The woman came down her stairs.

"Oh, they moved. They haven't lived here for years."

They.

I stepped off the porch and crossed the yard. The woman peered
out from under the hand when I reached her.

She said, "Damn, boy, that must hurt! What happened?"

"Wreck. The airbag saved me."

"Looks like you got your ass kicked is what it looks like."

I glanced toward Sadie's trailer.

"So she moved? We used to be close. I was hoping to see her and
catch up."

"Well, they've been gone a while now."

"I was gone, too. You know how it is. People lose touch."

She eyed me.

"You in prison?"

"I'd rather not say."

She said, "Mm."

I studied Sadie's mobile home some more.

"Know where they went?"

"I might."

She might and she didn't want to tell a man she didn't know.

I said, "How's her little girl?"

"You knew Anya?"

"Through Sadie. Never actually met the girl. Just from talking with
Sadie."

The woman turned her back to the sun and shook her head.

"That poor child. Oh my Lord. And after Sadie worked so hard to
straighten herself out. She blamed herself, you know."

The woman shook her head again and I wondered why Sadie blamed herself.

"For going to prison?"

"Well, yeah, for that, but I meant the little girl."

"What happened to Anya?"

"Her troubles set on."

"Her troubles."

The woman touched her head.

"Here. I thought it was drugs, Anya taking that stuff they take, but I don't know. She got the terrors. Wake up screaming and clawing herself. Burst into tears. I used to stay with her, you know, when Sadie was working. That child couldn't stay by herself. I never took money, though. She wanted to pay, but I wouldn't let her."

"I didn't know."

"Got so she wouldn't leave the house. I said, 'Sadie, you better make this child go to school,' but she didn't listen."

"This was all after I went away."

The woman shielded her eyes again and studied me.

"Don't be ashamed. You did your time, you paid your debt, that's all there is to it."

"When did Anya start having troubles?"

"Well, I don't know. She was prolly fifteen or sixteen, around in there."

Beller.

I said, "I hate to ask, but I'd really like to see how they're doing. Would you have their address?"

She turned toward her home.

"I'll have one in here somewhere. Let's get out of this sun."

Her name was Martell Dail. Her home was tidy and uncomfortably warm despite the hum of an air conditioner. She waved toward a small dinette table as we entered, told me to sit, and went into the kitchen.

"You want some water or a Seven-Up?"

"Water would be nice, thanks."

Ms. Dail filled a green plastic tumbler with tap water, handed it to me, and went to a short armoire in the living room. She knelt, pulled out the bottom drawer, and fingered through the contents.

I thought about what she'd told me and what I'd already learned.

I said, "Did Sadie and Charley get married?"

She stopped digging through the drawer and grinned at me.

"Charley Reed?"

I nodded, wondering why the grin.

She said, "You know Charley?"

I shrugged. Noncommittal and vague.

"A little. Not well. Met him around the same time I met Sadie."

Ms. Dail climbed to her feet and went to a window facing Sadie's mobile home.

"That's Charley's handiwork right there. He built her porch. Place was falling apart when Sadie bought it."

I nodded.

"How about that Charley."

"Her mama died, you know, when she was away. Left some money, not much, but a little. Anyway, Sadie bought the place. and let me tell you it was a dump. The steps were rotten. Wasp nests all along underneath, must've been hundreds. Charley got rid of them, walked right over here and killed a nest for me. I didn't even have to ask. Here, come take a look."

She headed back to the kitchen and went to the fridge. The door was covered by fading snapshots and cards held in place by little magnets.

"This is me and Anya after they moved in. See how cute? She was about twelve, I think. And this is Sadie here."

Ms. Dail touched a photo. Sadie looked a thousand years younger with bright, intelligent eyes and a happy grin.

"And this is Charley when he built the porch. I brought him a Seven-Up."

Charley Reed, the wasp killer, was toasting the camera with a Seven-Up. Smiling. I hadn't seen him well enough in the dark to recognize the man in the picture, but he looked exactly like the man Lori Chance described, a big man with a big square head and big hands wearing a faded *Born to Run* T-shirt and jeans. Martell Dail was a gold mine.

I said, "Does Sadie live with Charley now?"

"Well, I wouldn't know."

Ms. Dail returned to the drawer and went on as she searched.

"I liked Charley more than Sadie liked him is all I can say and I don't know why. Got himself straight and did right for himself. I heard he's real successful, him and his brother, own a good business and some properties."

How nice for Charley.

I said, "Sounds like you haven't seen him recently."

"Not since Sadie left. He came around an awful lot back then, trying to help them, I guess, but she ran him off or he got fed up. I don't know. I do know they were close, but Anya was Sadie's life, especially after her troubles started. Sadie lost her to the state once, did you know? The state took her."

"I knew."

"Sadie moved heaven and earth getting that child back."

I said, "Heaven and earth."

"I liked having them there, I did. Sadie worked herself ragged, but she always looked in when I was down. And Anya was so much fun until all this started. I felt so bad for them."

"You miss them."

"I do. Then they moved and that was that. She used to send cards and such, but not in a while."

Ms. Dail struggled to her feet and brought me a red envelope. The envelope had been slit open. A birthday card was inside, but I didn't care about the card. Sadie Given's return address was on the back.

"Could I copy this, please?"

"Oh, sure, you bet."

I snapped a photo of the address and another of Charley Reed.

Ms. Dail said, "You get over there, please tell'm Martell Dail said hi and give them my love."

"I will, Ms. Dail. Thank you."

I finished my water and walked to my car. I slid in behind the wheel and texted the photo of Charley Reed to Lori.

Know him?

Lori answered in seconds.

OMG YES!! He's one of them!

I texted again.

The men who threatened you? The big men?

Less than seconds.

YES!! The really big one! Asshole!
Where are you? R U OK?

I told her I was fine. I told her I had to go, but I'd touch base later. She responded with a line of hearts.

I closed the message window and studied the photo of grinning Charley Reed. I grinned back. The stitches hurt, but I didn't mind.

I said, "You're mine."

45

Joe Pike

Pike studied the salvage yard with his sixty-power spotting scope from beneath a dead tree on a small rise. Seven cars and a red Nissan pickup sat in a fenced parking area, but no black Challengers or brown Chevy trucks were present.

Four men used a tow truck to drag damaged cars from a long flatbed trailer. From the nature of their damage, the cars had been totaled in traffic accidents. Pike glimpsed three additional men and a woman inside the cavernous building. None of the men matched Cole's description of Charley Reed or the squints. The woman was only visible for seconds, but Pike saw enough to know she wasn't Anya or Sadie.

Pike pulled back to his Jeep and drove down to the salvage yard. He parked inside the fence and entered the building through the wide hanging doors. The ratchet of a power wrench sounded like an automatic weapon. A man with a large belly and a smaller man were disassembling a car. The smaller man glanced at Pike, but went on with his work.

A sign above an open door to Pike's right spelled OFFICE. Pike entered and saw the woman he'd seen earlier seated at a cheap metal desk.

Pike said, "Is Charley here?"

The woman said, "Nope. Why you need Charley?"

"I need a radiator for a 1953 Willys Jeep CJ. A parts guy down in L.A. recommended Charley. Said Charley could probably find it and he'd give me a fair price."

The woman leaned back, squeaking her chair.

"Wow. A '53 Willys."

Pike said, "Yes."

The woman shook her head.

"Man, I just don't know. We don't have any Willys parts."

"I could wait if he's due back."

The woman leaned forward and squeaked again. She pushed a white pad toward him and added a ballpoint pen.

"Leave your name and number. I'll see he gets it."

"I'll wait if he's due."

"Charley's off on a buying trip. He'll call. He's good about it."

She pushed the pad closer.

Pike left a made-up name and number and drove back to the rise. He was about to dial Cole when his phone buzzed. Elvis.

"I have another address for Sadie. It's recent."

"Woman here says Charley's on a buying trip."

"If this address is current, we might find out if it's true. I don't want to go in my car. They know it."

"Send your location. I'll pick you up."

Cole sent his location and Pike hustled to his Jeep.

46

Elvis Cole

The birthday card took us to an older residential glen nestled in the hills on the far side of Rancha. The area wasn't upscale or well-to-do, but the lots were large, shaded by oak and walnut trees, and offered plenty of room for RVs and the inevitable horse trailers. Most of the homes sat at the end of long, crushed-gravel drives. It was quiet. I liked it.

Pike and I followed a narrow street along the base of the glen to a small Spanish-style home with a dark tile roof and a sprawling walnut tree out front. A blue SUV sat near the tree. One of those gray metal sheds used for storing bug killer and gardening equipment sat behind the house on one side of the property opposite a detached garage on the other. A gravel drive led past the house through a carport to the garage. The garage door was open. I was hoping for a sign saying THE GIVENS LIVE HERE, but I didn't need it. Charley Reed's brown Chevy pickup was parked by the garage.

I said, "The big man."

"Third vehicle in back."

"Yeah. Maybe a van. People?"

"Negative."

We turned around and passed the house again.

A man with a bad limp and black eye was carrying a cardboard box to the SUV. He was big, but he wasn't Charley Reed. The last time I saw him he was wearing a Hawaiian shirt.

"Charley's brother, Christopher P. He was at the SurfMutt."

I caught a flash of movement past the edge of the house near the van.

"Someone's behind the house."

Pike said, "Let's get close. Neighbor on the right has good cover."

We parked two houses away and slipped from the Jeep.

The neighboring property was thick with prickly shrubs, azaleas, and big red manzanita bushes clumped between oak and olive trees. A drive curved between the shrubs to an older home with a goat pen behind it. Pike and I worked our way along the edge of the property to the pen and beyond it to a tangled manzanita with drooping red flowers. A black-and-white goat watched us pass.

The manzanita let us see the back of Sadie's house, Charley's truck, the little gardening shed across the yard, and the van. Her yard was dry and patchy, but a couple of oaks and pretty blue lilac bushes made it pleasant.

Pike said, "Corner window on the left. Someone moved."

I studied the windows but saw nothing.

"Sadie or Anya?"

"Couldn't tell."

A back door stepped down to a concrete patio shaded by a pergola with a faded canvas top. The van was parked on the lawn by the patio with its side open. Christopher P. limped from the house with the squint who rode shotgun in the Challenger and went into the garage. A plaster cast covered the squint's left arm from his elbow to his hand and the left side of his face was swollen and purple.

I nudged Pike.

"One of the squints. Looks like he got his ass kicked."

Pike offered a fist. We bumped.

The squint went back to the house a few seconds later, spoke through the door to someone inside, and returned to the garage.

Pike whispered.

"So we have two in the garage and at least one in the house."

I nodded at the brown truck.

"Might be Charley. Plus whoever else."

Pike glanced past me to the street.

"Your shadow."

The Challenger pulled into the drive and parked in front by the SUV. The driver squint got out and came up the drive. A large white bandage covered his right ear like an earmuff. It made him look lopsided.

Pike offered his fist again.

We bumped.

The driver squint went to the van and looked around as if he didn't know what to do. His passenger shouted from the garage.

"Hey, dumbass!"

The driver flipped the hair from his face and went into the garage. Charley's brother limped out, dragging a heavy black bag toward the gardening shed. The weight of the bag made his limp worse.

Pike studied me for a moment and I saw myself in his shining black lenses. He whispered.

"You good?"

"Let's do it."

The corner of Pike's mouth ticked and he slipped away, moving so quietly he might have been mist.

We didn't discuss it or plan it. We'd worked together so often for so long we knew what to do and what each other would do and we did it. Like being one with the other.

I counted thirty slow seconds, stepped around the manzanita, and walked toward the garage. I drew the Dan Wesson and let it dangle, watching the back door and the garage. The broken ribs and stiff back and the lump vanished. Adrenaline.

I reached the corner of the garage when both squints stepped out, heading for the house. The driver was closest.

I said, "Dumbass."

They turned.

I hit the driver in the forehead with the flat of the pistol, spun right, and swept the passenger's legs with a roundhouse kick. He went down hard with his feet in the air and a hoarse "*Oof.*" I hit him with the pistol two times fast, glanced at the driver, and saw Charley Reed's brother emerge from the garden shed.

Christopher P. stared at me for two heartbeats, as if he needed two heartbeats to understand. Then he opened his mouth to shout, but Pike appeared behind him, hooked his arm around the man's neck, and lifted.

Reed wasn't as tall as his brother, but he was a large, strong man. He clawed at Pike's arm and punched over his shoulders, trying to connect. Pike bent backward and lifted higher, squeezing hard to compress the carotid artery. Reed's feet left the ground.

I pinned the driver squint with a knee and watched the house.

Reed thrashed like a gorilla with a leopard on its back. He punched air and kicked. He thrashed and clawed Pike's arms. The kicking slowed. His hands fell limp. Pike slowly lowered him, keeping his arm locked around Reed's neck. He held tight.

Heartbeat.

Heartbeat.

Pike flipped him over and zip-tied his wrists and ankles. I zip-tied the squints and ran toward the back door. I reached it as the door jerked open and Charley Reed charged out like a rodeo bull exploding from a chute. He'd been huge in the dark when I couldn't see him, but he looked even bigger now—a good two-eighty easy. Both eyes were black from our fight and a lump like mine rode his left cheek, but the dark eyes and swollen cheek only made him look more dangerous.

Reed drove into me and we fell. I didn't try to get away. I pulled him close with my left arm, wrapped my legs around him, and pounded the side of his head with my pistol. I hit him as hard as I could. I hit him three times hard before he worked an arm between us and tried to push me away. I held on and kept pounding until Pike slammed into him like a blocking back and knocked him sideways.

Charley came up on all fours, wobbled to a knee, and Pike punched him in the throat. Charley fell forward and made a gakking sound. Pike twisted his arms behind his back and glanced at the house.

He said, "Go."

47

entered the house with my gun up, the lump pulsing like an angry heart. A dining room off the kitchen opened to the living room and a hall leading to two bedrooms with a shared bath. The furnishings were inexpensive and simple: a maple table and chairs for dining, and a couch, three chairs, and a coffee table for the living room. Half-empty bookcases stood against a wall with open cardboard boxes on the floor.

"Police! Is anyone in the house?"

I cleared their home, moving through the two bedrooms and shared bath quickly.

Boxes on the bathroom counter held medicines and toiletries. Clothes were on beds waiting to be packed and suitcases lay open on the floor. Nobody was hiding under the beds or in the closets. I found nothing belonging to Charley Reed.

Sadie's bedroom was messy with a cluttered dresser and night-stands and books scattered within the clutter. Anya's room was so bleak it seemed sterile. There were no framed photos or floppy stuffed animals or mementos or computers or any of the things you'd expect in a young woman's bedroom. Maybe those things had been packed. The only items left were two prescription bottles on her nightstand beside a lamp, a single bracelet tree on her dresser, and a large white poster on the wall with the words DON'T WORRY, BE HAPPY circling a huge yellow happy face. The words were from an old Bobby McFerrin song I liked, but something about the poster's empty, lifeless face above her bed disturbed me.

I went to the nightstand and checked the medicines.

Paroxetine and diazepam. Paroxetine was a big-league antidepressant and diazepam was an anxiety medication. Both were from a Mexican pharmacy in Rosarito and scripted by a Mexican physician.

I studied the bottles and thought about Martell Dail describing Anya's troubles, how she'd changed and woke screaming and burst into tears.

Pike called from the far end of the house.

"You good?"

"Clear."

Pike had zip-tied Charley's hands and ankles. We found duct tape in the garage to wrap his knees and mouth and did the same with his brother and the squints. We searched them as we bound them and took their wallets. When we finished, they looked like mummified sausages.

We stashed Charley's brother and the squints in the garden shed, carried Charley into the living room, and dropped him. He landed face down, hard. Pike pinned him with a knee. I nodded toward the hall.

"Back in a sec."

Pike pinned him harder.

I returned to the bathroom and upended the box of medicines. Zoloft, Paxil, Prozac, and lithium, all scripted for Anya. Most had labels from Mexican pharmacies in Tijuana, Rosarito, and El Refugio. Antidepressants and mood stabilizers. Antianxiety meds, alpha-1 blockers, six different sleep medications, and heavy-duty painkillers like oxycodone and tramadol; over-the-counter herbal supplements and cannabis gummies. The physician names varied, but every med in the box was scripted for Anya. I heard Bobby McFerrin's upbeat voice.

Don't worry, be happy.

I shouted.

"We good?"

"Good."

I returned to the living room and stood over Charley. Blood leaked from his hair in crooked red lines and puddled beneath his face. I toed his leg. I toed him harder. He struggled against the ties and tape, trying to see me, but looking up wasn't easy with Pike's knee on his back.

I squatted to let him see me. He glared and strained like glaring and straining would matter.

"Hey, Charley. Remember me?"

Charley arched and bucked and made a muffled bellow through the tape.

I went through their wallets while he watched and photographed the fronts and backs of their DLs. The guy who drove the Challenger was named Howard DeLeon Semple Jr. His passenger didn't have a driver's license, which maybe explained his role as the passenger. I emailed the photos to myself and peeled the tape from Charley's mouth.

Charley bellowed with a deep rumbling baritone.

"How'd you know my name?"

"I'm a detective, stupid."

"Where's my brother?"

"In the shed with the other morons."

I dragged a chair near the window and took a seat. Not close enough to be seen from the street, but close enough to see if someone was coming.

I said, "Where's Sadie?"

Charley bellowed again.

"Kiss my ass!"

He bellowed so hard a streamer of bloody spit hit the floor. I didn't raise my voice.

"She and Anya hit the road?"

"Kiss it!"

More spit. He strained so hard his face looked like mottled liver. The ties we used had a tensile strength of three hundred pounds. We used two ties on his wrists and two on his ankles. His wrists would break before the plastic.

I said, "Why does Anya take so much medication?"

Charley twisted in a fury.

"I'll kill you! I'll break your damn back!"

Pike snapped the heel of his hand into the back of Charley's head. Charley's forehead slammed into the floor and Charley closed his eyes.

I said, "Charley, here's the deal. I'm going to call the police. They'll come and I'll identify you and the assholes outside as the people who attacked me. You'll be charged with assault, assault and battery, aggravated assault, and—I'd be willing to bet on this—attempted murder. Sound good?"

Charley didn't react.

I said, "Tell me what happened. What's the story with Thomas Beller?"

Charley sighed. He didn't open his eyes or raise his head.

"I don't know any Beller. I don't know anything."

"Then why'd you try to stop me from looking for him?"

"I don't know what you're talking about."

"That wasn't you the other night?"

"I don't know anything. Not a thing."

I was about to ask again when a small gray hatchback turned into the drive and crunched toward the house. Anya and Sadie.

Charley heard the crunching and bucked to life, thrashing like a beached shark and bellowing like a bull.

"Run! Sadie, run!"

Pike cut off his air. Charley flexed and arched and purpled again, but the bucking stopped. I went to the hall and stood out of sight.

Sadie and Anya entered the kitchen from the carport. Sadie came first, carrying her phone in one hand and her keys in the other. A large purse hung from her shoulder. Anya carried two large In-N-Out bags filled with hamburgers and fries. Sadie set her phone and keys by the sink and shouted.

"Charley! Food's here! Where is everyone?"

I raised my hands and stepped to the door.

"Behind you."

48

adie gasped when she startled. Anya lurched sideways as if a wave hit her and dropped the hamburgers. Then she saw me and shriveled like the witch at the end of *The Wizard of Oz*, getting smaller as she melted.

Sadie saw Charley and Pike and snatched up her phone.

"Get out! Get out of here! I'll call the police."

I kept my hands up and offered the gentlest smile I could find.

"Call. It's all right. I'll tell them what I know about Thomas Beller."

Sadie shouted, livid with rage.

"You don't know anything! Leave us alone and go the hell home!"

"I need to know where he is and what happened to him."

Sadie waved her phone and shouted louder.

"We don't know any Thomas whatever! Now get out or I'll have you arrested!"

"Call. They'll arrest Charley for aggravated assault and attempted murder."

Charley looked at Sadie and Anya with calm eyes.

"Nothing to worry about, buddy. We don't know anything."

Sadie put an arm around Anya, glaring like she wanted to kill me.

"You threatened us. You've been stalking my daughter and scaring her. Charley was protecting her."

I offered a smile to Anya and meant it.

"I didn't mean to frighten you. I'm sorry if I'm scaring you now, but I think something bad happened between you and Thomas Beller."

Sadie jabbed her finger at me. Vicious.

"I will have you arrested for stalking and worse. Aggravated assault? How about attempted fucking rape? How about sexual assault? We will fucking ruin you."

Anya spoke so softly I barely heard her.

"No, we won't."

Charley rumbled, but the rumble was gentle.

"Baby girl."

Sadie gripped Anya closer.

"Shush! You stop!"

"I want to tell."

"Shush!"

I lowered my hands.

"Whatever happened, Anya, I'm sorry. It must've been awful."

Sadie jabbed again.

"You shut up. You don't know what you're talking about."

"You're feeding her antidepressants and anxiety meds from Mexico. You have boxes filled with books about PTSD. Something happened and it's killing her."

"She's fine!"

Anya looked down and made the small voice again.

"I'm not. I'm not fine."

A single tear dripped from Anya's nose. I saw it fall.

Charley rumbled, now to Sadie.

"Call the cops. Let'm arrest me, I don't care. You'll be fine."

Anya's voice.

"He knows and I'm glad."

Sadie held her closer.

"Shh. He's guessing. He has nothing but guesses."

Anya clenched her eyes like her head hurt.

"I can't sleep. I'm not right. This must stop."

"Shh. We'll be fine."

Anya looked up with hollow red eyes.

"We aren't. He *knows*."

Her blurry red eyes came to me.

"He's dead. His blood was all over my face and in my mouth and I can't tell anyone and we just went on like nothing happened. I can taste it. I still taste it."

Sadie slumped. Her face sagged with impossible sadness.

"Oh, Anya. No."

Anya wrapped her arms across her head, her eyes clenched tight.

"I took the ride. I knew better, but I did it and messed up everything. It was me. I did it."

Charley, the deep gentle rumble.

"Baby, no."

My mouth felt dry. I wet my lips.

"What happened, Anya? What did he do? Where is he?"

Sadie looked at me. Her sad eyes emptied and filled with something cold.

"Who was it you said you're working for, somebody's daughter?"

Charley rumbled.

"Buddy."

I said, "Yes. Beller's daughter."

"Imagine that. A daughter. And she hired you to find him."

Charley again.

"Buddy, c'mon now."

Sadie kept going.

"And what'd his baby girl say when she hired you, what a good father he was, what a wonderful man, how much she misses him?"

I didn't answer. My center grew cold and the cold spread down my arms and legs and my fingers tingled.

Charley rumbled at me now, a warning.

"That girl doesn't want this. Tell her you didn't find him. Leave right now for her sake."

Sadie's voice cracked, sharp as a gunshot.

"Anya wasn't spared! I did this and I will fix it!"

She softened when she looked at Anya and smoothed her daughter's hair.

"It's over, baby. No more lying. No secrets."

I felt my heart break for Traci and for them. Maybe it was the way Sadie smoothed Anya's hair and kissed her head and held her. I don't know. I'll never know.

Sadie held Anya, but she looked at me.

"You should've gone home, but no. You had to find him. Well, here he is."

Charley rumbled, a final plea.

"Buddy."

Sadie's eyes never left me.

"Tell his daughter this, Mr. Private Investigator. The wonderful daddy she misses so much, paying you good money to find, he tied up my baby, wrapped a wire around her neck, and was choking her to death when I found them. So I killed him. I killed him and I'd kill him again. I'd kill him every day 'til the end of days and I'd kill you for her, too. I'm this girl's mother and I killed him."

She never, not once, looked away.

Then Sadie Given told me the rest. It got worse.

49

Bad Mother, Part Two

Sadie saw a flash of light in the distant darkness and slammed on the brakes. The old Honda shuddered. Sadie watched for the flash again, but saw only dark beneath the stars. She shut the engine and turned off the lights, thinking she might see better. She climbed out of her car and stood in the road.

The light flashed again, a dim white square across the field, lit for a second and gone, a light within a car. Now a boxy shape resolved, a lighter shadow against the murky earth and within the flash a man behind the wheel.

A stab of fear hit Sadie as quickly as the flash and her heart clenched. Everything here was wrong. A vehicle in a lonely field so far off the road in the dark in the middle of nowhere meant only one thing.

Sadie didn't think. Anya was out there or not. She shouted.

"Anya!"

She expected the vehicle to roar to life, but nothing happened. They hadn't heard her.

"*Anya!*"

Sadie's only thought was Anya, driven by a gut-sick fear and rising anger that Anya had done something stupid and was out there RIGHT NOW with a mouth-breathing slug doing something even more stupid.

Sadie cursed and started across the field, then had a thought and returned to her car. If Anya was out there tongue wrestling some fool, Sadie wasn't going to take shit from the mouth-breathing slug who was screwing her baby daughter. She grabbed her phone and the ball-peen hammer she kept in the Honda and charged across the field. If that damn girl was doing the nasty, she planned to scare the shit out of them both.

Sadie stumbled, landed on the same knee she'd hurt earlier, and lurched to her feet even angrier. Today was NOT a good day.

She pounded across the field, getting closer and closer. The vehicle she'd thought was a car became a ghostly, pale van, parked facing to her left with the driver's-side window visible. Something was written on its side, but Sadie couldn't see well enough to read it. The interior was dark, but something moved in the window.

Sadie stormed directly to the driver's window, raised her hand to slap the glass, and stopped in a terrible instant. Frozen, as if she'd left her body. Frozen, her hand in the air, as if what she saw in the van could not be real. The driver was faced away from her, his broad back to the window. Beyond the driver, Anya thrashed in the passenger seat. Her wrists were bound with rope and a clear plastic bag was over her head. A cord was around her neck and the driver was pulling it tighter. Anya's mouth opened and her head whipped to the side. Sadie heard grunting and a muffled, gurgling moan. Frozen, until her soul screamed.

Sadie jerked the door open and swung as hard as she could. The hammer hit high on the man's shoulder. He lurched and started to turn. Sadie hit him again and then again. The hammer caught him on the back of the head and the side of the head, throwing blood like a dog shaking off water. She hit him as hard as she could, but the sonofabitch kept trying to get out. She caught him behind the ear, swung again, and caught the top of his head. The man slumped into the wheel. Sadie stopped, scared to move, waiting to see if she needed to hit him again. The driver hung over the wheel for a moment and slowly slid sideways into the dash.

Sadie said, "Baby!"

She raced around the van and threw open Anya's door. Sadie frantically tore off the plastic bag and the cord, all the while murmuring.

"Baby? Baby? I'm here now, baby. You're okay now. Baby, are you okay?"

Sadie couldn't untie the fucking rope. She dug at the knot, but the knot was too tight.

Anya was crying. She gave a shuddering gasp and nodded. She sobbed once and nodded again. Sadie hugged her and held her. The rope could wait.

Sadie said, "C'mon, let's get you out of there. Let's go. We have to go, baby, get up, let me help you down."

Anya turned to step from the van when the driver sat up like a ghoul rising from the grave and grabbed her. Anya screamed.

"No!"

Blood dripped from his face like a melting red mask. Sadie growled and swung hard again. The hammer sliced his forehead. Sadie climbed on her daughter and hit him again. She brought the hammer down and hit him and hit him. She hit him.

Anya shouted.

"Mom!"

Sadie stopped with the hammer overhead. Anya's face was streaked with blood. Her clothes were wet. Sadie saw herself. Her hand, her arm, and the hammer looked like they'd been dipped in paint. Her clothes were splattered with blood. Sadie backed from the van and pulled Anya with her. They fell. Sadie scrambled to her feet, pulled Anya farther from the van, and pushed Anya behind her. She raised the hammer, ready to strike if the man came after them.

Sadie waited, her heart pounding, chest heaving, and nothing happened. The man didn't move.

Sadie didn't know what to do. Her mind raced and nothing made sense. The sonofabitch was dead. Sadie Given had killed a man.

She glanced at her daughter.

"Who is he?"

"I don't know! I'm sorry."

"You don't know who he is?"

Anya sobbed.

"I'm sorry! He offered a ride. I'm sorry! I know better!"

Sadie dropped the hammer and held her daughter's face. She ran her hands over Anya's head and arms and hands, looking for cuts and wounds.

"Are you hurt?"

"He was going to *kill* me!"

"Does your throat hurt? Can you breathe?"

"I'm fine!"

Sadie thought, *Doctor, she needs a doctor, I have to take her to the hospital.* She glanced at the van.

I killed him.

She had to report it. They couldn't just leave. The man was dead. She had to call the police and tell them what happened. The police would come. They would come and when they entered her name in the system they would know. Sadie suddenly looked at Anya. She cupped Anya's face again and her sweet baby's face blurred as Sadie's eyes filled.

Sadie said, "I don't know what to do."

"Let's go home."

Sadie looked at the van. Anya was only fifteen. She was a baby. If Sadie had picked Anya up as she'd promised, this horrible thing wouldn't have happened. But Sadie had not picked her up. Sadie had fallen asleep. Sadie had been too stupid to set the alarm. Sadie had allowed her underage, unsupervised minor child to fend for herself after dark.

I am bad.

I am a bad mother.

A maelstrom of self-defeating, self-sabotaging thoughts enveloped her. The prison counselors had warned her. The meetings she attended three times a week all preached the dangers of negative self-talk, but here, now, in the dark with the van and Anya, the maelstrom was overwhelming.

She was an ex-con with a criminal record who had killed a man, an ex-con with a criminal record who allowed her underage child to run around after dark, an ex-con pathetic excuse for a mother who'd been declared unfit as a parent once and lost her child to the state. Once. The police would notify Child Protective Services. A CPS investigation might find her unfit again.

Sadie stared at Anya.

Anya said, "What?"

"I love you. You're my heart, you know? You're the world."

Anya said, "*What?*"

"I don't want to lose you again."

"What are you talking about?"

"We maybe shouldn't call the police."

"I don't care."

"We couldn't tell anyone."

"You have blood on your face."

Anya looked at herself.

"Is it his blood? Do I have blood in my hair?"

Anya raked her fingers through her hair, saw the glop on her fingers, and vomited.

Sadie held her.

"We'd have to keep this secret and secrets are hard. You understand, baby? Secrets are hard."

Anya wiped her mouth, saw smeared blood on her hand, and threw up again.

Sadie's thoughts spun faster. The van was a bloated, beached whale basking in starlight. Her fingerprints were all over it. Someone would see it sitting there and report it and the police would come whether she called them or not. They would print the van and know what she'd done.

She shouted.

"Fuck!"

Anya burst into tears and heaved again.

Sadie's eyes went from the van to Anya and back to the van.

She needed help. Anya needed help.

Sadie took out her phone, brought up a number, and called.

"Answer, answer, answer. Please answer."

Charley Reed answered, his deep, rumbling voice as smooth as velvet.

"Been a while, buddy, but I like seeing your name in the caller ID."

Charley had always called her "buddy," even when they were just stupid kids. Sadie couldn't help herself. She sobbed when she heard his voice and cried as she spoke.

"I did something bad, Charley. I need help. I stepped in shit and I need your help."

Charley Reed had loved her since he was nine years old. His velvet voice came back gently and even more reassuring.

He said, "Are you all right?"

"Not really."

"Where's Anya? Is Anya there?"

"She's here."

"Is Anya all right?"

"No. I don't know. Something bad happened and I'm really scared. I have to fix it."

Charley said, "Whatever it is, I'll help. Tell me where you are and I'll come. I will help you fix it."

"I'm scared."

"I know, but I'm here. That's why you called. You know I'd do anything for you and that girl."

"I know. Thank you. I'm sorry."

"Where are you? I'll come help fix it and whatever else you need. We'll fix it."

Sadie and Anya waited for Charley in the Honda. Anya sat with her arms crossed, rocking as if she was anxious. Sadie murmured how much she loved her and asked a few questions, but Anya barely replied. After a while Sadie stopped. She didn't know what to say.

Charley arrived a few minutes later and Sadie led him to the van. She told him she wanted to make the dead man disappear. Charley thought this was a terrible idea. He didn't argue with her about it. He explained how he felt. The smart move was to call the police and let it play out straight up. She was saving her daughter and defending herself from a homicidal psycho freak when she killed him. No cop in his right mind would charge a mother for saving her child, no prosecutor would prosecute if the cops were stupid enough to charge her, and no jury on earth would convict her. Best to deal with it here and now, get past it, and walk away clean.

Sadie refused. She was adamant. The idea was set in her mind before Charley arrived. The dead man had to go.

Charley didn't argue. He had come to help, so he heard her out. The two of them stood by the van for a while, neither speaking, until Charley tipped his head toward the Honda.

"Okay. Take her home and I'll get rid of him."

Sadie said, "By yourself?"

"Don't worry about it. Go."

"Now wait. What are you going to do?"

"Get rid of him."

"How?"

"Best you don't know. Buddy, I only have a few hours. Let me get to it."

"I killed the sonofabitch. I don't want him popping up somewhere."

"He won't pop up. I got it figured."

"That fucking van has my fingerprints all over it."

"I got it figured, Sadie. Do you trust me?"

He almost never called her Sadie.

She said, "Yes. How can you even ask? Of course I trust you."

His eyes filled then and he looked away. He didn't speak until he got control of himself.

He said, "Then trust me, buddy. I owe you."

An old anger flashed. She hated when he brought it up, him owing her.

"Stop."

"I'll never be able to pay you back. Not by this or anything."

"Shut up. Stop it."

He got control of himself and cleared his throat.

"Then trust me. Best for us and the girl if what you know stops here. If you don't know, you can't tell, right?"

She nodded.

"Then from here on is mine. I'll do what I do and whatever I do will go to my grave. Nobody will ever know. Nobody will find him. You don't have to worry."

Sadie glanced at the Honda. She was worried and scared, but Charley had come. He had always come, every time since they were kids. *Look at him!* She looked at him, there in the dark. Big as a mountain, big as a damned bear, blotting out the stars. He needed a great huge body for his great huge heart.

Sadie grabbed Charley Reed's shoulders, pulled herself tall, and kissed him. She gave him a single, long, hard forever kiss. Then she went to her car and drove Anya home.

Sadie never asked Charley about the dead man again. She didn't know how Charley handled it or if anyone else was involved. Sadie wondered sometimes, but she didn't ask. She trusted Charley and Charley was good at his word. The dead man and his van disappeared and Charley never—not once—brought it up. He never mentioned that night again or told anyone what he'd done until the day he told Elvis Cole.

50

Elvis Cole

adie told the story in a flat monotone until she reached the part where Anya's head was in a plastic bag. She reached the bag and fell silent. Then she continued until she finished, kissed Anya's head, and whispered into her hair.

"No more secrets now. We'll get you some help. We'll tell whoever we need to tell."

She kissed Anya again, but her eyes returned to me, cold and resentful.

"His little girl will be proud, so you run tell her you found him."

Pike was as still as a Roman statue. The lump throbbed. I had expected them to claim Beller raped or abused Anya in some way, and I had been prepared to believe it, but her story of plastic bags and strangulation was so crazy weird I told myself she was lying or deluded or talking about someone else.

I said, "You saw Thomas Beller strangling Anya. You saw him doing this."

"I didn't even know the man's name until you told me, but yes, he did and yes, I killed him for it."

Anya said, "Yes, sir, he did."

I took out my phone and brought up Beller's photograph.

"This man?"

Anya said, "Yes, sir."

Charley rumbled.

"She made it up. Can't be proved by her or anyone. Not a word she said."

Sadie glanced at him, tired.

"It's done, Charley. I've told him and I'll tell whoever else. We can't keep living like this."

Anya stood.

"I can prove it. I'll show you my books."

Sadie watched Anya leave, then lowered her voice.

"She journals. Journaling is good for the PTSD. It's all in her books."

Anya returned with a box of thick spiral notebooks and gave me a notebook with a pink marbled cover.

I said, "You wrote about what happened?"

"Him. What he did. Me. Mostly my dreams. I don't sleep so well. I have nightmares."

Pike said, "I don't sleep."

This was the first time Pike spoke. Everyone in the room looked at him.

Anya said, "You have nightmares?"

"Yes. I don't remember them, but yes."

Anya nodded.

"I wish I didn't remember mine."

I flipped a few pages.

Her journal was filled with handwritten entries and drawings, the entries written in blue ink or black or green. Most of the drawings were red. The paper was worn and the entries appeared to have been written over a period of time, but a journal wasn't proof. Anyone could write anything and claim their wildest fantasy or nightmare was real.

"How many journals do you have?"

"What's here in the box. Seven or eight, I guess, but this one was the first. I wrote a lot about what he did in this one."

She looked at Joe.

"Do you journal, too?"

"I run. Running's my journal."

"I'll have to try it."

I flipped more pages and saw drawings of monstrous men with huge heads, big teeth, and hammers crushing their skulls. I read a passage, skipped ahead, and read another. I skipped again, read more, and felt dull. Anya hadn't made these things up. They weren't fantasy.

I thanked him for going out of his way. He said taking me home was more fun than killing time in a parking lot. He had a long drive home and hated driving in traffic so he'd been waiting for the traffic to die down. I asked what's a long drive? He said he lived in Glendale and asked if I knew where it was.

This had been Thomas Beller's excuse to his wife. Anya could not have fabricated this. She could not have known he lived in Glendale. I looked from Anya to Pike to Sadie.

She said, "What?"

"Where's his body?"

"No idea."

I turned to Charley.

"What'd you do with him?"

"Kiss my ass."

"Where's his van?"

"Up your ass. In there deep."

The car crusher at his salvage yard could've crushed Beller's van into two cubic yards of scrap. The van could've been shipped to Asia with hundreds of other crushed vehicles.

Anya said, "What's his daughter like?"

Her question came from a place so removed from the moment I hesitated. It took several seconds to answer.

"She's nice. A little younger than you. She likes to bake."

"Is she married?"

"No. She isn't married."

Anya seemed to consider this.

"I'm glad she's nice."

I didn't know what to say so I went to the window. Outside, the shady ground was dappled with yellow sunlight. The yellow shapes reminded me of Traci's backyard. Her patio beneath the blossoming pear was dappled with light the morning Traci asked me to find her father.

I turned back to Sadie and felt lost. Like a swimmer at sea who couldn't see land. This would come out and Beller would be linked to Traci. I would have to tell her, but I didn't know what to say. A journal wasn't proof even if it was true. I was angry.

"You didn't think to call the police?"

"Of course I did. I'm not stupid."

"You should've called."

Sadie wiped her face with her hands.

"If I got do-overs I'd do over my life. I was scared."

"Listen. If what you've said is true, this was a justifiable homicide, not murder. You wouldn't have been in trouble."

Her face flushed.

"I *know* what I should've done. Anya had marks from the wire all over her neck. She had bruises. But I was so damned—"

Sadie fell silent and Anya continued for her.

"Mama got in trouble once and lost me to the state. She was scared they'd take me again."

Sadie's eyes flashed hard, then softened with embarrassment.

"I was scared. I did what I thought was best."

She looked at Anya.

"Didn't work out so great, did it? I'll make it right. I swear I'll make it right."

I said, "What are you going to do?"

"Get a lawyer. Find a shrink. Whatever I have to do."

I looked at Pike. Pike shrugged, the shrug asking what I wanted. I didn't know. I felt more tired than I'd ever felt. Maybe the concussion had caught up to me.

Anya said, "Will my mama go to jail?"

"Not if you tell the same story. All they'll have is what you tell them."

I didn't say it, but the odds were good the police wouldn't believe them. People confessed to crimes all the time and sometimes those crimes were real, but sometimes they weren't. Cops tended to ignore confessions with no supporting evidence, but this involved an actual missing person who Sadie would identify as Thomas Beller. This might interest the police long enough to link Beller to his famous daughter and then the media would drive the story.

Charley rumbled.

"For covering up? For not reporting it 'til now?"

"No DA in his or her right mind would bring the charge."

"How about me? Helping her with it. Accessory after the fact."

I went to him and squatted low.

"You're on the hook for me."

I stood, looked at Sadie and Anya, and went to the box of journals. I flipped through a second journal and saw more drawings, the big heads, the monstrous teeth, the tiny stick-figure sketches of a girl with her head in a plastic bag. The lump pounded.

I showed Anya the photo of Beller again with a last-ditch desperate hope she'd say Beller wasn't the guy.

"*This* man in *this* picture is the man who attacked you?"

"Yes, sir."

"He abducted you and tried to murder you like your mother said?"

"Yes, sir. He'd done it before. He showed me."

My head hurt. I was tired. I didn't understand.

"Showed what?"

"Pictures of the other girls."

Everything changed in the instant of her words.

Pike moved. Just a bit. His glasses gleamed like obsidian shields.

I said, "Pictures of what other girls?"

"They had plastic bags over their heads like me. He showed me before he put the bag over my head. Then he took my picture. He said, 'Here you go, now you're pretty like them.'"

Sadie kissed Anya's head.

"I saw the flash. I saw that flash across the field and I got him. I got him."

Sadie's eyes filled and she shook. The shaking started deep and grew harder until she buried her face in Anya's hair.

Charley rumbled.

"You're the finest woman ever lived."

I said, "Anya. How many pictures did he show you?"

"Five or six. I don't know. I didn't want to look."

"He showed you photos of young women with plastic bags over their heads."

"Uh-huh. His girls, he said. He collected girls. He liked to watch them die, he said."

The lump and the tiredness and the pounding headache faded.

"These girls, did he tell you anything about them? Their names? Where they were from?"

"Just stuff like 'See how pretty they are, let's get you ready and you'll be pretty, too.' Like that."

I walked to the window and back. I stared at Sadie, then Charley.

"What did you do with his stuff, destroy it?"

Charley didn't answer. I turned to Sadie.

"Did you see the pictures?"

"I didn't go in his van. I pulled Anya out and got the hell away. I thought he'd wake up and kill us."

"Those women had families. Their families want answers."

"What are you talking about, families?"

"The photographs. If those women were his victims, the police could've identified them. Their murders would've been solved."

Sadie wet her lips.

"I didn't know. I never thought."

She looked at Charley and her voice grew tight.

"Charley! What did you do with him?"

Charley answered Sadie, but he was watching me.

"Made sure nothing would come back on you, like I said."

"Did you keep anything from that van? Did you?"

Charley rumbled, but now it was a mumble.

"I don't know. Maybe."

I toed him hard.

"You either know or you don't know, stupid. Did you?"

"I didn't go in his van. I don't know what was there."

Sadie said, "If we can help those families, we'll do it. I mean it, Charley. Imagine if Anya was one of those girls."

The rumble.

"I gotta look."

I toed him again.

"You kept something of Beller's?"

"I'll look."

"Let's go look now."

"Not so easy to get to. Gonna take a while. Especially if I find my-self arrested."

"Something that would prove what he did to Anya?"

Charley's rumble came slowly.

"You're damn right it will."

Sadie said, "You get it."

I studied Charley for a moment, then looked at Sadie and decided.

"If you want a lawyer to help you, I can recommend one of the best. He's represented me."

Sadie looked surprised.

"You would?"

"Give me your number. I'll speak with him first and let you know."

I squatted by Charley.

"If you disappear or get stupid, I'll file a formal complaint naming your brother and Sadie as co-conspirators. You might be in the wind, but I'll make everyone else's life hell. And I will find you."

"I ain't going anywhere. And I'll do what I said."

"Look."

"I'll look."

"Look fast."

I glanced at Pike. Pike clipped the plastic ties from Charley's wrists and ankles.

I picked up the notebook with the pink marbled cover and turned to Anya.

"I'd like to read this. May I borrow it? I'll bring it back."

"You can take them all, if you like. I don't care."

"I may have questions. Are you okay talking about this?"

She glanced away and shrugged.

"I don't care. If it helps."

I looked at Sadie.

"You okay if I call to speak with her?"

"Yeah. Yes, I am. Thank you."

Sadie gave me her cell number written on a blue slip of paper.

I took the journals and we walked to Pike's Jeep.

51

We were almost at the Jeep before Pike spoke.

"You okay?"

"It's a lot to get your head around."

"Yes."

And what'd his baby girl say when she hired you, what a good father he was, what a wonderful man, how much she misses him?

The whine was back, a distant singing between my ears. I tried to picture myself telling Traci.

I said, "'Hi, Traci, your dad tried to strangle a girl and showed her pictures of his other victims.'"

Pike said, "Maybe they weren't."

"Weren't what?"

"Victims."

"You don't believe her?"

"I believe her, but he could've shown her pictures from a porn site. Freaks use fear to feel powerful."

The street was quiet. Dust motes and pollen drifted from the trees. It was hot.

I said, "Bad for Traci either way."

"Yeah. And you."

We reached the Jeep and Pike drove me to my car.

He said, "Want company tonight?"

"Got the journals, but thanks."

I climbed out with the journals and Pike hesitated.

He said, "Think I'll keep an eye on them."

"You going to stay?"

"In case they change their minds."

"Good idea."

I watched his Jeep disappear, looked at the journals in the box, and felt empty.

I called a criminal defense attorney named Charlie Bauman as I drove home. I did not mention Traci or Traci's involvement. After setting it up with Charlie, I called Sadie and told her to expect his call.

She said, "I can't believe you're doing this."

"Me neither. Let me know if Charley Reed comes up with something helpful."

"I will."

I hung up without saying 'bye. Petty.

Anya's journals were on the seat beside me with the lurking presence of a tumor. I thought about Traci and Anya and felt as if I had stepped into a life I didn't want. Sadie and Anya were credible and their claims, real or not, provable or not, would be investigated. I had to warn Traci, but I told myself maybe I shouldn't until I had some actual facts about her father. I went back and forth about it until I realized I was looking for an excuse not to tell her. By telling her, I would break her heart.

Time doesn't pass when you're trapped in your head. I didn't know how long it took to get home, but I pulled into the carport at twilight. I wanted to wash and change clothes, but I didn't. I used the bathroom, made a cup of coffee, and took the journals to the couch.

Anya wrote about her encounter with Thomas Beller over and over, each entry a little different from the others, but all describing one or more parts of the same event. Repetitive writing was a technique used to relieve stress and mute anxiety. Every time she wrote was an effort to kill the demon. She had written a lot.

Anya had not known his name. Throughout the entries in all the notebooks, she referred to him as "the man" or "he."

No single entry described the entirety of their encounter from beginning to end and most contained self-critical descriptions of herself. *I'M STUPID! I SUCK! I'M SUCH A LOSER!* These entries left me sad. Anya's rage had been directed at herself.

Her impression of Beller when he offered to give her a ride was of a kind, nonthreatening man who seemed nice. *"If you're heading home I'd be happy to give you a lift. It's awful dark out here."* He didn't press when she hesitated. *"All right then, you get home safe."* She'd changed her mind and climbed in. *STUPID! STUPID!*

Anya wrote she'd never accepted a ride from a stranger before. *It was kinda exciting.* She'd told herself, *I'll jump out if he tries anything!* She liked him right away. He asked about her and was so easygoing and friendly she relaxed.

Then Beller turned right when he should've gone straight.

He grabbed my neck and slapped me really hard. He pushed me down. He said, "Stay there or I'll hurt you bad." I cried and prayed. Mama was right. Don't accept rides! Strangers are monsters.

The following three entries described what happened after he pushed her down. *I was so scared! I didn't know where we were going. I knew he would rape me and do things. I was scared it would hurt. I wanted to jump out. I should've jumped. What's wrong with me?* She prayed he wouldn't hurt her and felt ashamed for not jumping. *I'M A STUPID COWARD MORON!*

Reading her entries was painful. I kept seeing the thin, hollow-eyed young woman I knew and the girl she would have been ten years earlier. I heard the words in her voice as I read. I took a bathroom break, dumped the coffee, and poured two fingers of bourbon.

The next entry contained a microanalysis of his facial expressions, his gestures, and how calm and ordinary he appeared. *Normal is a mask! How could I not see?* She was on the floorboard when she heard him say something. *I thought he said something to me, so I looked. He was on his phone. He saw me looking and smiled. I hid my eyes.*

I wondered if this was when Beller made the final call to his wife, so I checked. The timeline and call records showed no calls made or received at this hour. The mystery phone again. I made a note and kept reading.

The ride got real bumpy. I knew we'd turned off the road and I knew I'd die. I prayed so hard. Please don't let it hurt. She heard him say, "Here we go." The van stopped bouncing, the engine died, and he grabbed her arm. "Get up." She knew.

He pulled me up by my hair. I tried to get out, but he slapped my head real hard until I stopped.

Once she stopped struggling, he gave a friendly smile. *He looked like Santa without a beard.* He said, "Here, I want to show you something." He showed her photographs of young women with clear plastic bags over their heads. *I could see their mouths wide open. They were screaming.* Then he'd said, "Let's get you ready."

Ready.

My glass was empty. I added another finger, drank it, and added two more. Five fingers seemed appropriate.

I put the journals aside, went upstairs, and checked the lump. Lovely. I showered, went down to the kitchen, filled a ziplock with ice, and held it on the lump. The cat wasn't home, but the lump was good company. We thought about the women with bagged heads. We wondered who they were, and when and where they were murdered.

The lump said, "Their cases were never solved, you know."

The lump was smart.

It said, "And we don't know what he did with their bodies. Their families might not know they're dead. Maybe they went out one day and never came home."

The bourbon made my eyes water. I wiped them and blew my nose, but they kept leaking. Maybe gin would be better. I added a finger of gin to what was left of the bourbon and called Lucy. Her voice was sleepy when she answered, but warm.

She said, "Hey, baby. It's late. Are you all right?"

"What time is it?"

"After two."

"I'm drunk."

"I know. What's wrong?"

"I found him and it's bad. I want to tell her I couldn't find him. Leave it at that and walk away. Leave him among the missing. I don't want to tell her. I don't want to tell anyone."

"Baby?"

"I love your voice."

"You called to tell me. That's why you called. So you can tell me."

Lucy was smart like the lump.

I told her about Anya and Sadie and the van and what they said happened in the van and the women with plastic bags over their heads who might or might not be his other victims and what would happen to Traci when word got out. My eyes watered as I told her. The gin was as bad as the bourbon.

Lucy said, "You can't unfind him."

"Traci's my client. I like her and I work for her. I should protect her."

"You want to protect her, but you know you can't. That's why you hurt."

I tried to take another drink, but the glass was empty.

Lucy said, "Baby?"

"I'm here."

"The pictures of those other women might not be real?"

"It's possible they aren't. I hope they weren't."

"But they might be real?"

I drank again, but the glass was still empty.

I said, "Yeah. Yeah, they could be real."

"Possible is enough. Those women, they need you, too."

"I know."

"Their families need you."

I was sleepy. My head dipped.

I said, "I know."

"Fall asleep with me. Don't hang up. Fall asleep while I'm with you. Sleep."

"I'm here."

"Sleep."

My eyes closed. I slept.

52

Lori Chance Sanchez

Lori's last customers that night before she closed were two shit-faced women, who rolled up in a white Mercedes-Benz and stumbled through the door giggling. Lori watched them from her fleece cocoon, thinking, *Look at these two.* The makeup, the long orange nails, the belly jelly spilling out of stretchy jeans with big honking diamonds on their fingers.

The first woman pulled up short to get her bearings, the second crashed into her, and they fell in a laughing, drunken heap.

Lori said, "You vomit, you're cleaning it up."

The women climbed to their feet, wheeling and waving for balance.

The second woman squinted to focus.

"We want beer. Do you have beer?"

Lori said, "How in hell did you drive fifty feet without crashing that car?"

The first woman scowled at the floor.

"Your floor tripped us. We could sue."

Her friend remained focused on the mission.

"I think the beer is over here."

They wobbled to the cooler, made their selections, and staggered back to the counter, each with a six-pack of Pabst Blue Ribbon tall boys.

The second woman, who arrived first, plopped her six-pack on the counter and looked around, head tipping and craning like a parrot.

She said, "Why is it so cold?"

"My fuckhead boss. Will this be all?"

The first woman arrived and added a second six-pack.

"Tell your fuckhead to fix the floor. I could sue. My husband sues the ass off people all the time."

"Is that how you got that Mercedes?"

"You're goddamned right. Tell him."

Lori rang them up.

The first woman, the one married to the lawyer, pried a wallet from the way-too-tight pants.

"I got it."

She fumbled with the wallet and slapped a credit card on the counter. Lori had heard about cards like this, but had never seen one.

"Is this an Amex Black card?"

"You're damn right. We got so much money I shit green."

Lori processed the transaction in silence and watched the two women drive off in a car worth more money than she could make in ten years. She felt low. Lori couldn't get ten bucks from her exes and this lush had a Black card.

Life sucked.

The time was six fifty-four. One hour and six minutes until closing. Lori watched the parking lot, praying she wouldn't have any more customers, praying some meth head tweaker wouldn't stumble in and stab her to death.

Ten minutes to eight, her mother called. Lori rolled her eyes as she answered.

"What?"

"Where are you?"

"At work. What do you want?"

"Sometimes you go out."

This was her life. Day in, day out. Dealing beer to drunken lushes, freezing her ass off all alone, and getting calls from her mother.

"I'm at work. What do you want?"

"I thought you'd be home by now."

"It's only ten to eight. Jesus Christ, what's wrong with you? You know what time I close."

"Tonight's my show."

Her mother watched a singing competition, same time every week. The show aired live so the audience could vote for their favorite singer and see who won in real time. Her mother voted. Which meant Lori had to be home in time to keep her son out of her mother's hair.

Lori said, "I know. I didn't forget. Eight minutes and I'm out of here."

"Don't forget. Don't meet some man and go drinking."

"I should be so lucky."

"You'll come straight home?"

Lori hung up.

A Black Amex card and a white Mercedes.

What am I doing wrong?

Lori locked the door and flipped the sign at seven fifty-six. She counted the register cash, fed the bills through a slot into a cheapo metal box only her fuckhead boss could unlock, and let herself out the back.

She struggled into her car and headed home.

A small white sedan sat at the exit from the superstore, waiting to turn with its blinker on. Lori passed the car and it pulled out behind her. She paid the car no mind. Lori was thinking about her mother and the dumbass stupid show and wishing she had a life.

53

Wendi Nicole Chance
Lori's Mother

Wendi Chance watched her three-year-old grandson, Lawrence, buzz through the living room like an airplane. He swooped, he turned, he made noise, and the little shitass never stopped moving.

Wendi said, "Settle down. It's almost bedtime."

It was eight thirty-five. Wendi was propped on the couch with her feet up, beat-to-hell tired from chasing Lawrence all day and looking forward to her show. She sipped her gin and tonic and set the glass in a puddle. Wendi was angry and getting angrier each time Lawrence zoomed past.

"Stop it or I'll get the switch."

Lori should've been home twenty minutes ago. She should be getting her noisy-ass child ready for bed so Wendi could watch her show in peace. Lawrence didn't go down easy. He raised nine kinds of hell.

Wendi snatched up her phone and called Lori. If that girl made Wendi miss her show, Wendi would kill her.

Voice mail.

Wendi started right in.

"You don't even answer? Which bar are you at? If you're not home by nine I'll put this boy outside."

Wendi stabbed the END CALL button and tossed the phone aside.

Disgusted. Lawrence veered into the dining room and zoomed through the kitchen. Wendi watched him zoom and felt a million years old.

She said, "C'mon, boy. Let's get you ready for bed."

Lawrence zoomed away.

At eight fifty-two, Lori still wasn't home and Wendi was getting worried. Lawrence was in bed, though he wasn't asleep. He jumped up and down like his bed was a trampoline, bouncing back and forth from head to foot. Jump jump jump, jump jump jump. Endless.

Wendi turned off the light, left a crack in the door, and returned to the living room. She called Lori.

Voice mail.

"I'm getting worried and I don't like this."

Wendi thought, unsure what to say next.

"I put him in bed, but he isn't down. He wants you. You might think about him next time."

Wendi hesitated, then ended the call.

Her show started at nine o'clock on the dot. Wendi sipped the g&t as the familiar opening played, but Wendi wasn't paying attention. She went to the window, hoping to see approaching headlights, but didn't see a damn thing.

She said, "Shit."

At nine-fifteen she phoned Lori again.

Voice mail.

"He better be rich. He better be damned good-looking is all I can say, you putting me through this. Call me when you come up for air. I don't care how late. Lemme know you're all right."

Wendi lowered her phone.

At nine-thirty, Lawrence walked into the living room, crying. His face was all crumpled and tears shimmered in his eyes.

He said, "I want Mommy."

Wendi bent toward him and opened her arms.

"She'll be home soon. She's just late, is all. Come be with Grammie."

Lawrence came closer, but didn't stop crying. He pointed at the door with his little chubby hand, eyes all red and his nose all snotty.

"I want Mommy."

Wendi lifted him in her arms.

"She might be coming right now. Let's go see."

Wendi unlocked the front door and stepped outside, bouncing Lawrence to soothe him. The air was chilly. Nothing moved in the distance.

Wendi said, "Well, I don't see her just yet, but she'll be home soon."

Wendi bounced Lawrence as she searched the far dark.

"She's on her way. I know she's coming."

Wendi bounced the boy. She watched for Lori, hoping to see her coming. The night was still. She didn't see Lori. Nobody was coming. Nobody came.

54

The Kill Car

The first gold of dawn kissed the eastern sky as the kill car slid past the empty plain of the shopping mall. They didn't stop. The driver wanted to see the flower shop.

The witness gave them names. Anya. Sadie. The same names were written in the detective's file, but the file didn't explain their role. Now he knew.

The girl was Anya.

The driver had never known her name. He hadn't thought of her in years, but here she was, his most terrifying, gut-churning nightmare now real, a victim who survived.

How are you still alive?

What happened?

Who did you tell?

He said, "Stop. It doesn't matter."

Only one thing mattered now.

He said, "We have to find her."

The kill car whispered, soft.

"Yes."

PART FOUR

55

Elvis Cole

The morning sun painted my living room with nuclear yellow panels. I didn't pull the drapes. I wanted the light to burn through my hangover.

The cat was watching me.

I said, "I have to call her."

He rubbed against my leg and walked away.

I pulled off my clothes in the kitchen, put on a pair of unwashed shorts I found in the hamper, and went out to the deck. The sun was blinding and my head hurt, but not from the concussion. I tried to center myself, taking slow deep breaths, letting them out, then I hit it hard: stretches, crunches, push-ups, dips. I powered into tae kwon do and kung fu forms without pausing, kicking and spinning across the deck until my muscles burned and drops of sweat stained the deck like a freckled path. Punishment.

I drank half a liter of water, showered, and dressed. Pike called as I tied my shoes.

I said, "Did they run?"

"Unloaded the SUV and the van and broke down the boxes. Sadie went out a little after six and came back with what looked like pizzas. The squints took off about eight-forty. The brother left at a quarter to ten. Everybody else stayed."

"Even Charley."

"All night. Still there."

"Thanks, brother. I guess we're good."

I didn't feel good or not good. I finished tying my shoes, and went down to the kitchen. I wasn't hungry, but I scrambled two eggs. When the eggs were scrambled, I threw them out and called Traci Beller's phone. Dina answered.

"Hi, this is Dina, Traci Beller's assistant."

"Elvis Cole. I need to speak with her."

"Um, Kevin's picking us up. She's getting ready."

"I need her now."

"I'll have her call you right back."

"Now. Tell her, Dina."

Traci came on the line three minutes later.

"Hey! Good morning! How's your face?"

"I need to see you. It's important."

Traci hesitated. She heard the tension in my voice, so I tried again. Calmer.

"It's about your father."

"What? Is he dead?"

"I'll come over. We should speak in person."

Now she sounded worried.

"I'm going downtown. We have a meeting."

Gentle.

"Cancel it, Traci. And get rid of Kevin and Dina. It'll be easier to talk alone."

"You really know how to scare a girl, don't you?"

I didn't say anything funny. I couldn't.

She said, "Give me an hour."

Delivering bad news went with the job. The runaway teenager you were hired to find, you find dead or turning tricks or addicted. The blackmailer you were hired to stop turns out to be the victim's spouse. The online scammer who conned a ninety-something couple out of their savings turned out to be their granddaughter. I had delivered plenty of bad news, but never news worse than this.

The midmorning sun washed Traci's home. Her bright green lawn shimmered. The blue bay windows glowed with an azure incandescence. The colors were so pure the little house seemed caught between this world and another, as if it were a perfect fantasy except for the AC van in the driveway. Phil.

I went to the door and rang the bell.

Traci answered, looking nervous as she let me in.

"I wish you'd told me on the phone. I feel like I'm going to throw up."

"Why is Phil here?"

She glanced toward the living room and lowered her voice.

"Kevin wanted to stay. He called Phil and told him you had news. Thank God my mother didn't come."

Kevin shouted from the living room.

"We're in here. What is going on?"

I looked at Traci and shook my head.

She looked trapped and miserable.

"I can't make them leave. Just tell us and get it over with. *Please.*"

She tugged me toward the living room.

Kevin was on his feet, irritated, and Phil was on the couch. Kevin's eyes widened when he saw me.

"Christ, man, what happened to you?"

"I fell out of bed."

Kevin scowled and flicked his hand.

"Who cares? You've upset Traci and I don't like it. What could possibly be so important?"

Traci perched beside her uncle and Kevin remained on his feet. I focused on Traci.

"Remember Eric Zalway? From the Byers report?"

"Yeah, the hamburger guy. He talked to my dad."

"Your father went back later. A friend of Eric's on the evening shift saw him, so I spoke with her."

Phil scooted forward like Traci.

"Does she know what happened to Tommy?"

I stayed with Traci.

"Your father was at the SurfMutt for a long time. Almost two hours," she said."

Phil grunted, nodding.

"Yeah, okay. Waiting out traffic like he said."

Traci glanced at Phil, nodded with him, and came back to me.

"She saw him waiting. That's good, isn't it? Did you ask what time he left? Which way he turned?"

"She saw him offer a ride to a girl she knew from high school. A sophomore. She was fifteen."

Kevin's face soured. He glanced at Traci.

"If you're trying to make this sound sordid, congratulations."

Traci glanced from Kevin to me and wet her lips.

"So? He was being nice."

I leaned toward Traci, wishing I could be any other place or earth saying something other than what I was about to say.

"Not according to her. She's twenty-five now. I found her and spoke with her and her mother."

Kevin rolled his eyes, cutting me off.

"Here it comes! Let the rape allegations begin. For shit's sake, man, this is ludicrous."

I ignored him. I focused on Traci and said what I said only to her and for her.

"This part is hard."

Kevin again.

"Just say it. Stop the drama."

"They told me your father overpowered her, drove to a field, and attempted to murder her."

Kevin barked a single sharp laugh.

"Bullshit. Are you insane, telling her something like this?"

Traci was shaking her head.

"Wait. They accused my father of what?"

Kevin wagged a finger.

"Your detective's a fraud. This is nonsense."

Phil leaned forward, his broad face dark.

"Who are these people?"

I didn't look away from Traci. I stayed with her and kept going.

"The girl's mother saw his van in a field. She saw her daughter inside and saw what was happening and stated to me she killed him."

Traci stood and raised a hand, the hand saying stop.

"I'm sorry, but no. Do you believe every crazy story people tell you?"

Phil stood with her.

"Now wait. She said she killed him? This woman murdered him?"

Traci kept shaking her head, back and forth, back and forth, her hand still in the air.

"I don't believe any of this. It's absurd."

Kevin spread his hands.

"Cole, seriously. Think. Half the cops in the state were looking for him. Georgina would've been called."

"This is why he's missing, Kevin. They didn't report it. They didn't tell anyone. They kept it secret, but now they're not. These allegations will be made."

Kevin lowered his hands and studied me.

"They smell Traci's money."

"They don't know I work for Traci."

"Then why not keep the secret?"

"The daughter suffers with severe PTSD. She should've been in therapy, but you can't do therapy unless you talk about what happened. The mother's coming clean so her daughter can get help."

Phil glanced at Traci then came back to me.

"You sound like you believe them."

I said, "They're credible. Zalway's friend puts the daughter in his van. I've read the daughter's journals. They're convincing."

Kevin's jaw tightened.

"Do they have any proof besides these so-called journals?"

Traci's mouth opened and she glared at him.

"You cannot be taking this seriously."

I answered Kevin.

"They claim they kept something from the van. I haven't seen it."

I focused on Traci.

"There's more. The daughter says your father showed her photographs of other girls he murdered."

Phil shouted.

"Shut your damn mouth!"

Kevin shouted, too, waving his arm again.

"Outrageous! I'll have these people arrested for extortion. I'll sue them for slander."

Traci stalked to the far end of the room.

"I'm done here."

Kevin went to Traci. His jaw flexed.

"They want money. I can meet with these people."

Traci said, "No."

"We'll find a number they like, make them sign a nondisclosure agreement, and bury this. No crazy claims going viral. No investors losing interest."

I went to Traci. I wanted to touch her, but I didn't.

"The police will investigate and the story will spread. You can't stop it and it will hurt."

Kevin said, "Shut up, Cole! Get out."

"But if it's true, if there were other victims, those women and their families deserve justice. Be the one who gives it to them."

Kevin flicked his hand again.

"You're talking nonsense. What does this even mean?"

I didn't look at him. I looked at her.

"I'll find out whether these victims exist and I'll try to identify them and you can bring it forward. Be the one who gives them justice."

Kevin shouted.

"No, you won't and neither will she! People won't buy muffins from a maniac's daughter. Set up a meeting. I'll cut a deal."

Traci looked into my right eye and my left and seemed to be searching for something she did not find.

She said, "You're going to do this anyway."

"I will. For them and for you. You know I'm right."

She took one step back.

"You're fired."

Traci turned and quickly left the room.

Kevin stalked to the entry and threw open the door.

"Tell those people we'll sue them. And we'll sue you, too. Get out. You're fired."

I left.

56

Phil called from the door and caught me at the street. He huffed from the little run across her yard.

"Listen, sorry I got upset in there. It's just—"

He ran out of words.

"I know. It's a lot."

The big head bounced up and down.

"Hell, yeah, it is. If you told me Tommy was a Martian, I'd believe it faster. I mean, this can't be."

"I hope it isn't."

He took a deep breath, blew it out in a whoosh, and glanced at the house.

"You gonna tell Georgina?"

"Nope, but someone should. You or Traci."

He stared at the ground for a moment before looking up.

"You really believe these people?"

"I believe they believe it. They're credible, Phil. Credible doesn't mean it happened or happened the way they say it happened, but the police won't ignore them."

"The police will want proof."

"Yes."

"You saw these journals?"

"I read them."

"Credible."

I nodded.

Phil shrugged, the big face dark again.

"Credible isn't enough. Call a man a killer, show me proof. Ruin memories of a man, you better be able to back it up."

Phil studied me for a moment.

"And all you've seen are journals."

"They say they have more. We'll see."

"But they didn't say what."

"Phil, I don't want to get into it now. If they produce something, I'll confirm whether it's real or not, and I'll let Traci know."

"I should meet these people. Feel them out."

"Not going to happen."

"Bet a buck they couldn't pick Tommy out of a lineup."

"They recognized his photograph. I don't want to get into it now, Phil. Please."

Phil took a breath.

"All right."

He stared at the ground again. He wasn't finished.

I said, "What?"

He glanced at the house again.

"Kevin makes a lot of money. He's worried about Traci's career and I am, too, I guess, but I care more about her. She loved her dad. She's worked her butt off to come this far."

He looked back at me.

"This turns out to be real, I'll need to help Traci and Georgina get through it."

I didn't say anything.

He said, "If the news is bad, let me know first. I'll break it to them. I'm family."

Phil walked back to the house across the sunny yard and I drove home, feeling bad and alone. The hero saved the damsel; he didn't destroy her. I wanted to save her. I wanted to save all of them.

57

nya's journals were even more disturbing the second time I read them. I skimmed for descriptions of the victim photos and scanned relevant pages. The photos were mentioned in most of her entries with little or no description, but sometimes a word stood out.

He said, "Here, look at this," and showed me this girl. Her head was in this bag. OMG so gross! He grabbed my hair and said, "Look, I collect little girls." He had these weird shiny little pictures. I pretended to look, but I didn't I didn't I didn't.

"Shiny" could mean they were glossy prints, but "little" made me think of instant-camera photos. In other entries, she described the picture as "square."

The bag was kinda foggy. Her mouth was a big black hole. I saw the hole and OMG, I knew I was going to die. She was screaming. I thought I heard her screaming but it was me.

Anya never described their hair color or complexion or clothing. Only the mouth of the young woman in the first photo. Screaming.

A line in a later entry reminded me of something Anya said.

Him, as he showed her the photos: *"See how pretty they are? Let's get you ready and you'll be pretty, too."*

Anya had written about this moment in more than half of her entries and most contained the same or a similar line.

"Let's get you ready and you'll be pretty, too."

"I'll get you ready and you'll be pretty like them."

"Lemme get you ready."

Getting her ready implied a ritual. Serial killers were often pattern killers, re-creating the same event over and over. Their victims were usually similar—young Anglo females, older Latinas, young Black males. They might be posed in similar ways or found in similar locations or bear similar wounds and their victims were almost always murdered like their other victims—strangled, suffocated, stabbed, or bludgeoned. Compulsion killers were creatures of habit. Their repetition was a signature.

I thought about it and called Sadie's number. I counted eight rings before she answered.

I said, "It's Cole. How're you doing?"

"Oh, yeah. Uh-huh. Good, I guess."

She sounded wary.

"I've read her journals. Something I'd like to ask. Okay if I speak to her about it?"

"Uh-huh. Sure."

I waited. She didn't put Anya on the line or say anything or hang up.

"Sadie?"

"Spoke with Mr. Bauman. We're going to see him tomorrow."

"Good. He's a good guy. A good attorney."

"Yeah. Seems like. Anyway—"

She fell silent again.

I said, "Anya?"

"I want you to know I appreciate this. Mr. Bauman, what you're doing, helping Anya. I don't know what to say."

"How about 'Here's Anya'?"

She gave a tight laugh.

"Here's Anya."

Anya came on the line. I told her I had a question and asked if she'd mind talking about what happened.

"I don't care. Sure."

"When he said, 'Let's get you ready,' how'd he get you ready?"

"He took off my necklace before he wrapped the wire around my neck. He said it looked nicer."

Her voice was flat, with no highs or lows or emotion.

"I am so sorry."

"It's okay."

Flat.

"Did he do anything else to get you ready, like change your hair or put lipstick on you?"

"No, sir. He just took off my jewelry, wrapped the wire around my neck, and put on the bag. The bag was last."

I said, "Jewelry. You mean your necklace?"

"No, all of it. My rings and studs and my bracelet. He took off the necklace last."

"The studs from your ears."

I saw it happening: the monstrous figure with big teeth from her drawings touching the ears of the stick-figure girl who was too scared to move. The lump burned. It felt so hot it must have glowed, but a frosty chill crept down my spine and up the back of my neck.

She said, "Yes, sir. He took them out."

"He removed your jewelry."

"Yes, sir."

"What'd he do with it?"

"My jewelry?"

"After he took them off. What did he do with your rings and brace-let and things?"

"Put them in a little envelope. It was white."

"Okay. Thank you, Anya. Thanks a lot."

I drank some water and used the bathroom. I opened the fridge, but

Traci's muffins were on the shelf. I went to the couch and called John Chen. He answered with the usual whisper, but sounded excited.

"I'm in Pacoima. Dude killed his mother with a blowtorch. Burned a hole through her skull. A freaking torch killer, right? You should smell the stink."

"Go someplace where we can talk."

"Dude. I'm at a crime scene. It's crawling with cops."

"Major Crimes keeps a database of unsolved homicides, don't they?"

He answered slowly, wondering what I wanted.

"Yeah. So does the CDOJ. Why?"

"I need to search for unsolved homicides with specific similarities."

His whisper tightened.

"No shit? A serial killer?"

"Depends on the search results."

"Hold on."

I heard him breathing and tell someone to get out of the way. The background was quiet when he spoke again.

"Okay, go."

"Anglo females murdered between twenty-five years ago until ten years ago."

"Here in our area?"

"California. Cause of death is strangulation and/or asphyxia, plastic bags on their heads, and jewelry removed from their bodies."

Chen said, "Hang on, hang on, I'm writing."

I stared across the wide bowl of the canyon while he wrote. A male red-tailed hawk floated past, his tiny head moving side to side. The feathers on the undersides of his wings were a pale mix of gold and brown.

Chen said, "Okay. Shit. Anything else?"

"That's it."

"The jewelry thing is good. Man, I'm all over it. I'll get back to you."

Chen was thrilled. Serial death had serious upside potential.

I wandered back to the kitchen and looked at Traci's muffins. I was deciding what to do when my phone rang. The caller ID read SADIE, but when I answered Charley Reed rumbled.

"This is Charley Reed. I'm here at Sadie's."

"Did you look?"

"Said I'd look, but looking's not so easy. Figured I'd show you and let you decide."

First words out of his mouth and he pissed me off.

"Do you have something or not?"

"Come out whenever you want, up to you, and I'll show you. I'm not discussing this in front of Sadie, but you come see, I don't care when, and tell me what you want to do. You want what's here, it's yours."

The headache was back in full force.

"Does Charlie Bauman know what you have?"

"Not yet, but he will."

"Will this help identify those women?"

Charley hesitated.

"It should, but I don't know. I cannot tell you it will, but it should."

I checked the time.

"I'll be there in an hour."

I held the dead phone, thinking about Charley's invitation. I wondered if it was legit or if he was luring me into another situation. "Luring" was a good word. I felt proud for using it. I called Pike.

"Charley Reed offered to show me what he has. I'm going."

"Want company?"

"Nope. Wanted you to know, is all. In case."

"Rog."

"I'll check in later."

"Rog."

"Be seeing you."

"Let's hope so."

Pike.

I packed up Anya's journals, made the long drive back to Sadie's, and found Charley Reed waiting for me.

58

The Kill Car

They passed the detective's home and found the carport empty. This did little to ease his fear.

"I should've left the tracker in his car. I don't like not knowing where he is. He might be just around the corner."

Rushing air carried the kill car's soothing hiss.

"You've done this a thousand times. You'll be in and out in no time."

"I know, I know."

The driver had faith in his skill set and tools. He could pick locks quickly and disable most residential security systems with the Wi-Fi and Bluetooth jammers he'd bought online. Once the Wi-Fi and Bluetooth connections were broken, devices couldn't talk to each other, which meant no alarms or recordings. This was how the driver entered homes while the people inside slept. He enjoyed creeping through homes in the dark and standing over people in their beds.

The kill car's hiss was calm.

"You're nervous. Nerves are normal."

The driver suddenly checked the mirror, certain the yellow car would be behind them.

"He could come home and catch me."

"He's close to catching us anyway. Remember what she told us. The girl and her mother?"

The thundering voice shouted.

RUN! GET AWAY! BEFORE IT'S TOO LATE!

The kill car whispered.

"If you run, you know how this will end."

They cruised along gentle curves on the quiet street. He found it peaceful.

"They'll find my body."

"You'll hang yourself or blow your brains out. You've always said so."

The driver had seen his fate play out. In the moments when paranoia consumed him, his thoughts filled with witnesses coming forth or newly discovered evidence and, always, his name and face on the news. He'd see himself on the run, living in his car or in frozen forests, surviving on snack food, rat meat, and tears as an army of police and federal agents surrounded him. And he'd seen his inevitable end.

BANG.

The kill car whispered gently.

"You shouldn't run. You don't need to run."

The thundering voice boomed.

RUN!

The kill car found a place to turn, and they headed back toward the detective's home. The sharp peak of its roof grew closer.

The kill car's voice was soothing.

"The detective did the work. Just go in, find it, and see what he knows."

The driver repeated.

"Find it. What if it isn't here?"

"We'll wait."

The house came toward them, larger and larger.

The driver's tongue felt scaled.

He said, "They have to go."

"Them. Him. Whatever he's found. We'll get rid of everyone who can hurt us and we'll be fine."

"Yes."

"You won't have to run."

"No."

They reached the house.

The driver said, "This is good. Stop."

The kill car stopped.

The driver got out with his tools and hurried to the door.

59

Elvis Cole

Charley Reed met me at my car before I got out.

I said, "Okay. Let's see it."

"Gotta take you there. You can ride with me, you want."

"Where?"

Charley hesitated, as if this was his last and final chance to hold his secret safe and saying the words wasn't easy.

"Where I left him."

"Beller's body?"

The front door opened and Sadie stepped out. She didn't look happy to see me, but she raised a hand.

She said, "Hey."

"Hey."

"You bring back Anya's journals?"

I handed the notebooks to Charley and he took them to Sadie. She accepted them without a word and closed the door.

Charley trudged back to my car.

"Yeah, Beller's body. You want to go or not?"

"I'll follow you."

"Okey-doke."

I stopped him as he turned.

"Charley."

I brushed my jacket aside to let the pistol peek out. He saw it and turned away.

"You won't need it. You're helping Sadie."

The brown truck led me north to Bell Canyon, then south to an undeveloped area in eastern Ventura County. The land was dry and colored like straw. Traffic was sparse. The drive would've been pleasant except it wasn't. The pavement ended and the road grew bumpy. Charley pulled over and I pulled over behind him. He walked back to see me.

"Your car's not gonna like this road. You might wanna ride with me."

I climbed into his truck and we bumped along over rocks and cuts without speaking or looking at each other. The land around us held nothing but scattered clumps of withered manzanita that looked dead even if it wasn't.

I said, "Is this where Sadie found them?"

"Uh-uh. Oh, hell no. They were on the other side way over by town. Not here. Nothing's out here."

"Except him."

Charley nodded without looking at me.

"Yes, sir. Him and his van."

"You kept his van?"

"I buried it. Him and his van."

"You buried his van."

"Yes, sir."

"A van."

"Shut the doors, put it on a flatbed, and trucked it out here."

I studied Charley Reed, trying to figure him out.

"Why didn't you kill me?"

He pooched his lips and kept his eyes on the road.

"I didn't want to kill you. I just wanted you to, I don't know, leave them alone. Go away. Shit, I don't know."

Them. Sadie and Anya.

His lips worked some more. He glanced over, squirmed, and seemed uncomfortable.

"You read her journals?"

"Yeah."

"I tried, once. I couldn't."

He glanced over again.

"Listen. Your medical bill? I'll cover it. Your out-of-pocket costs, whatever, I'll get it."

"You're something."

"I don't know what else I can do."

"How much farther?"

"Right up here."

The land tabled out at the top of a rise and we stopped at the edge of a field. Charley opened his door and stepped out.

"This is it."

I joined him. The field was covered with the same dead weeds, scrubby manzanita, and desolation.

I said, "What a fine place to dump a body."

Charley grunted.

"A hundred and sixty-two acres my grandpa left. I own it. It'll never be developed, the utilities don't cross my land, and nobody has a right to be here but me. Wasn't a chance in hell he'd be found."

I said, "Where?"

"Out here."

Charley led me into the brush.

"You actually buried a van."

"Trucked out my backhoe. I thought about crushing it, but then what? Sadie's prints were all over it and Anya's prints and God knows what else, plus the DNA. Anya's schoolbag was splattered with blood and brains. That van was a mess. I didn't go in it."

"The photos of the other women?"

"I didn't see any pictures or anything else. I didn't look. If it was in the van then, it's in the van now."

"You didn't check his body?"

"Hell no. I could see his damn brains."

"So you closed the doors, brought it here, and buried it."

"Deep. Anything that might lead back to Sadie was in the van, so I got rid of the van and everything in it."

I saw nothing around us until I did. Wide knobby tires had cut fresh tracks in the soil and crushed the brush.

Charley said, "This is him. May he burn in hell."

We reached a round hole about three feet across circled by a ring of fresh earth. A steel rebar cage like the kind used in footings jutted up out of the hole for maybe two feet.

Charley went to the edge and looked down. I looked down and saw something round, white, crumpled, and mostly covered by soil at the bottom of a deep hole.

I said, "Is that the van?"

"Crushed a little, but that's it. Sixty or seventy tons of dirt's been sitting on it."

I took out my phone and showed the photo of Thomas Beller's van.

"This van?"

He studied the picture and nodded.

"Bel-Jan Heating & Air. Yeah, that's it."

I didn't smell anything unusual. I couldn't tell if I was seeing a van or garbage from a landfill.

"How deep is he?"

"Twelve feet from the bottom of your shoes to the roof when I buried it. I measured the van and dug accordingly."

"Twelve feet."

"To the top. I dug down nineteen feet. Figured to put him down deep, what with coyotes and how they get after a stink."

I stared at him. You had to shake your head.

"Your brother help?"

"Nope. Didn't tell him. Still haven't."

"You did it yourself."

"Wasn't much to it."

"You actually buried a van."

Charley Reed looked at me.

"Now you know why I wanted you to see. Brought out my bore and backhoe, got down there, and saw the roof was crushed. My backhoe might rip this thing apart, but if you want me to dig it up, I'll dig it up."

I stared at the crumpled white metal at the bottom of the hole and wondered what was left. Ten years of ants and bugs and moisture and mold and seepage through the strata. I wondered what would be left of the photographs and whether the persons once pictured could even be recognized.

Charley said, "You're calling the shots. What do you want to do?"

The police would want to preserve the scene. They'd send criminalists to document the excavation and preserve the evidence and medical examiners to exhume the remains. Disturbing the scene without their involvement would taint the evidence and open these people to additional charges.

"When do you see Bauman?"

"Tomorrow afternoon. We're driving in to see him."

I wasn't in a rush anymore. The photos or whatever was left of them could wait a little longer. Waiting would give Traci more time to prepare and me more time to help her if she'd let me.

I said, "Talk to Bauman. Tell him what's here."

"You don't want me to dig it up?"

"Talk to Bauman. He'll know what to do."

I headed back to the truck. Charley followed behind and brought me to my car. Seventy-two minutes later I rounded the final curve toward home and saw two L.A. County Sheriff SUVs parked in front of my home. Their doors opened. Two uniformed deps slid from one vehicle and Detective Dan Carmack climbed from the other. Carmack watched me drive toward him with the sleepy eyes of a goldfish. He raised his hand to greet me, but he didn't smile.

60

wheeled into the carport and met them at their vehicles. The deps were rangy men with dark glasses, basket-weave holsters, and gleaming brass buckles. They looked like a recruitment poster. Carmack didn't offer his hand and neither did the deps.

I said, "Happened to be in the neighborhood?"

"Thought I'd follow up. How's your head?"

Carmack and his deps didn't drive from Rancha to ask about my head.

"Hard. Sometimes it's a plus."

The one dep said, "Most times not."

The other dep said, "True. Right now, it isn't."

I looked from the deps to Carmack.

He said, "Thought you might've remembered something. I've seen it, you know. A few days pass, the fog clears, people remember."

"Sorry."

"Like why they were at a particular place instead of bullshit about taking a pee."

"Take it easy."

"Like who beat the hell out of them instead of crap about drunks wanting to buy their car."

He was pressing. He had new information and I knew I wouldn't like it.

"Tell you what, Carmack. Hook me up or take off. We're done."

Carmack made a tight, brittle smile.

"We're not close to done."

He nodded toward my house.

"Let's go sit. I got bad knees."

I didn't move or respond, so he nodded again.

"C'mon. I get grumpy when my knees hurt."

I turned off the alarm, showed him through the door, and stopped. Papers and file folders were scattered across the dining table and the floor.

Carmack said, "You need a housekeeper."

The cabinets and drawers behind my dining table were open. The file box I kept on the shelf beside my printer had been dumped onto the table.

I stared at Carmack.

"Did you do this?"

"Don't be silly."

I checked my phone for alarm and motion alerts and found nothing. I remembered arming the house when I left, but now I doubted myself. Lucy, Joe, and I were the only people who knew the entry code.

I circled through the living room and ran upstairs.

Carmack shouted.

"Cole! Stay down here with me."

The bedspread was pushed up on the side as if someone looked under the bed. The closet door was open and clothes were pushed to the side.

Carmack called again.

"Cole!"

I hurried down. The sliders and the door to the carport were locked. The windows in the guest bedroom were secure. I returned to the dining room and scooped the scattered pages from the floor, but I didn't want to look through them with Carmack.

I said, "Someone broke in, Carmack. Someone searched my house."

Carmack watched me with the goldfish eyes. The eyes drifted to the files and floated back.

"Call the police."

I called my alarm company, told them I'd been breached, and asked them to run a systems check.

Carmack said, "Put down the phone, Cole."

I walked away, waiting for the check results.

Carmack followed me and gripped my arm.

"Hang up. Look at me."

I looked, but I didn't hang up.

He said, "Do you know a woman named Lori Sanchez?"

Carmack's expression and tone told me he knew the answer, but his jaw flexed and rippled with tension.

I lowered the phone.

"Yeah, from Camille's. Why?"

"Your card was in her purse."

Was.

A sound like faraway surf rose and faded. Carmack must've seen something in my reaction. The tension left his jaw.

I said, "Lori?"

"Her body was found this morning. Murdered."

I pulled a chair from the table and sat.

"At the store?"

He pulled a chair and sat facing me.

"Between the store and home. Her car went off the road. Damage wasn't bad, though, so we're not sure why. She probably started walking and somebody came along."

"Came along and murdered her? C'mon, Carmack, who would murder her? Why?"

"Road crew found her. I'll leave it at that."

Carmack leaned toward me, the goldfish eyes bulging.

"Her mother said she was spending time with you. This true?"

My eyes burned. I blinked and rubbed the burn.

"We flirted. Having fun. You know."

"Want some water?"

"I want to know what happened."

Carmack glanced down.

"Blunt force and I'll leave it at that."

I nodded.

"Lori told her mom she was helping you with a case. That one true, too?"

I wondered what else Lori told her mom.

"Yes. In a way."

"So you weren't shopping for a weekend getaway like you told me in the hospital."

I wanted to be honest but I had to be careful. The Givens would tell their story soon and the world would learn about Traci's father. Telling Carmack too much now would undercut the Givens and limit my efforts to help Traci, but I wanted Carmack to catch Lori's killer.

"A man named Thomas Beller disappeared from Rancha ten years ago. He was never found. The family had him declared dead, but they wanted to try again."

"Hence you."

"The ten-year anniversary is coming up. They hired me to find him."

"Have you?"

"I will."

"How does Ms. Sanchez fit in?"

"The last place he was seen was the SurfMutt. Lori worked the counter at the time. I interviewed her and she offered to ask her friends if they remembered him. They didn't, but yes, she helped."

Carmack and I stared at each other. We were both thinking, but we were thinking different things.

I said, "Why was her car was off the road?"

"We're looking into it. Maybe the boys who kicked your ass were involved."

Charley and his brother and the squint were with Sadie last night. Pike was watching them.

"No. I don't see how."

Carmack leaned forward again.

"Did Ms. Sanchez mention if anyone was bothering her? Someone who scared her?"

"What do you mean, scared her?"

"Creeped her out. Frightened her. A customer, maybe?"

"What are you saying, Carmack? What happened to her?"

"Someone angry. An ex-boyfriend or ex-husband."

The goldfish eyes floated in hazy water a million miles away.

"She worried about being robbed. Junkies and bandits, but nobody in particular."

"Where were you last night?"

"Here. And no, I can't prove it."

Carmack stood and headed for the door.

"Okay. That's it for now."

Carmack opened the door but hesitated. The goldfish eyes considered me.

"Thomas Beller. Did his family file a missing persons report?"

"When he disappeared. Yes."

Carmack turned and went to his vehicle. His deps mounted up. I gave them the finger, slammed the door, and called John Chen. He sounded wary.

"I couldn't check the thing, bro. The new tech's a plant. Harriet put her here to hawk me. I'm positive."

I was shaking. I tried to stop, but couldn't.

"A woman named Lori Sanchez was murdered out by Rancha last night."

"That's the sheriff again, bro, not us."

"Ask your sheriff buddy what happened to her."

"I don't have buddies."

I closed my eyes. Maybe closing my eyes would help. It didn't.

"Find out. Right away."

He lowered his voice even more.

"Is this connected to Melendez?"

"I don't know."

"To the thing?"

I opened my eyes and saw Joe Pike on the deck, watching me.

"I don't know."

I killed the call and opened the slider.

"How long have you been here?"

"Followed you from Sadie's. Saw the deps and waited until they left."

"From Sadie's? I thought you were at home."

"Couldn't let you go alone. Why was Carmack here?"

I tried to answer, but my mouth felt dusty. I glanced at the mess on the dining table and Pike saw the upended files.

I said, "Someone broke in."

Then I said, "Lori's dead. She was murdered last night."

Pike didn't move. He might have been staring at me or through me. I couldn't tell. Whatever he felt was hidden by more than lifeless black lenses.

Pike spoke so softly I barely heard him.

"When?"

"After work. On her way home."

Pike's head moved. Just a bit.

"Wasn't Charley or his brother. Who?"

"I don't know. Carmack wouldn't tell me much, so I called John. John will find out what happened."

Pike's head moved again. He stared at the table.

"The person who did this."

"I'll see what's missing, but I have to warn Traci first. I had to tell Carmack why I was in Rancha."

Carmack would return to his office and look up Thomas Beller's missing persons report to check my story. He might or might not link Thomas to his famous daughter, Traci, but he would contact the family to confirm my employment. Pike went to the table and gathered the pages and files.

He said, "Call. I'll get this stuff together."

I took the phone to the couch and called Dina.

"Hi, this is Dina, Traci Beller's assistant."

"It's me. Let me speak to Kevin."

"I was told they fired you."

"Yes, they fired me. Let me speak to Kevin."

"Traci's mad and really upset. Kevin's furious. But they won't tell me why. What did you do?"

"Dina, please. Put Kevin on. It's important."

Kevin came on, furious as advertised.

"If you think you're safe because you didn't sign the NDA, forget it. Your business card says 'confidential'—"

"The police know I was in Rancha looking for her father."

Pike finished gathering pages and went into the kitchen. Kevin continued ranting.

"The word 'confidential' is all over your website. Therefore—"

"I didn't tell them I worked for Traci or what I've learned about Thomas, but I had to tell them why I was in Rancha."

"*Therefore*, confidentiality is implied by you in any work arrangement, which means you breached your contract. We will sue you and we'll prevail!"

Pike returned with two bottles of Modelo, but he stopped in the door, waiting.

I shouted to cut Kevin off.

"KEVIN! I told them Beller's family hired me. They may call

Georgina, but I did not mention Traci's name. Don't lie to them and don't tell them more than necessary. I'm trying to help."

I watched Pike watch me.

Kevin was silent for several seconds. When he spoke again his voice was low, as if he didn't want anyone but me to hear.

"Cole, listen. These muffins she makes are good. People really do love them, but nobody buys her muffins because they're good. They're buying the friendly, fun, kinda-cool-but-not-so-cool-she-puts-you-off girl who makes them feel good. This is why investors will invest in her. Traci sells joy. They won't invest in death. This will ruin her."

My headache was back and hammering hard.

"Kevin. Did you break into my home?"

"What?"

"Did you enter my home? Trying to find out what I know?"

Kevin exploded, livid and loud.

"We will *own* your house! We'll own your *ass*! I will personally—"

I hung up. Pike came over and offered a bottle. I took it and he clinked his beer to mine.

He said, "Lori."

"Lori."

We drank to Lori.

The Beller replacement file was one of eight case files scattered on the table. The others were asset searches, pre-employment background checks, and a single fraud investigation on behalf of a defendant. All eight files were complete with no missing pages.

I said, "It had to be about Beller. Nobody would break in for this other stuff."

"Nothing's missing?"

"Nothing. Either they didn't find what they wanted or seeing it was enough."

"The alarm was on?"

"I'm positive."

Pike said nothing. He didn't move.

I sipped more beer.

"You hungry? I'll make something."

Pike said, "She was okay."

Lori.

"Yeah. She was something."

John Chen called while I cooked. His voice was low like always, but now it was careful.

He said, "Lori Sanchez. I didn't get much. My guy wouldn't talk."

I motioned Pike closer and put Chen on speaker.

"What did you get?"

"Her body was found at a trail head about a mile from her car. Way it looks, someone ran her off the road, grabbed her, and dumped her. My guy, he said it was bad."

"That's all he said, it was bad?"

"Freakish bad. They got a lid on, bro. Locked down tight."

"Anything on the killer?"

"Not as yet. Sorry, man. That's all I got."

I lowered the phone and looked at Pike. He seemed a million miles away, but then he spoke.

"Cook. Finish cooking. Push forward."

I cooked and we talked about Traci and Sadie and Anya and Charley, but, mostly, we talked about Lori. I pictured her wrapped in fleece and prayed her death and my investigation weren't connected. If they were, the connection was me.

We ate on the deck and sipped beers, but we didn't say much. Silence was often best.

The sun settled and the day gave way to night before Pike spoke again.

"You sure about the alarm?"

"I set it before I left."

Pike said, "Mm."

Gravel crunched as a car stopped and Pike was up with his gun out. We reached the door before the bell rang.

I checked the peephole and opened the door.

It was Traci.

61

Traci stood in the yellow glow of the lamp outside my door. She wore jeans, a baggie Cal State Northridge sweatshirt, and white sneakers. She drooped like a wilted flower and her eyes were sad. All of her was sad. Moths and bugs hammered against the lamp, reaching for something that didn't exist.

Traci said, "I don't know what to do."

"Come in."

I stepped aside to let her pass. She stopped when she saw Pike.

"I shouldn't have come."

Pike stepped close. He seemed to hover, looming above her in space as she stared at him. Pike offered his hand.

"Please stay. Joe Pike. I'm on my way out."

I said, "Joe's my friend and partner in the agency. Joe, Traci Beller."

Pike released her hand and glanced at me.

"Later."

He slipped past her and walked away. Traci glanced after him.

"He doesn't have to go."

"He's giving us privacy."

She glanced after Joe again and came inside.

"They were making me crazy. I had to get out."

I closed the door and we went into the living room.

"Have you eaten?"

"I can't."

"I have muffins."

She didn't smile or react.

"Want some water or something to drink?"

Ever the thoughtful host. Neither of us knew what to do.

"They won't shut up. Kevin, on and on with the lawyers. Uncle Phil and my mother and her bullshit. I couldn't stand it."

"I'm glad you came."

She crossed her arms.

"No, you're not. You're probably worried I'll start screaming and make a scene like Kevin."

"Scream. I earned it."

"I'm not going to scream at you. I'm past the screaming part."

"It's a lot to get past. You want to sit?"

She didn't sit. She glanced after Pike again.

"Does he know?"

"About your father? Yes."

"I don't believe it. I'm telling you right now I don't believe any of this and I'll never believe it, but I'm past the shock. I'm processing. I'm trying to process."

"I'm going to sit."

"I can't sit. I can't sit still. I can't—"

She looked at me and looked away. She uncrossed her arms and crossed them again.

"I can't tell anyone. I can't talk to my friends. I can't even talk about it with Dina. Kevin sent her home. I'm scared. How can I keep this inside?"

"Talk to me."

Her face contorted as if the pressure within her was painful.

"You're the only person I can talk to. I'm sorry."

"No."

I took her arms and leveled our eyes.

"I'm sorry, not you. Please don't be sorry. You don't have to be sorry or apologize to me for anything ever. It's me who's sorry. I'm sorry."

"I don't want to hate you."

"I don't want you to hate me. And I don't want to hate myself."

"I don't hate you. Yet."

She flashed the grin when she added the "yet" and dimpled. It was weak and not one of her best, but the crushing weight of my guilt lessened. I let go of her arms and stepped back.

"We can talk as much as you like for as long as you like or we don't have to talk at all. Whatever you like."

"Maybe not talking about it would be best."

"Fine."

"Can we just hang out?"

"You bet. I'm going to make eggs. Come in the kitchen."

I scrambled eggs with mushrooms and onions and made enough for both of us even though I'd eaten with Joe. Traci took a plate with eggs, but only picked at it. We ate on the deck, yakking about TV shows and movies and the family of raccoons who tapped on her French doors in the middle of the night. She didn't mention her father or the Givens and neither did I. I didn't tell her about Lori. I couldn't.

Lucy called at a quarter to ten. I saw her name on the caller ID.

I said, "It's my girlfriend. Do you mind?"

"No! Get it! She has the son who follows me?"

I answered the phone as I answered Traci.

"Yeah. Ben. He and his friends are total fans. Hey, Luce."

Lucy said, "Who's a total fan?"

"Traci's here. I told her Ben's a fan."

Traci got up and hurried into the house.

Lucy said, "Should I be worried?"

"No, ma'am. Not ever."

I turned enough to see Traci and lowered my voice.

"She went inside. I told her this morning. She's upset."

"I'm sure she is. It can't be easy for you, either."

"Nope, but I'm glad you called."

"I'm glad I called, too. I won't keep you."

"We're okay. She's still inside."

Traci was at the dining table, writing something. Then she stood, held a sheet of paper beside her face, and snapped a selfie.

"She took a selfie."

"You're kidding."

"She's coming back."

Traci came out tapping her phone and grinning. She dropped into her chair, leaned close, and shouted.

"Hi, Lucy! I hope Ben likes it!"

Lucy said, "What did she say?"

"She hopes he likes it. Hang on."

My phone buzzed. Traci had sent a selfie of herself holding up a little sign: *Shout to my boy, Ben, in BR! You rock, Ben!!!*

I forwarded the selfie to Lucy and told her to check her messages. She did.

"Oh my God, he'll die. Thank her so much!"

I looked over to thank Traci, but her grin was gone. Her eyes were sad again as she stared into the canyon. I signed off with Lucy and lowered my phone.

"She says thanks."

Traci nodded from far away.

"He should post it now. He'll get more likes. He won't get as many after."

I didn't know what to say. Maybe she and Kevin were right. Maybe this would cost her everything.

She said, "This girl, what's she like?"

"She's scared. Like you."

"Maybe it's a child abuse thing. Maybe she was abused when she was little and this is how she explained it to herself. I saw a special once."

Traci wasn't arguing and she hadn't said it to me. She was trying to make sense of something that would never make sense.

I thought for a long time before I spoke.

"You'll survive this. It'll be ugly; you're not wrong. But you'll survive it. I will help you survive even if you don't want my help. It's what I do."

Her eyes came to me slowly and seemed vague.

"I don't want to go home."

"Stay. You don't have to leave."

"I'm alone at home. I don't want to be alone."

"Stay."

"I don't think I can sleep."

"I'll stay up with you."

"I'm really scared."

"I'll stay up with you. Let's go in. It's cold."

We went inside and sat on the couch. We sat together but did not touch and did not speak again that night.

Traci slumped against my shoulder when she fell asleep at ten minutes after three the next morning. I did not move. I didn't want to wake her. My head dipped, but I'd told her I would stay awake with her and I did. I stayed awake until light flooded my house and the rising sun woke her.

62

Joe Pike

Pike walked to his Jeep past lit houses through chill night air. An occasional car passed, people going home or going out. A dog barked higher in the canyon. Earlier, when Pike saw the sheriff's vehicles at Cole's home, he had left his Jeep on Mulholland Drive. It wasn't far. Pike pondered Traci and Anya and Lori as he walked.

Having met Traci and touched her, she was real. Pike tried to imagine what she felt, learning these horrible things about her father. Pike pictured a desert maelstrom within her, howling winds sand-blasting Traci's inner self until it left her hollow. Pike felt hollow, sometimes. Anya probably felt hollow, too, but Pike sensed a strength in Anya. Anya was tough. Pike didn't want to read her journals, but if Anya decided to try running as therapy and asked him to join her, he would run with her. Pike felt he might learn something.

Pike reached his Jeep and drove to a twenty-four-hour self-service car wash on Ventura Boulevard. He washed the Jeep, wiped it down with towels he kept in the rear, and checked for spots. Pike buffed the Jeep's red skin until it gleamed. The Marines had taught him to keep his equipment and himself squared away. He did.

Pike lived in a condo he owned in Culver City. He lived alone, without pets or plants. Pike considered going home, but he wasn't hungry and needed nothing. He used the restroom at the car wash, then headed east on Ventura, rolling slow, considering Lori.

Thinking of Lori was difficult. The weight of her death felt like failure. She had refused a weapon, but behind the eye-rolling and complaints, Pike had sensed courage and a warrior spirit. She had probably gone down fighting. Pike wanted to believe it. He felt responsible.

Ventura Boulevard led to Cahuenga Boulevard led to Mulholland Drive. Three coyotes watched him pass the Hollywood Bowl. Pike turned on Woodrow Wilson and reached Cole's A-frame a few minutes later. Traci's little car still sat at Cole's house. Fine.

Pike parked nearby.

He wondered if the person or persons who broke into Elvis's home was the same person who beat Lori Sanchez to death. This person might return. Pike hoped he would.

63

Elvis Cole

was thinking about Lori and Carmack when Traci sat up and cringed at the brilliant sun. Her eyes were puffy.

"May I use your bathroom?"

"Down the hall to your left."

I gave her fresh towels and soap and a new toothbrush and toothpaste, then put on coffee and used the bathroom upstairs. I finished and saw Traci at the sliders, arms crossed again, staring at the canyon. She heard me and turned.

"What's her name?"

"Anya."

She repeated it.

"Anya. It's pretty."

Then she said, "I like your house. It reminds me of Lake Arrowhead."

"Yeah. Me, too."

"I'd like to meet her. We should meet, don't you think? Would it be okay?"

I didn't know if it would be okay or even if they should. Anya seemed fragile and the subject was raw for both of them. I thought they probably shouldn't, not without counselors and mediators and experts who could guide them.

I said, "I can ask."

"Okay. Great."

Traci suddenly glanced away as if she had second thoughts.

I said, "You don't have to meet her."

"I know. It's just, if he really did these things—"

She pushed her hands into her pockets.

"Anyway, you're right. About what I should do. I knew you were right yesterday, it's just—"

She shrugged.

"I should go."

I went downstairs.

"You're welcome to stay. I'll make breakfast."

"I can't. Kevin's called a thousand times. Even my mother. She thinks I've been kidnapped."

She rolled her eyes and I saw Lori.

"Text her."

"She doesn't trust texts. Kidnappers could be pretending to be me."

Her eyes rolled again. Lori.

I walked Traci to her car and saw Pike's Jeep at the far edge of the curve. He raised a hand. I waved back and Traci saw him.

"Is that your friend?"

"Joe."

"Has he been out here all night?"

"Probably."

She studied the Jeep, then slid into her car.

"Will you ask her?"

Anya.

"I will."

I watched her drive away, thinking about Lori and Carmack again. Lori had been run off the road and Eric Zalway had gone off the road. I wondered if they went off the road for the same reason.

Pike pulled forward and climbed from his Jeep.

I said, "She asked if you were out here all night."

"Your alarm didn't stop him. You needed a better alarm."

"So you're my full-time alarm?"

"I'm going to shower and grab some zees. If the dude walks in, he won't walk out."

Pike disappeared into the guest bath and I sat with my laptop at the table. A search for Eric Zalway's death produced one obituary and three short articles.

Eric Graham Zalway, age twenty-one, a recent graduate of UCLA, was killed on upper Malibu Canyon Road when his car plunged one hundred forty feet into a ravine. Zalway was the vehicle's lone occupant and the cause of his crash was unknown.

I noted the date. Eric had died two months and two days after Jess Byers interviewed him. This was also two months and two days after Eric learned Beller was missing and began telling his friends about their encounter. The Highway Patrol's Collision Investigation Unit would have investigated. I wondered what they found.

Frank Zalway's number was in my phone. The same quiet male voice answered.

"Mr. Zalway, this is Elvis Cole again. From the other day."

"I remember. About the missing man."

The voice mumbled behind him and Mr. Zalway responded.

"It's the man who called for Eric."

I pushed ahead.

"Did the highway patrol determine the cause of Eric's accident?"

Mr. Zalway hesitated before answering slowly and with care.

"He had not been drinking and he wasn't impaired. He wasn't speeding. His car was mechanically sound."

He stopped, and I knew Eric's father had said these things for himself, not me.

"They couldn't determine the cause?"

"He swerved."

His voice grew tight.

"They said he lost control, whatever that means. A rock fell or a deer crossed the road. Bullshit!"

The voice behind him mumbled.

Mr. Zalway's response was sharp.

"I'm not upset. He's asking about the accident."

I said, "He swerved to avoid a rock."

"Bullshit! These kids in their rice rockets go up there and drift those corners like LeMans. I've seen'm! But do the police stop them? No!"

"Was another vehicle involved?"

"They found so many skid marks the asphalt looked like a zebra. I saw it myself."

The voice behind him mumbled.

Mr. Zalway said, "They found paint on his car, but they couldn't tell how long it was there. Something about oxidation."

"Paint from another vehicle was on Eric's car?"

"White, they said. Not much. A little streak."

"Not enough impact to cause the accident."

"So they said, but people don't just swerve. Do you? Of course you don't."

"And nobody saw it happen."

"No. Nobody who stayed."

Pike came down the hall and went into the kitchen.

I said, "Thanks, Mr. Zalway. I'm sorry about Eric."

"Good hunting, Mr. Cole. I hope you find your man."

I lowered the phone and counted the dead. Eric and Lori both saw Thomas Beller at the SurfMutt. Now they were dead, Lori murdered and Eric from an unexplained vehicular accident.

Arturo Melendez had known I was looking for Lori and why. Now he was dead and also murdered.

Pike returned with a bottle of water and stretched out on the couch.

I said, "Eric, Lori, Arturo. A lot of people are dead."

"Don't be the fourth."

I thought about it more and called Charley Reed.

"I hear gangsters killed your boy Arturo Melendez. True or false?"

"Wasn't my boy. Way he died, man, it was awful, but I barely knew him. I don't know anything about it."

"Whose boy was he?"

"Howard."

The squint.

"I want to see Howard. Can you set it up?"

"Come on out. He'll be waiting."

I hung up and looked at Pike.

"You don't need to follow me."

"Wasn't. No need to set your alarm."

"Copy that."

I hit the road for Rancha.

64

The Kill Car

They lived in an area with few streets and only two ways in and out. Places like this were traps, but the address was written by their names, so he googled the address, studied a satellite image, and drove through the neighborhood counting cars.

The kill car hissed.

"We're invisible."

They counted two white Toyotas, a pale cream Stanza, and three white Honda Civics before they reached the house. The kill car was one of many; as invisible as a pebble on a beach.

This was comforting, but the driver remained vigilant. He wore a hat and sunglasses, the sunscreens were up, and he sat low in the seat. He drove slowly, but not slow enough to draw attention, and averted his face when they passed oncoming vehicles.

The kill car whispered.

"I love this."

The driver checked house numbers.

The kill car coached.

"Easy. Here it comes."

The driver slowed, but only a bit.

They floated past Anya's address like a sleepy shark enjoying the sun.

A brown pickup truck sat in the drive behind a small gray hatchback.

"See anyone?"

"Uh-uh."

The driver checked for people without seeming obvious about it. Someone might remember a man craning his head when the police asked them later. After the bodies were found.

"This will be easy."

They passed the house without slowing and didn't turn back.

"We'll get them. We'll get everything they have."

Pressure built in his head, so much pressure his vision blurred.

"I know what to do."

Driving past their home had been an excellent idea.

65

Elvis Cole

The traffic through Studio City was the usual nightmare. I was waiting for the light to change at Moorpark when Kevin called. His voice was grudging.

"I'm against this. I think it's a huge mistake, but I'll go along on one condition."

"Traci will fire you if you don't?"

"I want access to their so-called evidence before they go forward."

"Won't happen."

"Whatever it is they claim to have, including but not limited to this woman's so-called journals, I want it examined by experts. If the experts say they're legit, we won't fight these people. We might even be persuaded to help. But only before they go forward. That's the deal."

"They're not looking for a deal, Kevin. They're trying to put this behind them."

"They can put it behind them just as easily after I authenticate their claims. *Before* they go forward. *After* I lock down investors for Traci."

"Does Traci know you're doing this?"

"I'm not Traci's employee, Cole. I funded her brand when we set up her company. I own a stake."

"So this is about you."

"Me, Traci, and the people who work for us. Traci can fire me all she likes, but a piece of the profit is mine. I won't let these chiseling, hick frauds—"

I hung up. I thought about calling Traci, but didn't. Complaining about Kevin would add to her stress and make me look like a whiner.

I settled into a freeway groove and made good time.

Charley Reed's truck, Sadie's hatchback, and the Challenger were parked in Sadie's drive when I arrived. A giant cloud of oily, white mist blossomed from the Challenger's driver's-side window, telling me Howard Semple Jr. was slouched behind the wheel. I parked behind him and crossed the yard to Sadie's front door.

"How's the arm?"

Howard slouched lower and sucked his e-cig. He looked sullen.

Charley Reed came out before I reached the house. He glanced at Howard and kept the rumble low.

"Now, we don't mention what happened to Anya in front of Howard, all right? He doesn't know."

"Fine by me. How's she doing?"

"Better. You want to say hi?"

I hesitated. I wanted to say hi, but I hadn't decided whether I should float Traci's request. Maybe I should tell Charley and let them discuss it among themselves. Maybe I should let Charlie Bauman decide. Maybe I should stick my head in the sand and avoid the whole thing.

I said, "Sure. After Howard."

Avoidance was the better part of valor.

Howard got out of his car as we approached. He looked like a tall, squinty mantis with a leg in a sling. His forehead was swollen and stitched, but the curtain of hair hid most of the damage. He flipped the hair from his face, squinted, and the curtain fell again. He still looked sullen, but he also looked nervous.

"Whut?"

Charley rumbled.

"You're not in trouble. Mr. Cole wants to know about Arturo."

"Whut?"

A moron.

I said, "Do you know how Arturo died?"

"I didn't do it."

"His junk was cut off. He was hanged. The police think a banger did it over a woman."

Howard flipped the hair.

"'Turo didn't mess with gangs. That's bullshit."

"He did YA time."

"Stole a car. So whut? He didn't run with gangsters. They scared him."

"Did he have a girlfriend with ties?"

Flip.

"Shit. He didn't have a girl, period. Shit."

Smirk.

"Was he with you the night you jumped me?"

Howard glanced at Charley. Worried. Flip.

Charley frowned as he thought and shook his head.

"No, I don't think he was. Was he, Howard?"

"No, sir. I asked if he wanted to come, but he was scared. A cop came around asking about the missing man and him."

Howard glanced at me, the him.

"'Turo was kinda freaked about it, like maybe the cops were onto him. He wouldn't come."

Harold glanced at Charley.

"I said, okay, but you better not say anything. He said he wouldn't, but I don't know. He was scared."

I thought about what Ms. Melendez told Pike and Jaime, how she thought he'd gone with friends.

"Arturo left work on a bicycle."

"Bike's how he got around. Couldn't afford a car."

"The people he worked with thought he went home. Did he mention other plans?"

Squint. Flip. Confused.

"Plans for whut?"

"For after work. Getting together with friends. Catching a movie. Crochet class."

Squint. Shrug.

"Didn't ask. He wasn't coming with us, so fuck'm."

Lovely.

"Did 'Turo have enemies or owe money?"

"Not that I know, 'cept for who killed him. They really cut off his stuff? I thought someone made it up."

"They didn't make it up. What about drugs? Did he deal?"

"Nah. 'Turo? Nah."

The lack of explanation felt heavy. The weight was growing and pushing toward something ugly.

"Why would someone kill him like this, Howard? Who would do it?"

Howard squirmed. Squint, flip.

"Got no idea. It wasn't me."

Charley rumbled.

"Nobody thinks it was you, son."

I studied Charley, hoping for something I didn't find with Howard.

"Was Arturo involved with Beller in any way?"

"All I know, I told him to let me or Howard know if someone came asking about the missing man."

I reached further.

"Arturo didn't meet him or see him, that day at the SurfMutt?"

Charley shrugged.

"Ten years ago, he woulda been, what, nine? Even if, the missing man sure as shit didn't kill him."

I nodded, but the weight remained.

Anya appeared in the window. She smiled and raised a hand. I raised a hand back.

"How about I say hi?"

Charley said, "You done with Howard?"

"Yeah, thanks. Thank you, Howard."

Squint. Flip.

"You're welcome."

Charley rumbled.

"Let Howard out and come on in. Howard, go back to work."

I moved my car so Howard could leave and followed Charley into the house.

66

The boxes had been cleared away and their home was back in order. Anya and Sadie stood side by side in the hall and looked happy to see me. Sadie smiled.

Anya said, "Hey."

"Hey yourself. How're you doing?"

"Fine."

Sadie smiled at Anya, smiled at me, and nodded.

"She feels better. We all do. Just knowing things will be different helps so much."

I felt the difference and saw it. A lightness absent before. Less tension in the way they held themselves, less like coiled springs. They had a painful road ahead, but moving forward changed the landscape. I stood in their home with all of us smiling but I thought about Lori and Eric and Arturo Melendez.

Anya said, "We're going to see Mr. Bauman this afternoon. He's really nice on the phone."

"He's nice in person, too. Let me know how it goes."

"We're bringing my journals. He wants to read them."

"You okay with sharing them?"

"I don't mind. I have to get used to saying what happened."

Sadie nodded, encouraging.

"That's right."

Anya seemed at ease and comfortable. I decided to pass along Traci's request.

I said, "I was asked to give you a message by the woman who hired me. Would it be all right?"

Sadie stiffened, but Anya didn't. Anya cocked her head. Curious.

Sadie said, "His daughter?"

"I won't pass it along without your permission. It's one hundred percent your call. Either way is fine by me."

Sadie's eyes turned hard. She looked the way she looked when I drove away from the florist shop the day we met. Like she was willing to kill me.

Anya said, "What'd she say?"

The skin beneath Sadie's left eye ticked.

"I don't think this is a good idea."

Anya said, "You stop. I want to know what she said."

The eye ticked faster. I was sorry I'd brought it up.

"Maybe it's too soon."

Anya said, "Was the message for me or my mother? If it's mine, I want to know what she said."

Sadie was so rigid she looked brittle. Her jaw knotted and flexed. Her lips were as thin as blades.

She said, "All right."

I looked at Anya.

"You don't have to respond or answer, not now or ever. Whatever you want to do is totally up to you."

Sadie said, "Stop squirming and say it."

"She wants to meet you."

Sadie answered so fast her voice was a gunshot.

"We'll think about it. That's it."

Anya said, "I'd like to meet her."

Sadie didn't look at Anya.

"We'll think about it. That's our answer."

"Okay. I'll let her know."

Anya said, "Tell her I said hi."

Sadie glanced at Anya. Her face and tone softened.

"How about we talk about it?"

"That's fine. He can still tell her I said hi."

Sadie's shoulders relaxed.

"Of course. Of course he can. That'd be fine."

Charley rumbled.

"We gotta get ready."

Anya said, "Tell her."

"I'll tell her."

Charley and Anya showed me out. Sadie didn't.

The traffic thinned in Encino and picked up speed when I passed the 405. John Chen called when I hit Sherman Oaks, his whisper clipped and tight.

"I did the thing. Where are you?"

"On the freeway. Did we get any hits?"

"Not on the phone. The freeway where?"

"Sherman Oaks. I'm going home."

"I'll meet you."

The line went dead. Chen was gone.

I called Pike, told him Chen was coming, and rounded the curve to my house twenty-five minutes later. Chen arrived first. He and Pike stood in front of my home by Chen's shiny black Tesla. John Chen had never been to my home. I didn't know he knew where I lived.

Chen was tall, thin, and hunched like a question mark. He turned from Pike, clutching a large white envelope with both hands. John didn't wait for me to arrive. He walked out to meet me, faster and faster until he was running.

John stopped me in the street, raised the envelope, and shook it.

"We got hits, bro. A shitload of hits. This guy's a monster!"

Chen abruptly leaned closer, examining my face.

"My dude! Did someone kick your ass?"

We went into my house and John showed us the hits.

67

John followed us into the living room, rolling his head like a parrot to take in the high, peaked ceiling and the loft and the view.

He said, "Did you inherit?"

I wasn't in the mood.

"It was a fixer. What did you find?"

His expression was somewhere between awe and envy.

"You gotta get major 'tang up here, bro. This place is a panty-dropper."

"It's a house. Show us what you found."

Chen went to the table and pulled on a pair of black nitrile gloves.

"Thirteen cases; eight slam-dunk matches and five maybes. The Feebs have an in-house name for the guy. The Bagman. Because he bags their heads."

"I got it."

"Anyway, I printed relevant pages from each case."

He opened the envelope and tipped out the files.

Pike said, "Why are you wearing gloves?"

"Same reason I didn't send these from work—so Harriet can't trace this to me."

He glanced at me.

"And I'll take this envelope when I go, thank you very much."

"She'll know the database was searched from your computer."

Chen flashed a smug smile.

"No, she won't. I used her spy's computer. Set her nasty Mata Hari ass right up! Mess with The Chen, suffer his vengeance."

Chen squared the documents.

"The top pages show the vics as they were found. You ready?"

Pike crossed his arms. I nodded.

"Do it."

Chen laid out the cases in two neat rows along the length of my table, six on top, seven on the bottom.

I saw the first image and knew Beller killed them. Victim One looked exactly like the victims Anya Given described: A young woman with a clear plastic bag over her head and a ligature around her neck. Barrow, Leslie Lynne. Age: seventeen. I closed my eyes. When I opened them, Chen was staring at me.

"You okay?"

Pike said, "He's good. Keep going."

The most recent victim had been murdered eleven months before Beller disappeared. Her body was found in Riverside. Victim One was murdered fifteen years earlier. Two years before Traci was born.

"Were they all in or around Los Angeles?"

"More or less. Most were found on roadsides or empty lots. One was in a parking lot, another up by Zuma. He dumped them where he killed them."

"Took their jewelry?"

Chen picked up a case, flipped a page, and read.

"'Piercing holes on victim's left and right earlobes, right upper ear, and right nostral found empty.'"

Chen pointed out a word before he continued reading.

"Look. Idiot misspelled 'nostril.' Family states victim was last seen wearing multiple studs and rings. No studs, rings, or other jewelry found on or near the body."

Chen tapped the page.

"Nine of the thirteen were missing some or all jewelry."

"Four weren't?"

"We got maybes, like I said, but they're linked."

Chen turned the page and read again.

"'Ligature consists of three lengths of ten-gauge solid-core aluminum wire, thirty-two inches in length, twisted into a single cord.' The wire. Eight of these women were killed with identical aluminum wire, same gauge, same length, available at any hardware store, and always three wires twisted to make the ligature. He fucked up with the wire. The wire's how they got his DNA."

I stared.

"They have his DNA."

"They've had it since Victim Two, but he's not in the system. Couple of hairs were trapped when he twisted the wires together. So much for DIY, right?"

I stared at the photo of Victim Two. Lyman, Susan Joan, age nineteen.

Chen waved at the cases.

"He left DNA twice, Vic Two with the hair and Vic Five with blood. Jabbed himself with the wire. Otherwise, the dude worked clean and knew the police were watching. Which brings us to Six and Seven."

Chen picked up the sixth case, flipped a page, and pointed out a small square photo of a victim who looked identical to the others. Something about the photo felt different.

I said, "The killer took the picture."

"My dude! Correct. Snapped it with a Fuji Instant and left it on her body."

I stared at the small square image. Anya described the photos he showed her as square.

Chen put down Six and picked up Seven.

"He left a pic on Seven, too, which was taken with the same camera. He's only left the two. Guess photography wasn't his thing."

Chen laughed. Hyuk.

He held the page to show the photo of Victim Seven, but I didn't look.

I said, "They were alive when he took these pictures."

Chen studied me. Suspicious.

"The Feebs think so, yeah. Do you know something you haven't told me?"

The victims on my table seemed to be watching me. Their clothes and shapes were different, but their plastic faces made them all the same.

"I know who killed them."

Chen's eyes widened.

"No way! Who?"

"He died ten years ago."

Chen deflated, seeing the glory of bagging a serial murderer disappear. Then he shrugged.

"Well, closing cases is important. We button this many homicides we'll still be heroes. Who was the guy?"

Chen watched me like an owl atop a pole, waiting for the answer.

I said, "Lori. Was there contact paint from the other vehicle on her car?"

"Yeah. It was white. So what? If this guy's dead, what's he have to do with Sanchez?"

"I don't know."

"Do you really know who killed them?"

"I can't tell you. Not yet."

Chen smacked Victim Seven on his leg.

"Why not? I thought you were my friend."

"John, it's complicated."

"Fuck!"

He smacked his leg again, steadied himself, and placed the pages on the table.

"All right. Everything here is self-explanatory, but if you have any questions."

"I'll call soon."

He snatched up the empty white envelope, wadded it into a ball, and stuffed it into his pocket.

"Don't cut me out."

"I'll call."

"Make it up to me, bro. Lemme bring a chick up here."

Pike said, "Leave."

Chen stalked out and slammed the door.

Pike didn't read the reports. He didn't want to read them. I forced myself.

68

The Kill Car

The driver strained to see everything at once, Anya's house, the neighboring homes, doors and windows and yards, trees and shrubs and cars in driveways; a watchful neighbor might be anywhere.

The first three times they passed, the truck and hatchback were home. The truck was gone on their fourth pass. Now the hatchback was gone.

The kill car hissed.

"Move fast. We don't belong."

The driver parked, turned on the jammer, and tucked the jammer into his tool bag. He checked for neighbors. The driver dreaded this part the most, then and now. Leaving the kill car left him exposed, as obvious as a fly on a plate.

"Faster. You're wasting time."

He pulled a sheer nylon stocking over his head, tried to hide the ludicrous stocking with a floppy-brimmed hat, and quickly walked up the drive, pulling on clear vinyl gloves. He was terrified, but excited. He could do this and his nightmare would end.

The kill car whispered.

"You're The Man."

"I hope she's here."

"Me, too."

The driver opened the back door in forty seconds, entered the house holding a claw hammer, and called into hollow silence.

"Repairman. Hello? Door was open."

His pulse thundered, drowning everything but the kill car's whisper.

"Find the fucking evidence. Hurry."

He slammed through the house, throwing open cabinets and up-ending furniture. He searched the first bedroom and the second, dumping drawers, ripping clothes and boxes from closets, scattering books and overturning the beds in a mad desperate rage until he stood in a field of debris, sobbing and lost.

"Fucking Tommy. Fucking asshole. How did you let this happen?"

"Don't worry. Be happy."

A giant yellow face smiled from the wall.

"I'm dead. Dead. I gotta run."

The kill car whispered.

"She'll come home. Let's wait."

The driver lifted the hammer. He slashed the claws across the smiley face.

69

Elvis Cole

Pike sat on the deck, staring across the canyon. I was at the table with dead women watching me. The cat appeared outside, circled Pike once, and jumped into his lap. Pike stroked the cat, but his eyes never left the far side of the canyon.

I read.

The victim's photo on the cover page was the only crime scene photo Chen included in each of the thirteen cases. The murder books would contain dozens of close-ups, macro close-ups, and wide shots from multiple angles. The single photo was enough.

Summaries by the original case detectives followed, all describing similar scenes, similar victims, and similar deaths. The van and its contents lost their importance. They mattered, but I had my own photos now. The families of the dead would learn who murdered their daughters and the fate of the man who murdered them. I hoped it would bring them peace.

I put the reports aside and went to Traci's website. I wanted to see her father. Here was Tommy presenting a tray of hot-from-the-oven muffins to Traci, little Traci clapping her hands, Tommy with a wide Dad grin. I tried to find evil in his face but couldn't. The face of evil looked like anyone.

Each investigation, separate and apart from the others, ran its course and became a string of quarterly due diligence checks. This meant checking the FBI's CODIS and National DNA Index System. The responses received were always negative, but the two most recent contained a boxed notation I didn't understand.

```
Special Update: CODIS results revised
Ref # MM-60251-DJF
Contact: Special Agent Clemons Lawrence
```

The box contained no explanation, so I called Chen and asked what it meant. He shrugged it off.

"Probably changed a sampling protocol. They screw with the CODIS all the time."

"The results were revised. This makes it sound important."

"Dude. If they found a match, you would've seen your dead guy on the news."

"Can you find out?"

"No way! I'd have to ask them."

"So ask. You're The Chen."

"Ha ha. Fuck, she's coming. Gotta go."

Chen was gone. I took the sheet outside to show Pike.

"Know what this means?"

Pike glanced at the page.

"Ask them."

He followed me back to the table.

The first DNA sample was found on Victim Two, a twenty-seven-year-old waitress named Didi Beth Lyman. The dick who caught the Lyman case was a Harlan Rowly, but the case currently belonged to a D-III out of Valley Bureau Homicide named Sonja Flores.

I said, "Guess I'll start with Lyman."

Pike said, "Good choice."

Helpful.

I powered up a prepaid burner phone and called. A male voice answered.

"Valley Bureau. Detectives."

"Detective Flores, please."

"Which one?"

"Sonja."

I waited on hold until a woman came on.

"Detective Flores."

"Hey, Mike Lloyd with Channel Six News. We're doing a four-minute spot next week on the Bagman investigation."

Flores hesitated and sounded wary.

"What about it?"

"We were told the DNA results were revised. Does this mean you have new information?"

"Give me a number. I'll get back to you."

I gave her a fake number and hung up.

Pike said, "A for effort."

I tried a different story on the dick in charge of Victim Five's case next and still learned nothing. I got nowhere by pretending to be a victim's family member, an attorney representing a victim's family, an L.A. *Times* reporter, or a special assistant to the mayor.

Pike said, "You're pressing too hard. Relax."

"Would you like to do this?"

The corner of Pike's mouth twitched. Pike never smiled, but the twitch was close.

I glanced through the cases again, decided my first choice was the best choice, and googled information about Harlan Rowly, the dick who opened the Lyman case. His Facebook page told me he was enjoying his retirement in Colorado Springs. I called the L.A. FBI office and asked for Special Agent Lawrence.

"Special Agent Lawrence speaking."

I tried to sound older.

"This is Harlan Rowly. I was the—"

Lawrence cut me off.

"I know who you are. You opened the Lyman case."

"Yes sir, Didi Beth."

"When Jerrold said Detective Rowly, I knew your name right away. Pleased to meet you, so to speak."

Jerrold was the desk agent.

"Same here. I was hoping you could—"

"Still unsolved, sad to say. I assume you're calling to see where we are."

"I am. Some of them stay with you."

"I know, I know. Wish I had better news."

"What's this CODIS revision I hear about?"

Lawrence didn't respond. The time stretched, so I gave him a nudge.

"I keep tabs, I hear from friends. I keep hoping. Maybe I got worked up over nothing, but I had to ask. Hell, I don't even know what a CODIS revision is."

Lawrence cleared his throat.

"We have different extraction methods these days. Take Lyman. Back then, extracting DNA from hair required a follicle."

"We got his DNA from Lyman."

"You did, but hairs without follicles were found on several victims. Mostly broken shafts. Useless for sampling nuclear DNA, but we've been able to reexamine them. Turns out, shafts from a second individual were present on three of the victims."

Pike moved closer.

I said, "A second killer?"

"Duos happen. The Hillside Strangler, who was actually two people, Buono and Bianchi; Bittaker and Norris; Ng and Lake. If I'm right, the Bagman is—or was—the Bagmen."

Lawrence didn't laugh.

I said, "If I'm right? You don't sound certain."

"Well—"

Lawrence stretched the word.

"The second profile could be a contamination. Hair transferred by the killer, say, from someone he lived or worked with. Considering all the time that's passed, we may never know. Neither of these individuals have been sampled, but maybe one day."

"Maybe one day."

"Let's hope."

I killed the call and stared at Pike. A second killer flipped the landscape.

Pike said, "A murder buddy nobody knew about."

"A partner would explain Lori and Melendez. Even Eric Zalway. If this is the same guy."

"Maybe Lori or 'Turo can help."

I realized what he was saying and called Carmack.

He said, "Calling to confess?"

"Did you pull suspect samples off Lori Sanchez?"

"Not your business."

"What about Melendez? Get any DNA from his body or clothes?"

Carmack hesitated.

"Who's Melendez?"

"At the SurfMutt. C'mon, Carmack, you asked him about me. The kid who was hanged and mutilated. You don't remember him?"

"Stop it, Cole. I know the case, but I never met the kid. I sure as hell didn't question him."

The squint had told me a cop questioned Arturo about the missing man and me. Jaime had mentioned a cop, too.

"You didn't question him at the SurfMutt?"

"No, Cole, the only time I've ever been to the SurfMutt is when I asked those people if they knew who killed him. What's this to you? What does this have to do with Sanchez?"

I cut the call.

"If this other cop was the killer, Jaime can describe him. I need to find out."

"This guy is killing people connected to Beller. He might take a shot at Traci."

"Watch her. I'll tell them you're coming."

I gave him Traci's address and sped back to Rancha.

70

I called Traci from the car.

"This is Dina, Traci Beller's assistant."

"Is she home?"

Dina hesitated.

"Yes. She's on a Zoom with *Food & Wine*."

"Let me speak to her."

"She's on with *Food & Wine*."

"It's important."

"So is *Food & Wine*. Would you like to speak with Kevin?"

"A friend of mine named Joe Pike will be there soon. Traci's met him. Tell her."

"Joe who?"

"You can't miss him."

The SurfMutt was back in business with Donna taking orders in her yellow SurfMutt T-shirt and Jaime at the grill. A tall, pudgy kid who was probably Arturo's replacement hovered at his side.

Jaime saw me park and met me at the pickup window.

"Joe told me what happened. Damn, bro, you look like hell."

"Need to talk. Can I come in?"

"Yeah. Around back."

I joined them in the kitchen. Donna winced at my face.

"Ow. That must hurt."

Jaime glowered as he flipped a row of burgers.

"Hear about 'Turo?"

"Yeah. I'm sorry, man."

He made a surly shrug.

"He was in with those assholes kicked your ass. You find'm, lemme know. I'll help you deal."

"A detective was here the day I was jumped or the day before. You mentioned him to me."

Jaime nodded.

"Yeah. Dude asked about you. Wanted to know what you were up to. I didn't say shit."

Donna nodded with Jaime.

"Yeah. Something about the missing man."

"Did he speak with Arturo?"

Jaime put patties on buns and slid the buns to the new guy to dress.

"'Turo was busy. Dude comes here, we got a line."

Donna cocked her head, frowning.

"No. 'Turo went in back for something, I saw them."

Jaime scowled.

"Bullshit. Where?"

She gestured toward the back entrance.

"At the door. 'Turo took out the recycling. The cop stopped him. They were out here."

I said, "Describe the cop. What did he look like?"

I didn't expect much, just enough for an edge. The police could send a portrait artist.

Jaime and Donna glanced at each other. Donna shrugged.

"Kinda round. Heavy."

Jaime said, "Burly. The fat hands, a round face, all red here on his cheeks. Why?"

An empty coldness filled my chest. I saw the killer, then and there.

"Frizzy hair? Reddish?"

Jaime glanced at Donna. Donna nodded.

"Yeah. Short and kinda frizzy. Kinda bald."

Jaime moved closer, sensing something wrong.

"This cop, he wasn't a cop?"

"No. What was he driving?"

Donna answered.

"I thought it was weird. He wasn't in a police car."

"Was it white?"

"Yeah. A little white car. My mom had a car like it."

Jaime touched my arm.

"Bro. You okay?"

"I need to make a call."

I walked back to my car on unwieldy legs and sat without moving. Jaime and Donna watched me and traded concerned looks between slinging burgers and taking orders.

I went to Traci's website again. Here were Tommy and Phil and Traci, Tommy holding Traci in his arm while offering her a cupcake. Tommy had touched the cupcake to her nose, leaving a dollop of frosting. Phil was looking on, a wide, toothy smile splitting his round, ruddy face.

Sharing a cupcake with my Dad when I was three. My Uncle Phil, who was my dad's best friend, couldn't stop laughing.

I screen-grabbed the image, cropped Phil's face, and returned to the counter. Jaime and Donna saw me coming and met me at the window.

"Is this the cop?"

Donna said, "This guy's a lot younger."

Jaime said, "Yeah, that's him. What's wrong?"

I turned without answering and went to my car. Maybe Tommy's calls on the second phone were to Phil. Maybe he told Phil he was going to kill another victim and Phil tried to talk him out of it, like a sponsor from Psychopaths Anonymous. I did not believe this. Tommy probably offered a play-by-play and promised to share more trophies, only Tommy vanished and Phil never knew what happened. Then people began asking about Tommy and Phil felt threatened. Eric, five years ago, Lori now; anyone or anything that led to Tommy would lead to Phil. My hands shook.

I sent the photo to Pike and followed with a call.

"Are you at Traci's?"

"Yes."

"This is her Uncle Phil. Is he present?"

"No."

"He's the guy. If he shows, take him down."

"Done."

"I'll try to find him. Stay with Traci."

"Done."

I hung up and called Phil. I didn't know what I would say, but I called. His voice mail answered on the fourth ring.

I hung up and called Dina.

"This is Dina, Traci Beller's assistant."

"Has Phil been around?"

"No. Would you like his number?"

"I have his number. Is Kevin there?"

Kevin came on the line with his usual nasty tone.

"Who's this thug you sent? Why is he here?"

"Have you seen Phil?"

"What?"

"Phil. I'm trying to find him."

"So call him, for Christ's sake. I'm not his service."

The line went dead. I checked the time. Georgina would be teaching, but I called anyway. Her voice mail answered.

"This is Elvis Cole. Please call when you get this. ASAP. It's important."

Phil might be anywhere doing anything. I tried to figure out what to do. Call Carmack. Call Lou. If I was right, Phil was beyond dangerous. He had to be located and approached with caution. Everyone involved was in danger.

Everyone.

Sadie's address was in my new file notes. The person who broke into my home was almost certainly Phil. He hadn't taken the pages, but he'd seen them. Phil had Sadie and Anya's address.

I called Sadie and got her voice mail. She and Anya and Charley were seeing Bauman today. I hoped they were with him.

"Sadie, don't go home. Don't take Anya home. If you're home when you get this, leave. Beller had a partner. Leave right away and call me. I'm calling Charley."

My hands shook worse as I called Charley. His phone rang forever until his voice mail answered.

"It's Cole. There were two killers. Beller killed with a partner and he's here. If you're with Sadie and Anya, don't go to their home. He'll kill them. Call me."

I started my car and called Charlie Bauman.

"Are the Givens with you?"

"Nah, we finished an hour ago. You and I should—"

I thumbed Carmack's number as I pulled away from the SurfMutt.

"Dan Carmack."

"The Bagman was two killers. One was the missing man, Thomas Beller. The other murdered Sanchez and Melendez. Copy this address—"

"Hang on, hang on. The Bagman was what?"

I shouted over him, repeating Anya's and Sadie's names and address twice.

"Send your deps, Carmack. Roll fast or more people are going to die."

I racked the gears and raced through Rancha. Sadie and Anya didn't live far and I was close. I reached the scene before the police. I saw the blood first.

71

harley Reed's brown truck and Sadie's gray hatchback were in the drive. The house was quiet and appeared fine. Two women passed on bikes, one bent low to adjust a pedal.

I parked behind Charley's truck and ran toward the front door, but didn't reach it. The window I'd sat by when Pike and I waited for Anya and Sadie offered a view inside. Furniture was tipped on its side or askew and couch cushions were jumbled.

I ran through the carport and drew my gun at the back door. The knob turned and the door opened. Cabinets and drawers lay open and pots and pans and dishes littered the floor. A bright red smear led across the debris into the hall. I didn't call out or shout. I went in fast, room to room to room. Every room in the house was trashed.

I didn't find Anya or Sadie or Charley, but they'd been home. Sadie's big brown purse was in the hall. The blood trail led to her purse and a curved smear on the wall. It looked like a fan, spread to hide a face.

A crazy pressure filled my head.

He'd taken them.

Taking their bodies made no sense, but what made sense to a madman? He'd come for something and now they were taking him to it.

I left before the police arrived and raced for the buried van, following my map app into the hills.

Phil would've made Sadie or Charley drive. He would've made them drive slowly and do nothing to draw attention. I hit eighty, ninety, a hundred; riding the red line.

Charley had told me, "Best you ride with me, your car won't like this road."

The road hammered my car and me, shaking and slamming us over broken ground and ruts.

A small white car appeared at the top of a rise in the distance. Figures moved, walking away from the car, too far to see who they were. Charley for sure, big as a mountain, and Phil, shorter but wide and round. I might've seen a third, but they vanished too quickly.

Up on top, where the van was buried, there was no way to approach them without being seen. Phil would see me, but I didn't know what else to do. I powered ahead, screaming and swerving up the hill.

My car broke at the top of the rise. The left front wheel folded, the nose augered in, and the car slid sideways. I stumbled out, ran to the white car, and saw them crossing the field, Phil, Anya, and Charley, and they saw me. Phil had Anya by the arm, holding her close, with something in his free hand. I leveled my gun and shouted.

"Phil!"

Phil ducked behind Anya and shot Charley Reed three times—bapbapbap. Charley staggered sideways and tipped over.

Sadie reared up in the white car's back seat like a bloody apparition, soaked red and glistening, and pushed the door open. She shouted.

"Anya!"

Phil pressed the gun into Anya's side, edging sideways, maybe thinking he could get to the car and get away.

I said, "Calm down, Phil. Breathe. Just stop."

The gun flicked from Anya to me and he fired again. Bap! The shot sounded hollow, swallowed by emptiness on the flat, open field.

I didn't duck or roll or shoot back. Not with Anya between us.

I said, "C'mon, man, it's done. Don't make it worse. Please."

He fired again and the bullet snapped past. Close.

Sadie crawled from the car and pushed to her feet. Her top and pants were soaked with blood, but, damn, her eyes were fierce. Charley Reed coughed and rolled onto his side.

I said, "Phil."

Phil shoved the gun under Anya's jaw, angling toward the car.

"Get away! I'll kill her! I'll kill myself!"

The gun went to his temple, then back to Anya's jaw.

"I'll kill her first and then myself! I'll do it!"

I spread my hands.

"What would Traci say?"

He fired at me again. Bap!

The bullet tugged my pants, low by my ankle.

Charley Reed rolled onto his belly and pushed to a knee. Phil was focused on me and Charley was behind him.

I said, "Phil, tell you what. Let her go and drive away. I won't stop you. Just let her go."

Phil's face was livid and mottled. He shouted.

"Bullshit!"

He tried to kill me again. Bap!

Behind him, Charley Reed rose to his feet. He gazed down at the red on his chest and looked at Phil.

I heard Sadie before I saw her. She staggered up beside me, weaving and rigid and taught as a suture, eyes burning like molten steel.

"I killed that other sonofabitch and I'll fucking well kill you, too."

Charley Reed lumbered forward.

Phil heard him or saw the movement, I don't know which. He turned, letting Anya fall free, and shot Charley again, but by then Charley was on him.

Charley made a wet, gargling roar as he lifted Phil and slammed him down. The gun flew free. Sadie lurched forward, picked up the gun, and pressed it to Phil's head.

She said, "I'm killing you now and I'll kill you every day until the end of time, just like your fucking friend."

Bap.

I could have stopped her, but I didn't. I could've reached the gun first or taken it from her, but I didn't. I didn't want to.

I rolled Charley onto his back, pulled off my shirt, and pressed the wadded shirt to his chest. I told Anya to hold it and press on it hard. I would've called the emergency number, but I couldn't tell them where to find us, so I called Carmack.

He said, "We're at their house. What happened here, Cole? Where are you?"

I dropped a pin on our location and sent it to him.

"Here. I've got one dead, one bleeding to death, and one injured. Come fast, Carmack. Send people now and tell them to hurry."

Sadie and Anya leaned on the wadded shirt, pressing as hard as they could.

Anya was saying, "Don't die, don't die, don't die."

Sadie was saying, "Don't you die, Charley Reed, don't you dare die."

We saw their lights on a far hill before we heard the sirens. We watched them race toward us, but a sheriff's helicopter arrived first, spiraling down to land on the field. The side slid open and two deps and a paramedic rushed toward us.

They reached us in time.

72

The helicopter flew Charley to a hospital in Woodland Hills. I guess they had a helipad on the roof. Sadie had a deep wound on her chest where Phil Janley struck her with a claw hammer. An ambulance took her to the same hospital where I'd been taken. Anya rode with her mom. I wondered if she'd be seen by Dr. Sherman. I hoped so.

I phoned Pike on the ride in and told him it was done.

He said, "Anya?"

"It was bad."

"You?"

"Well enough. Hang in at Traci's, okay? I don't know how long I'll be here."

"I'm here."

Charlie Bauman told me not to talk to the police until he arrived. I didn't, though Carmack and I shot the bull and drank coffee while we waited. After a while, Carmack began to fidget.

He said, "Listen, I gotta grab a smoke. Wanna come outside?"

A smoker.

I followed him out to the parking lot. Carmack fired up and exhaled as if his execution had been commuted.

He said, "I should quit."

Then he looked at me, face serious.

"Kept some things from you about the Sanchez killing. She was bagged and strangled."

"Aluminum wire?"

He sucked more smoke and nodded.

"Piece of the same wire was used to bind her wrists. Way it looks, she was strangled and asphyxiated, followed by a blow to the head. Probably finished her off with the blow, but I don't know. We're waiting on the ME."

"What did you keep back about Melendez?"

He drew again.

"We knew it wasn't gang-related. The gang theory was cover to hide what we knew."

"The hanging was staged."

"Postmortem. He was dead ten or twelve hours before he was strung up. The mutilation was postmortem, too. The question was, why go to so much trouble?"

"He enjoyed it."

Carmack drew and exhaled a long plume.

"Yeah. He'd done it before and he enjoyed doing it. We knew we had a bad one and we didn't want to spook him."

He studied his cigarette and dropped the butt. He watched it bounce.

"Never thought he was this bad, though. Not like this."

Carmack crushed the butt and looked at me.

"We didn't get much off Melendez. A few fibers. If we're lucky, they'll match his car. But Lori Sanchez gave us scrapings here, here, and here."

He touched the first three fingers of his right hand.

I said, "From her nails?"

"Skin, maybe. Might be her own, but, man, I hope it's his. The labs are so backed up we might not get results for four or five months."

"That's crazy. Don't you guys have juice? Put a rush on it."

"All homicide dicks ask for a rush. Every sex crimes dick. The wait time on rape kits is almost a year."

Carmack wanted to close his case. Lori's mother and son would want closure, too. I thought about Lori, bundled in fleece, and hoped she wasn't cold.

"I know someone who can make it happen faster."

Carmack frowned.

"Who?"

"A friend. A criminalist with LAPD."

Carmack shook his head.

"We have our own people."

"I know and they're great, but will your people cut to the head of the line?"

Carmack eyed me.

"The head?"

"You'd have to cook up a reason for a cross-agency collaboration, but this guy will move mountains. You'll have the results by the end of next week."

Carmack eyed me more, thinking about it.

"What's his name?"

"John Chen. I'll introduce you."

73

We were still in the parking lot when Charlie Bauman arrived. Carmack, his watch commander, and a detective lieutenant from Los Angeles questioned me for about ninety minutes. The watch commander and detective lieutenant asked most of the questions. All three took notes.

The watch commander said, "Did you know or suspect Mr. Beller's history?"

"No. Not until I learned what happened to Anya Given."

The detective lieutenant stared for a moment.

"And you believe Ms. Given was not his only victim."

"The FBI believes him responsible for between eight and thirteen homicides. Internally, they call him the Bagman."

"Thomas Beller."

"They've had his and Mr. Janley's DNA for many years, but not their names. Matching samples weren't in the system."

"How do you know this?"

"Friends."

Carmack coughed. Smoker.

The watch commander said, "Was his family aware of this?"

"Not to my knowledge, no. Not until I told them."

The detective lieutenant glanced at his notes.

"This was his daughter who hired you?"

"Yes. Traci Beller. She was thirteen when he vanished. Attempts to find him were without result. The tenth anniversary of his disappearance is approaching, so Traci wanted to try again."

The watch commander grinned.

"Bet she's sorry."

Carmack's jaw flexed. The detective lieutenant pooched his lips. Neither responded.

I said, "What's wrong with you?"

The watch commander looked surprised.

"Hey! Watch your tone."

"She was horrified. This was her father and the father she knew wasn't this. You think he walked around the house drooling? She couldn't believe it. She didn't want to believe it. Would anybody?"

I looked at the detective lieutenant.

"I told Ms. Beller about the unsolved cases and she encouraged me to continue. She believes their families deserve the truth."

The detective lieutenant said, "Has Ms. Beller asked you to conceal or destroy the things you've found?"

"The opposite. She told me to report my findings to the appropriate agencies as quickly as possible."

"Have you?"

"I was still in the finding phase. This is the reporting phase."

The detective lieutenant studied his notes.

"Traci with a *y* or an *i*?"

"An *i*."

"It's familiar. I know the name."

He suddenly looked up.

"The Baker Next Door?"

The watch commander said, "No shit?"

I filled out a form with my contact information, watched a uniformed dep scan my DL and PI licenses, and left. Charlie Bauman gave me a lift to a car rental place in Calabasas. They didn't have many vehicles available, so I ended up in a green SUV that looked like a loaf of moldy bread.

I called Georgina as I drove away. She sounded irritated when she answered.

"Who is this?"

"Elvis Cole. I called earlier."

"Don't tell me you want to come here. I just got home. My feet hurt."

"Phil Janley is dead. He was killed this afternoon."

It took a moment to process.

"Oh my Lord. What happened?"

"A woman named Sadie Given killed him. Ten years ago, Tommy tried to murder her daughter. She killed Tommy, too."

"What's wrong with you? Are you high?"

"Traci doesn't know Phil is dead. She should hear it from you. She's at home, so go to her house and tell her. Do it now."

"Phil is dead?"

"Tell her. I'm on my way."

"Phil."

"Call Kevin. Tell him to be there, too."

74

I swung by my house for the case summaries John Chen provided. I didn't have a large enough envelope, so I put them in a brown paper grocery bag.

When I arrived at Traci's home, Pike's Jeep was in the drive. Kevin answered the door with Pike behind him. I thought Kevin would make a crack when he saw the bag, but he didn't. He turned away without a word and walked past Pike to the living room. I lowered my voice.

"Is Georgina here?"

"Told Traci about Phil. It went down hard."

I nodded, thinking Traci's day was going to get harder.

Pike said, "Your pants. A bullet tore your pants."

I looked at my ankle. I'd forgotten.

"I guess so. I should've changed."

When I looked up, Pike was watching me. He looked like he wanted to say something, but he turned away.

"They're in here."

Traci sat with Georgina on the couch, looking like a hollow version of herself, as if all the things within her that made Traci Traci were gone. I sat across from her and set the bag by my feet.

"I know what your father did and when he did it. I know who his victims were. If you want me to tell you, I'll tell you."

Georgina snapped.

"She doesn't need to hear this. Phil is enough for one day."

Kevin rubbed his head. He looked beat-to-hell tired.

"Tell me and I'll deal with it. Trace, your mother's right. Take some time."

Traci seemed to be looking at me, but I wasn't sure she was. A tiny smile touched her lips.

"Did Ben like the picture?"

I wanted to cry.

"You made his year."

"I miss my dad. I miss Uncle Phil."

Her eyes focused and she saw me.

"My father and Uncle Phil did this together?"

"In whole or in part, yes."

"Tell me what they did."

I started with Phil and her father's van. I told her what Phil had done and how he died and what I'd said to the police about her and the rest of it.

Kevin said, "The other victims? The women this girl claims she saw."

He meant the photos Anya saw.

I gave him the bag. He peered inside. I knew he saw the top photo. He didn't take it out.

"How many victims are we talking about?"

"At least eight and as many as thirteen. These are crime scene photos and summaries from FBI files. The photos Anya saw weren't taken by police, but these women were in the photos she saw."

Kevin stared into the bag.

"Eight. Thirteen. How long was this going on?"

"A long time. Years."

Traci stared at her mother.

"Did you know?"

Georgina's lips parted and she frowned.

"Of course not. How can you ask such a thing?"

I said, "The police will ask. They'll ask what you knew and when. They're going to ask."

"I didn't know about this. Murder? No!"

Traci said, "Is this why you got rid of Daddy's things? You knew?"

"No!"

"You must've known something. How could you not know?"

Georgina flashed with anger.

"Did *you*? You lived with him, too. Did you?"

They stared at each other with fragile, frightened eyes, frozen for a heartbeat. Georgina softened and touched Traci's hand.

"Of course you didn't and neither did I."

"I can't believe he did this."

"Neither can I."

Traci turned to Kevin and glanced at the bag.

"Let me see."

Kevin grabbed the bag close.

"No! Absolutely not!"

I leaned toward her.

"Traci. You asked me to determine whether Anya was telling the truth and identify the victims so their families could be notified. I have."

I looked at Kevin and said it again.

"I did what Traci instructed. These are those women."

Kevin was staring at me. He nodded.

"I understand. I'll handle it."

"What you do with this information is up to Traci."

"I'll handle it."

Traci said, "I miss the daddy I knew."

I tried to smile, but couldn't.

75

Kevin handled the situation as well as anyone could handle something this tragic. A public relations firm specializing in crisis management and "problematic situations" was hired within the hour. They spent the night drafting statements and, in the end, told the truth.

Traci Beller, The Baker Next Door, who millions of people adored, woke one day to learn her father was a monster. She was devastated, cooperating with the police, and issuing apologies and condolences to the families of his victims, as well as providing the evidence acquired by her investigator to the relevant police agencies.

The internet exploded. Details of her father's crimes appeared the next day. Including photos of his victims. Pictures of police at her home and her mother's home were common. Her shop in Venice was vandalized. Barbie dolls with their heads wrapped in kitchen wrap were thrown into her yard. All reference to and photos of her father were removed from her website and social media accounts.

Her business suffered. Traci took major hits. She soaked up more bullets than combat Marines, but I never, not once, heard her complain.

Investors vanished. Personal appearances were canceled. Three advertisers dropped her. She closed a store. It was bad. Worse in the beginning, but it began to get better. The national morning host who'd loved her invited her back, not to bake, but to talk about having her heart broken, to talk about the betrayal. Traci was amazing. Lucy was visiting when the show aired. We watched it together. Kevin told me it was the highest-rated, most-streamed segment that year, and marked her turnaround.

Traci began making appearances again, at first to talk about her family, but after a while, to talk about baking or whatever she wanted. Traci was a great guest. People loved her.

Thirteen weeks after the news broke, I was watching the cat stalk a moth on the deck when Traci called.

I said, "Hey. Come hang out."

"I still want to meet her. Think she would?"

Just like that. No preamble. Anya.

"Yeah, she would. She thought you might not want to because of Phil."

"I think we should. I mean, if she does, then yeah. No pressure. I don't want her to be uncomfortable."

"No pressure. I'll ask. She doesn't want you to be uncomfortable, either."

"She said so?"

"She said so, but I'd better ask. Maybe she changed her mind."

"You're not funny."

"I am Mr. Funny."

"Maybe sometimes."

I asked Anya the next day. They met at my house the following Saturday afternoon. Anya came alone in Sadie's hatchback and arrived first. She looked nervous and whispered when I opened the door.

"Is she here?"

"You're the first. Come in."

We were still at the door when Traci arrived, so we waited. Traci joined us, stopping a few feet away. Nervous.

"Hi. I'm Traci."

"Hey. I'm Anya."

Neither of them moved.

I said, "Come inside. Anyone for Scrabble?"

A riot.

We went into the living room. They were awkward, but also something else. Careful. Shadows played on their faces as they looked at each other; flickers revealed things I'd never know. They stood as if they were on the edges of cliffs, maybe searching each other for something.

Traci said, "I don't know what to say. I'm sorry."

Anya said, "You're not him. You're you. Don't ever think you're him."

They stared, not moving. Their eyes filled.

I opened the sliders to the deck.

I said, "Why don't you sit out here? I'll stay inside."

They went out and I closed the door. I sat at the dining table and watched them. I couldn't hear them, but I wondered what they were saying. They knew things nobody knew. They'd felt things nobody else had felt or would want to feel. When they looked at each other, they saw someone only they could see. They shared something no other people shared. They had so much to say. I watched them speaking and wondered what they said. I still wonder.